HOW MUCH WILL
A MAN GIVE UP?

"You've said," the bearded man opened, "that I could do whatever I wanted with your wife." Even though Carol was moving up and down on him, his voice was even, level. "Was that true, Ray? Was that absolutely true?"

Somewhat belatedly, Ray remembered what he'd said while the women were undressing. "Yes," Ray agreed. "Yes, I did say that, didn't I?"

"Yes. Did you mean it?"

"Well—sure." His frown deepened. Maybe a little prudence was needed here, he told himself. "What'd you have in mind, Karl?"

Karl smiled as if he'd been waiting for that question. He let go of Carol's breasts, and both his hands went down to the floor alongside the chair, reaching under his piled clothing. When they came out, he was holding an ornate-hilted four-inch dagger in one hand and a small revolver in the other.

"I want," he said softly, "to kill her, Ray. . . ."

—fr█████████████████████████n Watkins

Edited by Jeff Gelb with Michael Garrett

Hotter Blood*
Hottest Blood*
The Hot Blood Series: Deadly After Dark*

Edited by Jeff Gelb with Lonn Friend

Hot Blood*

Edited by Jeff Gelb

Shock Rock*
Shock Rock II*
Fear Itself

By Jeff Gelb

Specters

By Michael Garrett

Keeper

*Published by POCKET BOOKS

THE HOT BLOOD SERIES

DEADLY
After Dark

**Edited by Jeff Gelb
and Michael Garrett**

POCKET BOOKS

New York   London   Toronto   Sydney   Tokyo   Singapore

An *Original* Publication of POCKET BOOKS

POCKET BOOKS, a division of Simon & Schuster Inc.
1230 Avenue of the Americas, New York, NY 10020

ISBN: 0-671-87087-4

First Pocket Books printing November 1994

10 9 8 7 6 5 4 3 2 1

POCKET and colophon are registered trademarks of Simon & Schuster Inc.

Cover by Gerber Studio

Printed in the U.S.A.

Copyright Notices

To Sharon Garrett and Terry Gladstone,
who get our hot blood boiling

CONTENTS

CONTENTS

FOREWORD

GOTHICA/EROTICA, OR, OF SEX AND HORROR

Forrest J. Ackerman

SEX—how, when, where, how much, etc.—has it crept into the crypts of horror fiction, added spice to the genre? Red-blooded erotica vs. blue-nosed puritanism in pulps, hardcover short stories and novels, art, motion pictures, every form of entertainment— what is the history of the infiltration of the sensual into the supernatural? How did the nature of horror, from fiction to films, come to nurture what is sometimes euphemistically referred to as curiosa? This is not a learned essay, fraught with psychological phraseology, but a lighthearted gambol through the erotic domains of de Sade and Masoch, Phil Farmer and Fay Wray, meant to be as enlightening as the tales that follow are frightening.

Books

Was a nineteen-year-old girl in 1818 the first to inject a subtle hint of eroticism into a Gothic novel? If so, the book was *Frankenstein,* its author young Mary Wollstonecraft Shelley. Subtle hints and sexual innuendos are to be found in this legendary work.

Certainly by 1970, in Calga Publishers' *Adult Version of Frankenstein,* eroticism unbound was at the core of the "updated" work. As the preface explained, "Limitations were imposed on the [original] book by the puritanical mores of the day. Powerful censors substituted *uncovered* for naked, *extemity* for leg, *charms* for breasts, *strawberries* for nipples, *thing* for penis, *stones* for balls, *place* for cunt, *occupy* for fuck." But suppose, the preface postulates, that the restrictions of the time had been lifted, that the episodes, descriptions, adventures, dialogue and vocabulary—"especially where sexual in nature"—were no longer blue-penciled by a bluenose censorship. "Dr. Frankenstein, the creator of the monster, is himself beset by the dilemma of a bride-to-be whose erotic appetites are such as to provide him with the tortures of the damned." Adapter Hal Kantor envisions:

> Their lovemaking [Victor and Elizabeth] was as the storm that raged outside. Naked, she was like a goddess. First soft and gentle, they delighted to the sensations of each other's flesh. And as the delights caught hold, it was wild and with a fury that neither knew they contained.

The storm was the stage for Victor's initiation into the secrets of sensuality. Elizabeth begs him to touch her—all over, everywhere. He complies and "almost maniacally fell upon her body, moving his hands and lips and tongue and fingers down and around and across her flesh. Probing. Caressing. Touching. Tasting. Feeling, exploring curves and arcs and orifices as if born into a new universe." As the storm increases in its intensity, so in direct proportion does the fury and the ecstasy of their love-making. "Bolt after bolt crashed and rocked around the castle, casting eerie and shaking shadows against the gloomy walls." Gothicism *cum* cum!

Time and again in the 191 pages that constitute the sexually explicit retelling of *Frankenstein,* sequences of increasing kinkiness are described, eventually going far beyond the eroticism of lesbianism into the depravity of bestiality and child molestation (both latter acts by the Monster).

In 1897—*Dracula.* Irishman Bram Stoker, then fifty, offered the world its most enduring vampire novel. And his hot Irish blood boiled over in one sequence when eroticism conjoined with vampirism. The three vampire brides of Dracula approach Jonathan Harker, the guest in one of the bedrooms in the Count's castle.

All three had brilliant white teeth that shone like pearls against the ruby of their voluptuous lips. . . . The girl went on her knees and bent over me, simply gloating. There was a deliberate voluptuousness which was both thrilling and repulsive, and as she arched her neck she actually licked her lips like an animal, till I could see in the moonlight the moisture shining on the scarlet lips and on the red tongue as it lapped the white sharp teeth. Lower and lower went her head as the lips went below the range of my throat and chin and seemed about to fasten on my throat. Then she paused, and I could hear the churning sound of her tongue as it licked her teeth and lips, and could feel the hot breath on my neck. . . . I could feel the soft, shivering touch of the lips on the super-sensitive skin of my throat. . . . I closed my eyes in languorous ecstasy and waited—waited with beating heart.

Now let us time-travel forward to that moment in 1976 when neophyte author Anne O'Brien Rice burst upon an unsuspecting world with the most alluring vampire novel of modern times, *Interview with the Vampire,* which quickly shot up to bestsellerdom (presumably by word of, er, mouth). Wendayne Mondelle, my late wife the university professor, quite an erotic lady in her heyday, was mesmerized by the power of this woman's erotic passages. Example:

She was very like a child, though clearly a full-grown woman. Her breasts though small were beautifully shaped beneath her blouse, and her hips though narrow gave her long, dusty skirt a sharp, sensual angularity. Her beauty was heart-breaking.

And later:

And slowly he drew the loose string from the gathers of her blouse. The cheap fabic opened, the sleeves slipping off her narrow, pink shoulders; and she clasped it, only to have him take her wrists and thrust them sharply away. The audience seemed to sigh in a body, the women behind their opera glasses, the men leaning forward in their chairs. I could see the cloth falling, see the pale flawless skin pulsing with her heart and the tiny nipples letting the cloth slip precariously . . . tears coursing down her blushing cheeks, her teeth biting into the flesh of her lip . . . The blouse slipped to her waist. A murmur moved through the titillated crowd as her small, round breasts stood exposed. . . . On the warm, rising air I could smell the perfume of her skin, hear the soft beating of her heart. . . . She was looking into his eyes now, and her pain bathed her in a beauteous light, a light which made her irresistibly alluring. . . . I could feel her skin, feel the small, pointed breasts, feel my arms caressing her . . . the drawstring of her skirt as she inclined towards him, her head back, the black cloth slipping over her hips, over the golden gleam of the hair between her legs—a child's down, that delicate curl—the skirt dropping to her feet . . . His white hand shone on her florid buttocks.

And so it goes. This was only a warmup for the continuous corruscating carnality in her trilogy bylined A. N. Roquelaure, which made the sensually sex-charged sufferings of *O* read like Little Bo-Peep shearing sheep.

I have (according to the count of four Los Angeles librarians sent over by the mayor's office) 50,000 books. Don't ask me if I've read them all—I've read every last word. (When I get a new book, I turn to the last page and read the last word.) But seriously: Though from 1929 till now I can't be expected to remember every book I've ever read, I seem to remember that in *Dream's End* by Thorne "Topper" Smith, 1927, and in Tiffany Thayer's *One-Man Show,* 1937, there were some steamy sequences augmenting the Gothic atmosphere. Eroticism and atmos-fear.

Weird Tales and the Pulps

I do believe it was in the pages of *Weird Tales* magazine, which began in 1923 and is being published to this day, that eroticism first raised its lovely head in the Gothic genre. Lo and behold, on the cover of the January 1931 issue is a vivid depiction of the following paragraph from the story "The Lost Lady":

Nude and fainting, a young girl was lashed face-forward to a pillar in the floor. Her feet were raised a foot or more above the cement, and round the pillar and her ankles was passed turn after turn a finely knit silken cord, knotting her immovably to the beam and forcing her entire weight upon the thongs which bit so cruelly into her white and shrinking flesh. Her arms were drawn around the post, the wrists crossed and tied at the farther side, but this did little to relieve the strain upon the cords encircling her.

A vicious whipping ensues, erotically arousing to all flagellation fans among the readership—of which there must have been many, as this was but the first of numerous whipping scenes to appear in the "Thrashing Thirties."

Apologies, anti-chauvinistic feminists, the readers of *WT* seemed to enjoy the erotic thrill of a woman being whipped.

In September 1934 *Weird Tales,* Hollywood writer Mindret Lord told it like it was in "Naked Lady": "In this jaded age, sex appeal is important. Important? It is everything! The public waters at the mouth at the very mention of nudism or Mae West."

September 1935 featued a cover that will live in infamy—the anti-erotic Canadian cover of *Weird Tales* on which the breast of the naked "Blue Woman" had censoriously been removed by air-brushing, leaving her as flat-chested as a man! The first time a mastectomy was ever performed on a magazine cover!

In January 1936 *Weird Tales* treated its lesbian readers (and the many closeted men who enjoyed words about or pictures of women with women) to a cover featuring two beautiful 99-percent-naked women in a wrestling match. The text that matched:

> Birth-nude, across the prostrate body of the man they faced each other. . . . Agnes' lissome body was perfection's other self. From slender, high-arched feet to narrow, pointed breasts and waving golden hair she was without a flaw, as sweetly made and slender as a marble naiad carved by Praxiteles.

The Return of Frankenstein: 1940, and a sex-charged horror periodical called *Terror Tales* was in its twelfth volume. It had been spewing forth bust and lust tales of horror for several years, and in its May issue one of its regular contributors titillated readers with "Test-Tube Frankenstein." A couple of chapter heads set the scene: "Abomination in the Boudoir," "A Moon and a Girl and a Horror."

Her hands loosed the belt of the sheer, wrap-around negligee, began slipping the garment from one shoulder. In spite of me, my breath caught in anticipation. This utter loveliness—I must concentrate all my attention on the pale dream of June's nearly unrobed figure. Here was heaven, however narrowly saved from the taint of hell. With some quirk of modesty she had half turned her back while slipping the pink negligee lower. It crumpled about her waist. I gasped with near pain at the beauty of her.

Twenty-seven years later the principal reason to view Terence Fisher's Hammer film *Frankenstein Created Woman* was to appreciate in action the curvaceous star Susan Denberg, who, if I recall correctly across a gap of a quarter century, was at the time a recent Playmate.

In the same 1940 issue of *Terror Tales,* Russell Gray's "Mistress of the Dark Pool" was accompanied by illustrations featuring one completely clothed woman menacing a totally naked one on a cliff. The story delivered what it promised in the way of erotic scenes. In "The Book of Torment" by Harrison Storm, sexual sadism was excused in the name of witchcraft. Madame Louise de Guibourg, a tall, proud, brunette beauty accused of being a witch, was stripped naked and subjected to the usual painful pleasures pleasing to a torture-happy inquisitioner. And so it went, story after story, issue after issue, year after year. The magazine might more rightfully have been titled *Sadistic Sex Stories.*

But wait! In order to sate the appetites of the erotically aroused readership of the forties, there was a companion periodical: *Horror Stories*. The February 1941 issue, volume 10, touted "Dracula's Brides" on the cover. The blurb in the table of contents told that the ever-popular Wayne Rogers, who had tackled the subject of Frankenstein in *Terror Tales* the year before, was back for an erotic bout with the King of the Vampires. "Every night hundreds of jaded thrill-seekers flocked to the Club Dracula to witness the impersonation of the famed vampire seeking the blood of a young maiden." In the midst of the story is an announcement, "In the history of Mystery-Terror fiction, there are two outstanding names—Dracula and Frankenstein. You all know Dracula; but don't miss 'Spawn of Frankenstein,' appearing in next month's issue of *Horror Stories*."

But the end was not yet. The literary (?) appetite for blood and bosoms, castles and cringing maidens, helpless ladies and the lash, erotic lovers and naked nymphos, ghosts and gossamer-gowned girls, undraped and violated virgins—this fictional hunger for fear-fraught sexual adventures was not completely fulfilled by the two perversion-pandering periodicals. How does *Spicy Mystery Stories* grab you?

It grabbed a feverish following in the forties with exotic covers to match the erotic interiors. It continued—and its companion, *Spicy Adventure Stories*—until its contents reached Fahrenheit 452 (the temperature at which blood boils) and it became too hot not to cool down and morphed into a somewhat less racy *Speed Mystery*.

Today that erotic era of horror fiction magazines is one commanding premium prices among pulp collectors. Three-figure quotes are not uncommon for the more desirable issues.

Movies

Let us turn now to the erotic in horror films. This is a subject with which I must be about as familiar as a witch's familiar, having been a devout cinephile from the age of five and a half in 1922. The first time I remember anything erotic in a horror film was in the Rouben Mamoulian/Fredric March Academy Award–winning *Dr. Jekyll and Mr. Hyde* of 1932. In *Dark Romance: Sexuality in the Horror Film* (McFarland), the author, David J. Hogan, describes the sequence in that film that gave sixteen-year-old me wet dreams. He speaks of Dr. Jekyll's great attraction to Champagne Ivy (Miriam Hopkins), a sexy prostitute. After, as a doctor, he has examined bruises on Ivy's back inflicted by another man, she "coyly suggests that Jekyll turn his back so that she may undress. In a moment she is sitting in her bed, barely covered and obviously naked. One bare leg is provocatively thrust from beneath the covers. Jekyll sits next to her and they kiss. . . ." This was highly charged stuff, the scene's sexual electricity. Yes, across a gulf of more than half a century and three years, four months, and twenty-nine days of World War II army service in between, I still cherish that scene. "Come back, woncha?" invites Champagne Ivy. Anytime, Ivy, for either sham pain or, as Theodore Sturgeon put it, real pain.

A year later, before the censors got to it, comely Fay Wray was getting peeled like a grape by a naïvely curious King Kong, and the same year, a love captive of Count Zaroff (Leslie Banks) in *The Most Dangerous Game* narrowly escaped rape at the hands of the mad hunter whose philosophy went something like "First the kill, then the woman."

The same year that Fay Wray became the sexual pawn of Kong, the king of Skull Island, Charles Laughton was up to skullduggery on the *Island of Lost Souls.* There (inspired by H. G. Wells) he scientifically sped up evolution to the point that animals became the manimals they might have become naturally after millions of years of mutations. And among the males was one womanimal, Lota the Panther Girl. The feline femme of futurity was the late Kathleen Burke, the subject of a nationwide search to find a believable woman to play the part. While I personally preferred a runner-up, Lona Andre (i.e., I found her more sexually attractive), Kathleen admittedly exuded an aroma of a pantheress in heat.

The year 1935 brought *The Hands of Orlac* (original: Conrad Veidt) to the screen in its first talking version as *Mad Love,* introducing Peter Lorre in his first American role (he had made an international hit earlier as the child murderer in Fritz Lang's classic *M,* a movie about an amputated but still murderous hand). Pop-eyed and bald-headed, Lorre as the sinister surgeon Gogol had googoo eyes for Colin (Frankenstein) Clive's wife, the beauteous brunette (with us yet and till the time of his death Fritz Lang's next-door neighbor), Frances Drake. "Gogol," says Hogan, "seems caught in a sexual trap," suffering from unconquerable desires that have driven him insane. Forty-six years later the hand with a mind of its own was back in a variant version of the perennial Orlac plot. This time simply titled *The Hand,* the disembodied, murdering member belonged to Michael Caine. Director Oliver Stone's script, adapted from Marc Brandel's book *The Lizard's Tail,* included some nudity amidst the gory crudity.

In 1936 the vampire theme surfaced again with the late Gloria Holden as Countess Marya Zaleska, *Dracula's Daughter,* repressing a bit of lesbian lust for nubile actress Nan Grey.

In 1946 France exported an enduring classic, *La Belle et la Bete,* with Jean Cocteau guiding Jean Marais as the Beast (himself the epitome of male beauty) through the mazes of this French fairy-tale fantasy of elegant irreality, diaphanous amour, and sexual subtlety. To quote the ubiquitous David Hogan, "Beauty (Josette Day) is able to come to grips with the Beast's powerful sexualty, maintaining her composure after realizing that she is being observed in her chambers, and allowing the Beast to lap water from her cupped hands. The latter scene is so highly charged with eroticism that one is left breathless."

In 1954 the first of Universal's trilogy of Beauty and the Beast films, *agua caliente* style, *The Creature from the Black Lagoon,* introduced "Blacky LaGoon," who constantly got cold water thrown on his erotic attraction to a heroine not of his species.

In 1955 *Cult of the Cobra* produced what Simone Simon's *Cat People* promised. Faith Domergue (*This Island Earth*) portrayed a shifty snake goddess who changed her shape (a shape-shifter) into that of a beautiful woman whom David Hogan characterized as "every boy's masturbatory wish-dream" (unfortunately I was thirty-nine by then), "lush of figure and wet of mouth, with sultry dark eyes and a sibilant way with consonants."

Richard Matheson in his 1956 novel *The Shrinking Man* more poignantly examined in print the dilemma of his protagonist's shrinking, er, manhood than he permitted himself the next year in his screenplay *The*

Incredible Shrinking Man. Incidentallyd, there is a hilarious story concerning my late friend the director, Jack Arnold, and his solution for making huge water drops (as compared to diminutive doll-man Carey) photograph realistically. When the accounting department raised eyebrows over Arnold's bill for a carload of condoms, with a straight face he explained they were "for the customary cast & crew party!" The comptroller, at first staggered by the enormity of the quantity, suggesting an all-night orgy at the studio, roared at the joke when it was described to him how Arnold, by experimentation, had discovered that water-filled condoms shot at slow-motion speed gave the perfect effect of giant water drops!

Dracula rose from his coffin in 1958 in the persona of Christopher Lee, who reprised the role seven times, six in the Hammer series. An examination of *Horror of Dracula; Dracula, Prince of Darkness; Dracula Has Risen from the Grave; Taste the Blood of Dracula,* et al., would be worthy of an entire chapter. Suffice it to say sex had come to play an important part in each picture, with lots of fleshly lust for lickable ladies in addition to bloodlust. In *The Satanic Rites of Dracula,* vampire Valerie Van Ost got done wrong when staked below her exposed bare breast. Dracula, the Lee way, enjoyed encarmined lips for thirteen years before turning in his cape, fangs, and bloodshot contact lenses.

In 1961 Oliver Reed crossed the Big Pond in *Curse of the Werewolf* and had the ladies in the audience swooning over his (wolf)manly hirsuteness. Same year *The Mask* arrived (with 3-D portions) from Canada, sex and death intermingled in intimate detail. The same year also saw Henry James's famous novella *The*

Turn of the Screw turned into an unforgettably subtle fright film of evil, *The Innocents.* Martin Stephens, the youngster who the year before scored a hit as the albino-haired Midwich Cuckoo with the huge dark eyes in *Village of the Damned,* returned as the adolescent who caused audiences to gasp when he planted a very knowing kiss on the shocked lips of his governess, Deborah Kerr.

In 1962's *Journey to the Seventh Planet* the gimmick was something similar to what I devised for Catherine Moore's "Yvala" (my title) in the February 1936 *Weird Tales,* whereby every man's distaff desire was materialized by a sentient plant with evil intent.

Shirley Jackson's famous novel *The Haunting of Hill House* became a classic ghostory in 1963 as *The Haunting.* Julie Harris and Claire Bloom shared a sapphic attraction for each other, their conduct being the catalyst for the creation of a psychic maelstrom within the walls of the house they inhabited.

In 1965 exotic Barbara Steele, age twenty-seven, was whipped on her bare back in *Nightmare Castle,* a genuine evocation of Gothicism.

Stephanie Rothman, female director, appeared upon the scene in 1966 with *Blood Bath,* a kind of Misery of the Wax Museum with female models getting murdered and desanguinized and then having their bodies painted.

French director Jean Rollin began rollin' out a sex-vampire genre all his own in 1967 with *Le Viol du Vampire* (*Rape of the Vampire,* if my high school French serves me right), treating viewers to the sight of a semi-clad vampiress supine on the tiger-skin upholstery of her hot car. Sado-masochistic imagery abounded in the follow-up, *La Vampire Nue (The*

Nude Vampire). Le Frisson des Vampires (The Shudders/Shivers/Thrills of Vampires) exhibited evil sexuality. *Vierges et Vampires (Virgins and Vampires)* I never saw, but I assume the virgins didn't last very long.

One of the delights of my life was taking the Austrian auteur, Fritz Lang *(Siegfried, Kriemhild's Revenge, The Weary Death),* to see *Rosemary's Baby* in 1968. Like myself a fan of the female form, Lang had failing eyesight that unfortunately did not permit him to see clearly, even though we sat in the front row, the rape sequence with the nude figure of elfin Mia Farrow violated by the Devil.

I suppose it had to happen eventually. If so, 1969 was the year for it: *Dracula, the Dirty Old Man.* He did his dirty work with lotsa bare-breasted babes. The film that revealed the thirsty count was gay was 1969's *Does Dracula Really Suck?* (co-billed with *Hollow My Wienie, Dr. Frankenstein*). And somewhere in the aarghives of vamporn lurks *Gayracula.*

Filmmakers discovered Elizabeth Bathory. Eliza-*bath* was a real-life woman with a hemoglobin habit which she indulged to excess from 1600 to 1610, during which time she kidnapped and killed hundreds of peasant girls and reputedly bathed in their blood, believing that between the ages of forty and fifty the literal bloodbaths would keep her young and beautiful. In *Daughters of Darkness,* 1970, Delphine Seyrig essayed the role of Bathory, who, together with a lesbian companion, lured a young honeymooning couple into erotic interactions, first voyeuristically and then as active participants. Bathory was back the next year as *Countess Dracula,* with Ingrid Pitt pittilessly murdering virgin maidens for her sanguinary Oil of Olay treatments. Admirers of feminine epidermis got their eyes full as ravishing Ingrid permitted herself to be photographed totally au naturel, baring a pair of the most beautiful breasts ever to grace the screen in any genre, topping a figure of most pulchritudinous proportions. Across a gap of nearly a quarter of a century, I express my personal gratitude for that treat, inspirational Ingrid!

For a second time in 1971 pneumatic Ingrid Pitt as Carmilla (from J. Sheridan LeFanu's acclaimed novella of the same name) allowed loving looks at her luscious body in *The Vampire Lovers,* a smorgasblood of bare breasts and sapphic soul-kisses. The same year Jimmy Sangster's sanguinary *Lust for a Vampire* sexposed the blood-dripping bare bosom of Scandinavian actress Yutte Stensgaard as Mircalla (Carmilla spelled sideways) who bit her way through a girls' school. Before year's end. Mircalla was back (in the vampiric vessel of Katya Keith) in a bitch-hunting spree by fanatical witch-hunters. Breast-beating was replaced by breast-biting and frontal nudity was brought to the fore before "The End" appeared upon the screen. The year 1971 also saw the return of Stephanie Rothman helming *The Velvet Vampire,* with vampiress Diane LeFanu (ooh!) attempting to initiate young innocents into the wicked world of perverse eroticism.

A soft-porn version of Oscar Wilde's classic was imported from Italy in 1971, *The Secret Life of Dorian Gray,* starring luscious morsel Marie Lijedahl and offering enticing acres of naked female flesh to boot— if one was the kind of brute with a private passion for booting bare beauties.

In 1972 Martine Beswicke steamed up the screen in

Dr. Jekyll and Sister Hyde. If memory serves me right (at seventy-seven I might have incipient Old Timer's Disease), this version treated audiences to a glimpse of Martine's magnificent mammaries.

In the extraordinary, perversely powerful *Wicker Man,* 1973, a paganistic island pulled all stops out in hedonistic celebrations of the body as naked teenagers cavorted uninhibitedly in fertility rites and a beautifully bare Britt Eklund drove a puritanical man up the wall as she bumped and ground against the thin partition separating his tortured flesh from her birth-naked body.

The 1974 British import *Vampyres* once again was heavy on the lesbian theme with kinky romance in an old dark manse. Same year Udo Kier, a latter-day Conrad Veidt, starred in *Blood for Dracula,* with four virgins awaiting his, er, coming.

In 1980 Stephen King's *The Shining* reached the screen via the direction of Stanley Kubrick, and while not as erotic as *A Clockwork Orange,* it did have its moments, notably the glorious goddess arising naked from the bathtub. ('Twas after the tub that the rub came in.)

Joe Dante's *The Howling* (1981) included one of my cameos but unfortunately as close to anything erotic as I got was a set of Tarot cards. However, Elisabeth Brooks as a licentious lycanthrope had a nice roll in the sand with a fellow werewolf. The orgasmic gasps on a scale of one to ten rated a ten. The only way the lycanthropic lay could have been more play-tonic was if it had been directed à la deep thrope.

The same year John Landis's *American Werewolf in London* broke more werewolfic ground and also injected erotic elements. Jenny Agutter, who had been seen partially naked in *Logan's Run* and totally buff in *Equus,* showered with David Naughton in the Brit bit-film, and the couple exchanged caresses and wet kisses and engaged in some fond fondling beneath the bed sheets.

The same year *Ghost Story* introduced Alice Krige, a South African actress with a singularly perverse brand of sexuality reminiscent of Barbara Steele and Martine Beswicke. Alice got her licks in at one point by seductively licking one of four young men on the face. With her they didn't have a ghost of a chance.

It is one of my personal tragedies that the original *Cat People* was made before an R-rated film would have permitted a viewing of the undoubtedly pulchrinudinous Simone Simon in all her purry feline femininity. Alas, no celluloid legacy of Simone, Marlene, Sari Maritza. Danielle Darrieux, Lona Andre, Anna Sten, Arline Judge, Toby Wing, naked as Nature intended them . . . but we did get lucky in 1982 when Nastassia Kinski, ever ready, willing, and able in mundane movies to display her wares (though to date never in a were-wolfilm), graced and spiced the remake of *The Cat People* with her unclad beauty. The sight of this naked cat-woman ought to have been enough to make a catatonic snap out of his nap!

In 1983, Barbara Hershey graphically became the victim of *The Entity,* an erotic ectoplasmic rapist who pursued her from bathroom to bedroom and worked its wicked will upon her willy-nilly, palping her persimmons, tweaking her nips with what Claude Rains might have characterized as his "little invisible fingers." This was the year that my discovery, Bobbie Bresee, shambled forth in horror raiment from the *Mausoleum* as a she-demon with a ferocious little

sentient monster-head protruding from each breast
. . . but not before her Monroesque mammaries and
eye-tractive bod had been tastefully displayed in their
non-monsterrific munchability. In the ensuing decade
Bobbie has been in demand nationally and interna-
tionally as a Scream Queen at horror film festivals.

Other actresses who have climbed the ladder of
sex-cess wrong by wrong (the Mae West syndrome) are
today's pre-eminent Scream Queens Brinke *(Teenage
Exorcist)* Stevens, Linnea "Wiggly" Quigley, Michelle
Bauer ("the most drop-dead beauty with a perfect
body"—Joe Bob Briggs), femme fatale Monique
Gabrielle and a dozen other doozies who are flat
where it flatters and curved where it matters and don't
mind presenting a fair derriere for a spanking or a
nude torso (and moreso) for a soaping in a shower
scene or a rub-a-dub-dub in a hot tub, clad only in an
aura of horror from the Gothique to the Grand
Guignolesque.

Bram Stoker's *Lair of the White Worm*, 1988,
contrasted breathtakingly beautiful nudes (queenly
Princess Catherine Oxenberg? Amanda Donohoe?)
with the squamous horror of the huge malignant
non-human menace of the vermicular variety.

In most recent times, Anne Parillaud appetizingly
paraded stark naked around her boudoir in the opening sequence of *Innocent Blood* (my 43rd screen
cameo; as the main male vampire makes off with my
automobile: "That's my car!"). And I can't tell you
how candidly I envy John Landis when the script-
tease required him to direct the most sensually seductive scene I've ever witnessed in seventy-two years of
moviegoing (move over, *O, And God Created Woman,
Basic Instinct, Ecstasy, Lash of the Penitente, Sex and*

Zen), when the heavenly hell-girl in all her totally naked glory (even though not even a pubic hair or aureole is showing) kneels on the bed in a bondage position of do-what-thou-wilt-with-me-lover submission and presents her voluptuous and vulnerable body to the camera's caressing eye. How many times did you have to rehearse that scene, John? And if you ever shoot a similar one, what would I have to pay to be a creative consultant?

Well, that about covers it. Or uncovers it. Sex appeal seems now inextricably interwoven with hex appeal, curiosa with cloven-hoofdom, eroticism with mysticism, lust with horror. While ghosts, goblins, vampires, werewolves, zombies, headless bodies and disembodied heads, phantoms and wraiths are wraithing the hair on your head, today's purveyors of horror, whether in art, literature, or the cinema, seem by and, er, large dedicated to arousing that little "Herr" down there where manhood manifests itself, ensorcelling the male malevolence-fan with a bonus of erotic enticements, with an occasional wicked wink to the straight and/or gay female. If I have whetted your appetite to taste the terror-*cum*-titillation tales in this volume of the erotic *cum* the erratic, the terrifying thing in the attic, the frightmare of the beast cellar . . . well, that's what wet-dreams are all about. Pleasant (s)creams!

INTRODUCTION

Recall, if you will, those mystical days of sexual awakening.

Few opportunities presented themselves to make love—or just get your rocks off—in the comfort of a warm bed, unless your parents were away. More likely, you were at a drive-in, or a lovers' lane. And on those occasions when the folks returned early, or the flashlight man banged at your car window, remember how you felt? Your libido was iced by the first foreign sound. Your heart thumped against your chest as you scrambled to dress or hide. Your hormones were chilled by the panic of discovery.

Sex and fear. They meshed naturally in the good old days, and the same holds true today in the *Hot Blood* series.

This edition's group of writers provides further proof that sex and horror are a bottomless well that has not begun to go dry. Fresh ideas crop up in every story we read, from both new and established writers. One of the fascinations of editing this series is watching the horror field change with the times. We're seeing fewer vampire stories and more about psychopaths, fewer werewolves and more horny husbands cheating on their wives . . . with disastrous results. As readers, it puts the horror more squarely in our own backyards, living rooms, and, of course, bedrooms. As a result, the current crop of *Hot Blood* stories is closer to home than most we're presented so far. That ups their fear quotient, so . . . be warned!

To put it all in perspective, we are honored to present a personalized overview of the history of erotic horror, courtesy of legendary horror fan #1, Forrest J. Ackerman. We both grew up reading (and hiding from our parents!) dog-eared copies of *Famous Monsters,* passed from kid to kid (and which we are now passing on to our kids, much to their delight!). In his own inimitable style, Forry provides a unique look at the role of the birds and bees in horror in his "Forryword" to this volume. But of course, in Forry's world, the birds might be the size of Rodan and the bees could be a killer swarm migrating north from South America. Enjoy his unique vision and sense of humor in this edition of "Fahrenheit 452," as Forry terms the *Hot Blood* series.

So caress this volume and relax in your favorite chair or the backseat of your car—whatever turns you on—to experience a new rush of excitement. And, oh, by the way—*is this your first time?* Have you missed the earlier volumns of the *Hot Blood* series? If so, you're in for a real treat, not only between these covers, but also through the pioneering editions that await you at your favorite bookstore. If you've been with us since the original volume, you already know what to expect. In either case, rest assured more volumes are coming.

For us, and for thousands of readers the world over, erotic horror fiction is a particularly enticing piece of forbidden fruit, one we must return to now and again, to satisfy some primal urge as essential as sex itself. And it's an urge you can explore guilt-free.

So . . . indulge!

Jeff Gelb
Michael Garrett
January 1994

DEADLY
After Dark

THINGS OF WHICH
WE DO NOT SPEAK

Lucy Taylor

*H*it me," said Elaine.

I thought I hadn't heard her right.

"Hit me," she repeated. I stopped in mid-stroke.

She might as well have said the sheets were on fire. My penis slithered out of her like a clubbed snake.

Rolling off her, I stared at the cracked plaster and wondered why ceilings weren't routinely decorated with some groin-enlivening mural—Delacroix's *Rape of the Sabines* maybe or some nice nineteenth-century Japanese porn—something to provide spent males, or prematurely limp ones, some focus for contemplation other than their own untimely detumescence.

"Why did you *say* that?"

"That was Little Elaine."

"Oh, Christ, not that inner child crap."

I flopped onto my side, willing myself not to say anything more. I mean, I loved this woman. Even if I'd only known her for a few months, I loved her passion and her energy and the way she craved sex like some kind of cock-junkie, but sometimes her incessant psychobabble, pop psychology, Survivers of Lousy Childhoods Anonymous or whatever bullshit the shrinks on the best-seller list were hyping these days really got old.

After all, nobody has a perfect childhood, right? But you grow up and you forget about the bike you didn't get for Christmas or the dog that got hit by a car. You get down to the business of being a grown-up and you leave your childhood behind.

I stole a glance at Elaine. She appeared to be meditating on the area between her eyebrows.

"I *asked* you to hit me."

"That doesn't turn me on. I care about you. I want to kiss you and caress you."

"You don't get it, do you?"

"Evidently not. Care to enlighten me?"

"I don't want you to *hurt* me. Getting rough during sex doesn't have to mean anything sexist or sinister. It just adds to the rush, like going over the top of a roller coaster. My therapist says it's really Little Elaine, my inner child, who wants to be slapped. Little Elaine grew up with lots of yelling and screaming and hitting. She's addicted to chaos."

"Do you have any idea how stupid you sound when you talk about yourself in the third person? I feel like I'm in a ménage à trois, and one of us is underage."

"Fuck you, Matthew. You're just being a prick 'cause you lost your hard-on."

She flung the sheets aside and leapt out of the bed. Suddenly I felt very alone.

"I wish you wouldn't go."

My pecker wished it, too. Elaine was a dancer and

part-time fitness trainer. Her body radiated a fierce, androgynous energy. Riding Elaine, it was like making love to a lust-struck python. Now she moved about the bedroom, gathering up items of her clothing that had been cast about in a frenzy of libido that, given the present circumstances, now seemed sad and ludicrous.

"Elaine, I'm sorry."

"Look, I won't ask you again to do anything you're not up for—" She realized what she'd said, and we both laughed. At least it broke the tension, but she didn't stop getting dressed. "I have to leave anyway. Cory's probably sweet-talked the sitter into letting him stay up to watch MTV."

"Hey, tell Cory I got that backgammon set he wanted."

"That was sweet of you, Matthew. I will."

After Elaine left, I lay on the damp, sex-scented sheets, feeling angry and confused, marveling at the peculiar masochism of people who seemed to relish the rehashing of their traumatic pasts. I had always avoided thinking of my own family. Yet now, perversely, the memories came, each with its own distinctive sting, like an angry acupuncturist jabbing in the needles.

My father had died in '88, and Mom lived with my sister RuthAnn in Illinois. I called occasionally, but the mere sound of their voices was like hearing the language of a foreign land where one was once held captive. I had no wish ever to revisit it.

If Elaine's family had been drunken and violent, mine had been the opposite: quiet, pious, restrained. Grace before meals, Mass on Sunday. No alcohol, no swearing, no voices raised in either rage or exultation. Boundaries were rigidly observed and privacies respected.

Dad taught high school chemistry and coached football. RuthAnn, two years older than I, was a high school track star. I was a "brain" who could master trig but blundered about in gym class like a lobotomized brontosaurus, a timid tourist in my skin to whom the language of the body seemed as alien as Sanskrit.

Football was Dad's great passion. A winning team meant conversation at the supper table, a losing one evoked grim silence. Sometimes I couldn't help but wonder how he felt, coaching other people's athletic, strapping sons, then sitting across the table from his own plump, uncoordinated progeny.

Freddy Burton was older than I, an eighteen-year-old senior, but even pudgier and less athletic than I was. For that reason, I suppose, I tried to be his buddy. I'd invite Freddy over for dinner and watch him scarf down two desserts and hope Dad noticed how truly disgusting Freddy was, how his gut lopped over his trousers and his chins jiggled. I figured if I couldn't make Dad proud of me, at least I'd make him less ashamed.

Like that time I dislocated my shoulder in a sledding accident, and Dad drove me to the hospital. He didn't comfort me, but only said he hoped I wasn't going to cry. I nearly bit my tongue in half not crying.

I was thinking of that ride to the hospital when I fell asleep, and the old nightmare surfaced in all its terrible clarity:

My throat feels like I've gargled with Drano. The school nurse has diagnosed strep throat and sent me home. Now I stand at the foot of the stairs, looking up at my father, thinking maybe he's come home for lunch. He holds one hand out like a traffic cop and says, "Don't come up here."

But my room is upstairs, and my bed and my books. I have a sudden, urgent need to be there. To crawl in bed with a book and escape into a jungle of squiggly black bug tracks on a cream-colored page.

I start up the stairs.

"No," commands Dad.

A fierce heat radiates from above. My eyelashes feel scorched, my forehead burns. At first I think it's fever. But suddenly I understand—our house must be on fire! And Mom and RuthAnn! Where are they?

Now I remember a story I read about a boy who saved his family from a burning building. How I longed to be that boy, to be a hero better than any football star. To see the pride and gratitude in Dad's eyes, to be someone who mattered.

I rush up the stairs, oblivious to danger, determined to rescue Mom and RuthAnn, to make Dad proud.

Dad blocks my path.

No!

He grips my shoulders, forces me to meet his eyes. They gleam like pale, ice-encrusted stones.

He says, "Some things we do not speak of."

This was the nightmare from my youth, with Dad saying those words I always thought I had imagined, until the night Elaine asked me to hit her.

After that, it seemed as if I heard Dad's voice every time I closed my eyes.

On Saturday, Elaine couldn't get a baby-sitter for Cory, so I took the Lexington #6 train over to 8th

Street and walked up to Avenue A, stopping at the corner market to pick up steaks and a bottle of Chianti, some soda pop for Cory.

When I left the store in the early twilight, the neighborhood was already acrawl with people who looked as though a few hours hence they'd be filling up the local emergency room psych ward and drunk tank. A shopping bag hag waddled past me, babbling gibberish with the panache of a Pentecostal speaking in tongues. A slant-eyed hooker—some exotic mix perhaps of Chinese, Hispanic, and black—leaned a leather-clad hip in a doorway.

Rap music blatted from an open window. Across the street, a couple stood on the porch of a dilapidated walk-up, bickering in some language that sounded like corn popping. I could smell marijuana, hear curse words shouted, taste the grit and the swill of the city.

Dammit, how could Elaine raise her son in such a pit? Once the neighborhood had held hopes for gentrification, but tonight the little ragged clumps of street people, the pairs of sullen hookers, fouled it like the droppings of a million diarrhetic pigeons.

"Hey, mister!"

They were on me before I realized what was happening. A tribe of them, four half-naked boys, their complexions varying shades of brown and black and yellow. They sauntered over from a doorway, all sinews and skin, like scrawny wolves wearing tight jeans and sneers.

"You party, mister?"

The one who spoke was short with black, crafty eyes, the eyes of some wild, nocturnal raptor. His skin looked the color of dusk, all soot and smoke, and his neck was way too supple and long and unblemished to belong on a boy. His face bore a mocking smirk that I longed to rearrange with my fist.

"You talk, man?" said another. I glimpsed gold teeth, heard gum pop.

I elbowed my way past them, clutching my parcels.

"What you like, man? Blow-job? Hand-job? You like it in the ass?"

I reminded myself these were just kids trying to shock. Their high-pitched laughter sounded like Cory's the time I took him to an Eddie Murphy movie and, to my embarrassment, every other word was a four-letter one.

"Fuck you then. You ain't from this neighborhood. What is it? You a cop?"

I shifted the shopping bags to one arm and shoved the boy who blocked my way. He lost his balance, toppled off the curb. A stream of curses flew at me like darts. I reached Elaine's building and hurled myself through the door.

I didn't mention the encounter on the street, but when Elaine asked me to go back to the store for salad dressing, I pleaded fatigue. While Elaine worked in the kitchen, Cory and I played backgammon on the set I'd bought him. He was a bright boy, quick to learn. I watched him concentrate on his next move, brows furrowing, a small black mole on his left cheek accentuating the pallor of his skin.

The whiteness, the fragility of that skin made me think suddenly of the vermin I'd encountered on my way there. A sudden appalling image: Cory, a few years older, posturing and smirking, eyes bright with dope and menace, thumbs thrust into the pockets of his too-tight jeans, fingers angling down to form a V.

"Cory, does anyone ever bother you?"

He looked up, surprised. "You mean at school?"

"Or here in the neighborhood. You know, older kids."

"You mean like drug pushers? Child molesters? We took a course in that last year in school—'How to Be Street Smart and Safe.'"

"But *do* you feel safe around here?"

I made my move. Too fast, a blunder so obvious Cory had to think I was deliberately throwing the game.

"C'mon, Matthew. You can do better than that."

His move.

"Hey, look, I know this ain't—this isn't Fifth Avenue, and people get mugged here and all. But I can look out for me and Mom." He glanced behind him to make sure Elaine wasn't looking, then dug into his school bag and produced a set of nunchucks.

"Cory, you've got no business—"

But at once I saw in Cory's face the fear that I'd tell his mother. I knew that such a betrayal would mean a sure rupture in the friendship the boy and I were forming. So I nodded, respecting the trust he'd placed in me by protecting his secret.

Later, though, helping Elaine do the dishes, I voiced some general concern. "You really ought to move. It isn't safe to raise a child in this neighborhood."

"Cory's a tough kid. You should have heard what he said to the panhandler who cussed at me the other day. He's a tiger."

"He's only twelve years old, Elaine. He needs protection."

"From what?"

"Christ, Elaine, don't tell me you don't see the kind

of hoodlums that hang out around this neighborhood. Why, just tonight on my way here, there was a gang of toughs who . . ."

But then the implications of what I was about to tell her struck me, and a queasy, seasick feeling roiled liquidly in my guts. What if there was some significance in the fact that the young thugs had chosen me to waylay? What if the street kids had sensed something in me that even I was unaware of?

Elaine was staring at me strangely. "What happened, Matthew? You look sick."

"There was a younger kid, that's all," I quickly lied. "They roughed him up a bit. I put a stop to it."

Later, after Cory was tucked in bed and we'd made love, we lay with only our fingertips touching, letting the sweat dry off our bodies. Elaine's bedroom was stuffy, airless. A ceiling fan turning dissolutely overhead stirred air that seemed the temperature and consistency of tepid porridge.

Elaine stroked my hand. "Cory likes you. You're good with him."

"Cory makes it easy. He's bright and well-behaved. I don't know how I'd be if he were a brat."

Elaine turned on her side, pressed against me. Her skin felt hot and slick. She caressed the damp hair off my face, explored between my legs. A dangerous heat radiated off her. She moved against me, her belly muscles flexing. She was wet when I pushed inside her.

"Matthew? Did you hear me?"

She'd murmured something in her "naughty" voice, her Little Elaine voice, but I hadn't listened.

"Suppose I was a brat—"

9

Her words knifed through the sex-trance.

"—and I'd been bad?"

I tried to get into the spirit of this without losing my concentration, without letting my mind leave its dark, preverbal rapture. "I wouldn't let you watch *Sesame Street*."

"I mean *really* bad."

"Put you up for adoption?"

"Matthew, please." Elaine stopped moving, but her internal muscles were at work, pumping, milking. "Punish me."

"You haven't done anything wrong."

"Pretend."

I wasn't good at fantasy. Whatever the appeal of make-believe, I'd tried to leave it behind in childhood.

"Elaine, I can't get into this."

"Of course you can."

(I *mustn't*.)

"I don't know what you want."

"You do."

(I *do*.)

She gazed up at me, hungry-eyed.

"Hit me," cooed Elaine, all honey and heat.

"Elaine, this scares me. . . ."

My erection was reacting like a Popsicle thrust toward flame. I tried to reconnect with sensuality by caressing Elaine's nipples, kissing her.

Elaine sucked my lower lip between her teeth, bit down. The pain was like an ice pick up the ass, unprecedented, scalding. I tasted blood.

"Christ!"

She lunged at me. I fended her off, pinning her arms above her head, but it felt like she had twice as many joints as an ordinary woman and three times the strength. She broke my grip on her wrists and flailed at me with long acrylic nails.

I knew this was Elaine's idea of a game, but suddenly I felt terrified, like I was battling for my life.

I did what she wanted.

A timid blow at best. Yet a smile of relief and lust and, yes, even childish triumph spread across her features.

God help me, I wanted to hit her again.

Not just hit her, but pound her face until her nose shattered, until her eyes were fleshy slits echoing the larger wound between her legs, her cheekbones like crushed eggshells, and then I'd work her over down below, starting with her penis—

Penis?

Shame flayed me. I muttered "Damn you," got out of bed, and headed for the bathroom.

I knelt beside the toilet, my dinner perilously close to retracing its original route. The hand with which I'd struck Elaine still tingled.

Elaine tapped on the door.

"Matthew? Matthew, listen. You didn't hurt me. Matthew, are you okay? What's wrong?"

But how could I answer her, when I truly wasn't sure? And how could I go to sleep, when I knew what I would dream?

I've left school early, sent home with a sore throat. Dad's car is in the driveway, but he isn't in the kitchen or the den, so I start up the stairs to look for him.

This time Dad doesn't stop me. A cold dread ices my stomach, and I try desperately to wake myself up, but it's as if I'm trapped in the dream, drowning in it, and I have to go on.

On the threshold of my parents' room, I hesitate. I've never intruded here, not even when I was five years old and woke up screaming, convinced the silhouette of the neighbor's cat outside my window was a bloody-fingered corpse, freshly self-exhumed, scratching at me outside the glass.

I give a timid knock before entering, but the room is empty.

Isn't it?

From the bathroom that adjoins their room, I hear sounds. The door's half open, so I peek inside.

And almost blurt out "excuse me," because isn't that what you say when you catch someone on the commode, except the toilet seat Dad's sitting on is down, and Freddy Burton's head is bouncing up-down, down-up on his lap.

Dad looks at me, but doesn't disengage. It's as if the head is growing out of my father's crotch, a gross and bloated cancer complete with jug ears, sprouting from his genitals.

"You bastard!" I shout. "You bastard, I'm going to tell!"

I shut the door and run.

Outside, a light snow's falling. I run until my lungs hitch. Then I walk until I'm able to run some more. It goes like that, until I'm numb in every part of me except my heart, the part that hurts the most and that I cannot deaden.

Anger keeps me going long past the time my lungs and muscles scream to quit. What brings me home at last, though, is something else, that most exhausting of emotions, shame. I feel that I will choke on shame, because, as the anger recedes, what's left stranded on the shore of my soul isn't disgust or rage or revulsion, but something much more terrifying: black envy of the boy my father's used. Envy and, God help me, desire.

Part of me would like to die, to be found frozen in the snow, my corpse mute accusation far worse than any words.

Instead, of course, I opt for warmth over melodrama. I hide out at the mall until it closes, then slink home.

Mom and Dad and RuthAnn are finishing supper. Mom looks up and says, "Thank God! We were about to call the police," but I know that's just to scare me. Then Dad takes me into the den and unbuckles his belt. I know this ritual well, know what's expected. I lower my jeans and briefs, brace myself against Dad's desk. My testicles curl up so tight I can feel them press my kidneys.

"Say it," says my father.

I can't. My throat feels cauterized.

"Say it!"

The belt hisses down, strikes the desk chair.

"What do you want? Say it or I'll make it worse."

The words dribble out of me like tears.

"Hit me."

"So I can hear you!"

"Hit me!"

I have to say it each time, before each stroke, even when I'm crying too hard to get the words out in any coherent form.

After it's over, my father says, "There are things

13

that decent people never speak about, Matthew. And if you ever threaten me again, I'll make it worse for you. Much worse."

And that is all he says about it. Ever.

I knew I shouldn't go back to Elaine's apartment, not with the weight of those memories. But on the phone, she purred and promised enticements so seductive my cock lifted like a charmed snake, while in the background, I could hear Cory urging me to come over so he could beat me again at backgammon.

A humid drizzle was falling, leaving the streets sodden, rain-slicked as I came up out of the subway.

Before I even saw them, I heard their voices. The sharp, mocking chatter of parrots, curse words interspersed with bright, harsh snaps of Spanish. Three of them were huddled under the rain-sagging awning of a fruit stand. Eyes glittery and feral, voices like little shards of glass, snipping at arteries.

"Where're your groceries tonight, man?"

Snickers, hoots.

The skinny one canted a hip. Batting of lashes, slicking of tongue.

"Hey, man, whatchoo want?"

I wanted to bounce their skulls off the sidewalk and watch them splat open like dropped melons. They were evil boys who singled decent people out for prey, who imagined others shared their vile desires.

By the time I reached Elaine's door, I burned with indignation. I would call the police, report the hooligans for prostitution, harassment.

Elaine greeted me wearing a little see-through teddy with cutouts in strategic places. "What's wrong?" she said.

"Those damned boys out on the street. They're hustlers. I'm going to call the police."

"Matthew, calm down. Can't it wait?" She took my hand and kissed the knuckles, the inside of the wrist. Her palms felt hot, as though she'd warmed them over a stove.

"I sent Cory to the store," she said, and she led me toward the bedroom, where we made love with all the fervor of the first time, or maybe Elaine made love and I just fucked, I couldn't tell. I only knew I didn't want to look at her, that every time I closed my eyes I saw the vile faces of the street hustlers.

Elaine clutched at me.

"Hit me, Matthew. I've been bad."

She bucked beneath me. Our bellies slapped together, sang of sex. She moaned, "I can't . . . come . . . if you don't. . . ."

"Then don't come."

"Damn you. Do it."

"No."

I can't. I won't. I *want* to.

Elaine stopped moving. We were suddenly no longer joined. The urgent, hormonal energy that a moment earlier had galvanized my penis simply vanished, and with it went my hard-on.

"Jesus, Matthew, not *again.*"

"So understanding, aren't you?"

"Okay, you've got a problem."

"Yes, I do."

She got out of bed, grabbed her robe. I came around the bed to intercept her.

"Elaine, I don't want to . . ."

hit you

"Maybe you'd better leave."

But I did.

I did what she had wanted all along.

Suddenly she became small and light, almost weightless. My blow was openhanded, but she flew backward, struck the wall, did not slide down, but blinked, astonished, *hurt,* but after the first time, it was easy, fun, like so many evil things, and the next blow spun her in another direction, against another wall.

"Matthew, no. Stop!"

This time she didn't rise so fast. Her mouth was bleeding. I grabbed her by the hair, flung her across the bed.

Straddled her.

Her eyes took on a bright, uncomprehending terror. The next blow made her scream. My fist rose up, as powerful and potent as I wished my cock to be, but I didn't hit her. Something struck my back. Feet thumped me in the kidneys.

"Let her go!"

I tore my hand lose from Cory's grip and caught his wrist as he wielded the nunchucks. They clattered to the floor, and I pinned him. In the pale light, I could see anguish on his young boy's face, the skin so pale, like marble, eyes black and fierce with rage. A lovely face, the pink mouth opening like the sweetest of promises.

Then the room went dark as Elaine grabbed the bedside lamp and swung the plaster base against my head.

Neon pain, Times Square inside my skull. Elaine and Cory fled. I heard the lock turn inside the bathroom door and stumbled toward it.

"Matthew, go away. If you try to break the door

down, I'll scream fire so loud everybody in the building will come running."

"But I . . . it shouldn't end like this. Elaine? Cory. Cory, talk to me."

"Go to hell, motherfucker!"

Elaine shushed the boy. "Don't make him any crazier." Then, to me, "Just go. You've terrorized me and my son enough."

I leaned my head against the door. It felt like I was standing outside that other bathroom door again, the door behind which Freddy Burton knelt at my father's feet, head bouncing up and down, and I wished it had been me. Me. I knew I wasn't supposed to cry, but I couldn't remember why not.

Before I left Elaine's apartment, I found Cory's nunchucks on the floor and took them with me. He was too young to have such a dangerous possession anyway.

Then I went looking.

I didn't have to go far. Two of them were lounging up against the wall of Elaine's building. Passing a bottle back and forth in a bag, stoned and sultry-eyed as heat-struck snakes.

I motioned to the one with the curvaceous white throat and the blank, executioner eyes.

"You still want to party?"

The worst part was he didn't look surprised.

I let him lead me to a room in a squalid walk-up used by hustlers and crack addicts. There were just the three of us tonight, though, me and the boy and Cory's nunchucks.

He wasn't shocked by what I said I wanted him to do. Perhaps he'd played this role before. Perhaps other men had asked such things of him, men who cherished the seductiveness of pain, the cleansing power of suffering.

After I gave him his instructions, he stood behind me, in the shadows, while I braced myself against the wall. But I could sense the bunching of his muscles, the gauging of the force he'd use on that first downward blow. My dick stiffened in remembrance of that place I once thought I'd escaped forever, my childhood.

And the words came like a long-forgotten prayer: "Hit me."

MR. TORSO

Edward Lee

Ol' Lud knew he was givin' 'em purpose by what he was doin'. This was God's work accordin' ta the books he'd read, and Lud believed it might fierce, he did. Yessiree, he thought. That's gettin' it. He gandered cockeyed down at Miss August outa *Hustler*. As purdy a blondie as he'd ever seen. Ooo, yeah. Awright, so sometimes it took awhiles. Sometimes he had trouble gettin' the ol' crane ta rise, but jiminy Christmas, at sixty-one what fella wouldn't, ya know?

What'd these gals be doin' otherwise? Gettin' diseases an' all, smokin' the drugs, gettin' cornholed by fellas. 'Stead Lud was helpin' 'em ta be what The Man Upstairs intended 'em ta be, an' givin' ta those without what they'se wanted fierce. And acorse paid fer. Ya know?

Lud's mitt needed ta jack hisself up a tad longer 'fore he'd be able to get it, so's he stared on at Miss August, one mighty purdy splittail with that velvety lookin' snatch on her an' that dandy pair of rib-melons. Yessir!

But it wasn't that he was no preevert or nothin' by's doin' this everday. He was puttin' some real meanin' in these gals' lives, just like the books said. He was givin' 'em purpose.

Once he was able ta pull hisself a stiffer an' get to it, he wondered what the gal in the August centerfold'd look like without any arms an' legs on her. Problee not too good, he reckoned.

But acorse sometimes God's work weren't purdy.

Tipps was contemplating the tenets of didactic solipsism and its converse ideologies when he disembarked from his county car. Positive teleology? Tipps didn't buy it. It had to be subjectively existential. It has to be, he thought. Any alternative is folly.

County Technical Services looked like scarlet phantoms roving the darkness. Sirchie portable UV lamps glowed eerily purple. The techs wore red polyester utilities so that any accidental fiberfall wouldn't be confused as crime-scene residue by the Hair & Fibers crew back at Evidence Section. But Tipps, in his heather-gray Brooks Brothers suit, already harbored a clear notion that TSD was wasting their time.

The moon shone like a pallid face above the cornfield. Tipps walked toward the ravine, where red and blue lights throbbed. Maybe, by now, these south county guys were getting used to it. A young sergeant rested on one knee with his face in his hands.

"Get up," Tipps ordered. "You're not a creamcake, you're a county police officer. Start acting like it."

The kid stood up and blinked hard.

"Another 64?" Tipps asked.

"Yes, sir. It's another torso thing."

Mr. Torso, Tipps thought. That's what he'd come to think of the perp as. Fifteen sets of limbs dumped on county roads like this over the past three years. And three torsos, all white cauc feems. The perp yanked their teeth and did an acid job on their faces, hands, and feet. Tipps ordered up the new g/p runs on all the parts but thus far to no avail. K-Y Jelly and sperm in the three torsos; the sperm typed A-pos. Big deal, Tipps thought.

"Down there, sir." The cop pointed into the lit ravine. "I'm sorry, I just can't hack it."

This is getting to be a hard county, Tipps told himself, and he descended toward TSD's lights. Techs crawled on hands and knees with flash-hats. Field spots had been erected; they were looking for tire indentations to cast. "Mr. Torso strikes again," Tipps muttered when he glanced further. At the culvert, two more techs were pulling severed arms and legs out of the pipe. Then a figure seemed to drift out of the eerie light. Beck, the TSD field chief.

"So we got another torso job," Tipps said more than asked.

Beck, a woman, had thick glasses and frizzy black hair like a witch's. "Uh-huh," she replied. "Two arms, two legs. And another torso that doesn't match with the limbs. What's that total now? Four torsos?"

"Yeah," Tipps said. The torso lay off to the side, white slack breasts depending into its armpits. The stumps, like the others, looked healed over. The face was an acid scab.

"I'll know more once I get her in the shop, but I'm sure it's just like the others."

The others, Tipps reflected. The previous torsos had

been crudely lobotomized, according to the deputy M.E. A hard pointed instrument thrust up through the left anterior eye socket. Eardrums punctured. Eyes glued shut. Mr. Torso was shutting down their senses. Why? Tipps wondered. "Do another g/p run," he said.

Beck half smiled. "That's been a waste so far, Lieutenant. We're never gonna get a records match on a genetic profile."

"Just do it," Tipps said.

Beck's sarcasm dissolved when she looked again to the ravine. "It's just so macabre. This is the sixteenth set of limbs he's dumped but only the fourth body. What the fuck is he doing with the bodies?"

Tipps saw her point. And what in God's name, he thought, is the purpose behind all this? Tipps felt strangely assured of that. His philosophies itched. He knew there was a purpose.

Ol' Lud's purpose, acorse, was ta get the gals knocked up. Then he'd wait till they dropped their rugrat an' he'd sell it ta folks who couldn't have critters of their own. An' he wasn't profiteerin' neither —he'd use the green ta pay the bills and give the leftover ta charity. Nothin' wrong with that.

Acorse he had ta do the job on the gals first. Seemed only proper an' humane like, to relieve 'em of the mental turmoil. An' he'd cut off their arms an' gams so's they could get by on less viddles and so's he wouldn't hafta worry 'bout 'em gettin' away. Ol' Lud poked their ears 'cos it didn't seem right fer their jiggled brains ta be hearin' things an' gettin' all confused, and same fer gluin' up their eyes. These gals didn't need ta be seein' stuff. And 'cos he felt for 'em he jiggled up their brains a tad just like the way his daddy'd do years ago when some of the cows an' hogs got too feisty. See, all ya do is stick the carvin' awl up under a gal's eye socket till ya hear the bone break, then ya give the awl a quick jiggle. Wouldn't kill 'em, just messed up their brains so's they couldn't think. "'Botomized 'em," daddy called it. Lud didn't need fer the gals ta be thinkin' things an' all. That'd be cruel considerin' they couldn't see or hear nohow, an' couldn't walk no more or pick stuff up. Acorse, he had ta be careful doin' the jiggle. See, a coupla gals kicked on him after awhiles, so's that's why Lud always disinfected the scratch awl now, so's no bad germs'd get up into their noggins. Yessir, Lud felt mighty bad about the four so far that died, but what could he do, ya know?

So he dumped 'em. Yanked out their pearly whites with a track wrench, an' burned up their kissers so's the cops couldn't recanize 'em and maybe figure out how he was nabbin' 'em.

Lud had 'em all rowed up in the basement, twelve of 'em. He'd lay each of 'em in a pig trough with one end cut out so's their lower parts'd kinda hang out over the edge. That ways all Lud had ta do was drop his drawers standin' right there when he gave 'em some peter, and they'se could whizz an' poop without makin' a mess of theirselfs 'cos Lud kept a milk bucket under each trough. He fed the gals three squares daily, good cornmash an' milk an' healthy stews 'cos he wanted nice *strong* critters ta sell. An' the gals could swaller and chew just fine 'cos Lud didn't pull their choppers unless they up an' croaked on him on account he seed on CNN one night 'bout how the coppers could 'denify dead folks by comparin' their teeth with dental records or some such.

Lud's routine was monthly. That's why he had twelve gals, ya know, one fer each month. Fer instance, right now it was August, so's that's why he this very second had his peter in the August gal. He'd give it to her 'least three times a day, ever day fer the whole month. That way it'd stand ta reason she'd be good an' preggered by the time September rolled around. Then acorse he'd start givin' it ta the gal in the September trough. An' when he wasn't dickin' 'em, or gettin' 'em viddles or washin' 'em up, he'd go upstairs an' check out the city paper classified fer folks lookin' fer a critter ta 'dopt. Lot of them folks was rich and they'd pay good scratch with no questions asked rather'n wait a coupla years ta get a critter legal like through the 'doption agencies. An' in his spare time, Lud'd kick back an' read his favorite books 'bout the meanin' of life an' all. He liked those books just fine, he did.

Only problem was the task of gettin' it on with the gals. See, sometimes it took awhiles ta get his peter hard enough ta give 'em a good pokin' on account it was no easy thing fer any fella ta keep a stiffer when the gal was, like, ya know, didn't have no arms or gams. An' worse was the noises they made sometimes whiles Lud was tryin' ta get his nut, kinda mewlin' noises an' another noise like "gaaaaaa-gaaaaaaaa" on account of 'cos Lud had jiggled up their brains. Yessiree, downright unappealin' they was ta look at an' listen to which is why ol' Lud'd put one of the girlie centerfolds on their bellies so's he had somethin' inspirin' ta gander whiles he was givin' 'em some peter.

Lotta times too he'd go limp right in 'em an' pop out, like right now with this red-hair gal in the August trough. "Dag dabbit!" Lud cursed 'cos Lud, see, he never took the Lord's name in vain. Couldn't get a nut out noways like that! So pore Lud stepped back from the trough with his pants around his ankles so's he could jack hisself back up but meantimes the K-Y in the gal's babyhole'd get gummy. See, 'fore Lud got ta dickin' a gal he'd have ta give their box a squirt of the K-Y on account the gals couldn't get wet no more theirself 'cos of the brain-jiggle he gave 'em. But like just was mentioned, see, that K-Y up there'd go gummy sometimes just like right now with this red-hairt gal, so's Lud'd have ta kneel down an' hock a lunger right smackdab on her snatch ta wet her up again, all the whiles he's jackin' his peter. It got right frustratin' sometimes. "Ain't got all blammed day ta be beatin' my peter 'front of a torso!" he hollered aloud. "Jiminy Christmas! Can't keep a good stiffer, can't hardly come no more!" Acorse when such things happened ta cause Lud ta pitch a fit, he'd let hisself calm down an' get ta thinkin'. Shore, it weren't easy sometimes, but this was God's work. He oughta be grateful—lotta fellas his age couldn't get a stiffer at all no more and they'se shore as heck couldn't have out with a nut. The books made it clear ta Lud. It was The Man Upstairs Hisself who'd called on him ta do this deed an' by golly there weren't no way he was gonna fail The Man Upstairs! God's work weren't always easy, weren't supposed ta be.

So Lud gandered down real hard at that girlie centerfold of Miss August, pretendin' it was her in that there trough 'stead of this red-hairt gal with no arms or gams goin' "gaaaaa-gaaaaaa!" an' he was jackin' hisself real hard an' fast eyein' them purdy centerfold hooters and that nice paper cooze an—"

Yeah, lordy!" he celebrated 'cos there his peter went finally gettin' hard again. "Yeah oh yeah! Here she comes, August!" he promised an' just as ol' Lud'd have his nut he stuck his peter back inta that stump-sided red-hairt snatch an' got a good load of his dicksnot right up theres in her baby-makin' parts.

"Gaaaaa! Gaaaaaaaa!" went the gal's droolin' mouth.

"Yer quite welcome, missy," Lud replied.

Next morning Tipps's Guccis took him up to the city-district squadroom where some newbies from south county vice swapped jokes.

"Hey, how's a torso play basketball?"

"How?"

"With difficulty!"

"Hey, guys, you know where a torso sleeps?"

"Where?"

"In a *trunk!*"

The explosion of laughter ceased when Tipps's shadow crossed the squadroom floor. "Next guy I hear telling torso jokes gets transferred to district impound," he remarked, then he moved on to his office.

The sun in the window blinded him. Tipps didn't want the answers most cops wanted—he didn't give a shit. He didn't even care about justice. Justice is only what the actualized self makes it, he reflected. Tipps was obsessed with philosophy. He was forty-one, never married, had no friends. Nobody liked him, and he didn't like anybody, and that was the only aspect of his exterior life that he liked. He hated cops as much as he hated bad guys. He hated niggers, spics, slant-eyes. He hated pedophile rings and church coteries. He hated God and Satan and atheists, faith and disbelief, yuppies and bikers, homos, lezzies, the erotopathic and the celibate. He hated kikes, wops, and Wasps. Especially Wasps because he himself was born a Wasp. He hated everybody and everything, because, somehow, that nihilistic acknowledgment was all that kept him from feeling totally false. He hated falsehood.

He loved truth, and the philosophical calculations thereof. Truth, he believed, could be derived only via the self-assessment of the individual. For instance, there was no global *truth*. There was no political or societal *verity*. Only the truth of the separate individual against the terrascape of the universe. That was why Tipps had become a cop, because, further, it seemed that real truth could only be decrypted through the revelations of *purpose,* and such purpose was more thoroughly bared in the *spiritual* proximity to distress. Being a cop got him closer to the face that was the answer.

Fuck, he mused at his desk. He wanted to know the *purpose* of things, for it was the only way he'd ever discover *his* purpose. That was why the Mr. Torso case fascinated him. If truth can only be defined on an individual stratum via one's conception of universal purpose, then what purpose is this? he asked. Tell me, Mr. Torso.

It had to be unique. It had to be—

Brilliant, he considered. Mr. Torso was making effective efforts to avoid detection, which meant he was not pathological nor bipolar. The m.o. was identical, painstakingly so. Nor was Mr. Torso retrograde schizoaffective, ritualized, or hallucinotic; if he were, the psych unit would've discerned that by now, and so would the Technical Services Division. Mr. Torso,

Tipps thought. What purpose could there be behind the acts of such a man?

Tell me, Mr. Torso.

Tipps had to know.

Lud always 'ranged ta meet 'em out in the boonies, with phony plates on his pickup. Old lots, convenience stores an' the like.

"Oh thank God I can't believe it's true," yammered the blueblood lady when ol' Lud passed her the fresh, new critter. The critter made cute goo-goo sounds, its pudgy little brand-spankin'-new fingers playin' with his new mommy's pearl necklace. She was crying she was so et up with happy. "Richard, give him the money."

Lud scratched his crotch sittin' back there in the backseat of this fancified big lux seedan, one of them 'spensive kraut cars was what he thought. But the gray-hairt guy in the suit gave Lud a bad look. Then, kinda hezzatatin' an' twitchy, this fella asked, "Could you, uh, tell us a little bit about the mother?"

She's a torso, ya dipstick, Lud thought. An' it was my spunk that preggered her up. But what'choo care anyways? I got'cha what ya wanted, ain't I? Jiminy Christmas, these rich folks!

"I mean," the suit said, "you're certain that this arrangement is consensual? I mean, the child wasn't . . . abducted or kidnapped or anything like that, right?"

"No way this critter here's kitnapped, mister, so's you's got nothin' ta worry about." Then Lud felt the fella could use a reminder. "Acorse, no questions asked is what we agreet, weren't it? Like ya said in yer ad, conferdential. Now if yawl gots second thoughts, that's fine too. I'll just take the little critter back and yawl can sign back up at the 'doption agency, acorse if ya don't mind waitin' like five er six years."

"Give him the money, Richard," the lady had out in a tone o' voice like the devil on a bad day. Women shore did have them some wrath now an' again. "Give him the money so we can take our baby home! And I mean right now, Richard, *right now!"*

"Er, yes," mouthed the new papa in the suit. "Yes, of course," and then he passed ol' Lud a envelope full o' hunnert-dollar bills, stuffed like ta the tune of twenty grand. Lud shot the folks a smile. "I just knows in my heart that yawl'll raise yer new critter just fine an' proper. Don't ferget ta teach 'im ta say his prayers ever' night, an' make shore he's raised in the ways of The Man Upstairs now, ya hear?"

"We will," said the suit. "Thank you."

"Thank you thank you!" gushed the new mommy all silly-face happy an' teary-eyed. "You've made us very happy."

"Don't'chall thanks me 'smuch as The Man Upstairs," Lud said an' scooted outa the big lux kraut seedan parked at the Qwik-Stop. 'Cos it's Him that called me ta do this, he thought. After the rich folks left, Lud hisself drove off in his beat-ta-holy-hail pickup, thinkin'. He had work ta do tonight. What with that skinny-ass brownyhead dyin' on him yesterday (Lud figured she musta got some bad germs up in her noggin when he jigged her brain, and that's why she didn't live long) he had ta swipe hisself a new gal an' get her torsoed up 'cos the June trough was empty now. Acorse, 'fore he did that he figured he best git home ta that red-hairt August gal ta lay some afternoon peter on her, get some good spunk up her hole.

After all, Lud had future orders now, and it didn't seem fit ta hafta keep God's work waitin'. An' he also's knew, from his fav-urt books, that The Man Upstairs kept his mitts off the world itself, ever since Eve put her choppers ta that apple, so's there was physerology in play too which was why ol' Lud knew he hadda get his dicksnot up the girl's hole many times a day as he could manage so's she'd be shore ta get preggered up just fine.

Tipps wore the morgue's ghastly fluorescent light like a pallor; he could've passed for a well-dressed corpse himself, here in such company. Jan Beck, the TSD field chief, set a bottle of Snapple Raspberry Iced Tea on a Vision Series II blood-gas analyzer. "Be with you in a minute, sir," she offered, matching source-spectrums to the field indexes. Tipps wondered how she applied her own conceptions of truth to her overall assessment of human purpose. Did she have such an assessment? She histologized brains for a living, autopsied children, and had probably seen more guts than a fish market dumpster. What is your truth? he wondered.

"Your man wears size eleven shoes."

"That's great!" Tipps celebrated.

"Ground was wet last night." Beck chewed the end of a fat camel's-hair brush. "Left good impressions for the field boys." Rather despondently, then, she closed a big red book entitled *Pre-1980 U.S. Automotive Paint Index.* "I checked every source index we got, and it's not here."

"What's not here?" Tipps queried.

"Oh, I forgot to tell you. When he backed up to the ravine last night, his right rear fender scraped the culvert rim. I ran the paint residuum through the mass photospectrometer. It's not stock auto paint, so I can't give you a make and model. All I can tell you is he drives a red vehicle."

Tipps felt delighted. Finally they had a real lead. . . .

Beck continued, sipping her Snapple. "And that g/p run you asked for? Well, you hit pay dirt this time, Lieutenant. We gotta positive match with the state CID records index. Torso Number Four has a name. Susan H. Bilkens."

"Why the hell's she got a genetic-profile record?"

"She's a whore, er, was. Six busts, five city, one county. Pressed charges against her first pimp last year so the city asked her for a g/p material sample. The pimp cut her up a little, they hoped the g/p sample would match blood on the pimp's clothes." Beck let out a humorless chuckle. "Too bad it didn't wash in court, fuckin' judges must be out of their minds. But at least it gave us the girl's name for a rundown."

"Susan H. Bilkens," Tipps repeated. He appraised the naked torso on the stainless steel morgue platform, which came complete with a removable drain trap and motorized height adjustment. The torso's acid-burned face more resembled a mound of excrement, and her y-section had been stitched back up like a macabre zipper. "You said she's a hooker?"

"*Was* a hooker, that's right." Another chuckle. "She's just a dead torso now. Worked the West Street Block, the dope bars, till she shitnamed herself with the pimp thing. For the last year she was turning her tricks at a truck stop up on the Route."

"This is . . . wonderful," Tipps intoned.

"The postmortem gave us more of the same. Teeth

manually extracted shortly after death. Eardrums ruptured, eyes glued shut with cyanoacrilate, aka Wonder Glue. Minor insult across the lateral sulcus in the frontal lobe. He lobotomized her just like the others. Oh, and I was able to match her body with the arms and legs we found in Davidsonville four months ago. You ready for the bombshell?"

Tipps looked at her.

"Tally this up, Lieutenant. Like I said, we found her arms and legs *four months* ago."

"I heard you."

Beck sipped her Snapple. "When she died she was *two months* pregnant."

Two months pregnant, he recited, motoring down Route 154 in his unmarked. It seemed spectacularly . . . hideous. With each revelation, Tipps felt beckoned to unveil Mr. Torso's conception of human truth, and, hence, his empirical purpose.

Mr. Torso, Tipps thought. I'm going to get you, buddy, and I'm going to find out.

Not only was Tipps a conclusionary-didactic nihilist, he was also a proficient investigator. A records check dropped the prostitute's life into his lap: twenty-five years old, Caucasian, brown hair, brown eyes, 5'5", 121 pounds. Tipps wondered how much she weighed *without* her arms and legs. Since she had been run off the red-light block in town, she worked a truck stop near the county line called the Bonfire. Truck stops were the first places banished prostitutes fled to, and there was only one in all of south county.

He parked between two Peterbilt semis at the end of the lot. The little dive of a restaurant glowed beyond, peppered with minute movement in its plate-glass windows. Tipps sang a tune in his mind, with a slight lyrical modification—"Eighteen Wheels and a Dozen Torsos"—scanning the Bonfire with a small pair of Bushnell 7x50's. In the binocular's infinity-shaped field, he could see them in there: unkempt, nutritionally depleted, desperate. Most, he knew, were clinical drug addicts, their only human purpose in the universe being to cater to the axiomatic and primordial male sex drive in exchange for crack money. They fluttered about the restaurant interior, fussing with corpulent truck drivers whose stout arms provided tattoo tapestries. Some of the girls dawdled outside, hidden amongst the gulf of shadows.

Tipps wondered about them, these sex specters. Did they even realize their place in the ethereal universe? Did they ever ponder such considerations as existential verity, psycho-societal atomism, tripartite eudaemonistic thesis? Do they ever wonder what their purpose is? Tipps wondered himself. Do they even have a purpose?

At once, Tipps sat up. The Bushnell's fine German optics easily revealed the dilapidated red pickup truck that pulled into the lot, as well as the long fresh scratch along the right rear fender.

Lud loped outa the Bonfire, wearin' the usual overalls an' size eleven steel toes, totin' a bag of mags. See, the Bonfire up 'fore the register had theirselfs a rack of the girlie mags and a lotta the September issues'd just come out. Lud never quite reckoned why, fer 'nstance, the September mags always come out third week of August, not that he much cared. Next week'd be time ta start gettin' his peter up inta that little blondie with the harelip sittin' all cozy an' limbless in the September trough. She had a nice set of milk wagons on her but a joyhole big enough ta take a hamhock. What'd fellas been stickin' up this gal ta get her so stretched out—their blammed heads?—or was she just born that way? Acorse bein' real big likes that'd make it easier fer her ta drop critters—Jiminy, big as she was she could problee drop a whole kintergarden at once! An' the lips 'round her snatch looked like a bunch of hangin' lunch meat er somethin'. 'Least she didn't make a ruckus like the gal in the August trough who Lud was gettin' a might sick of by now. See, that's why Lud buyed hisself new mags each month, ta open the centerfolds onta their bellies so's he could get his peter up proper an' come. An' on account of the June gal up an' dyin' on him an' his havin' ta dump her last night, Lud needed hisself a new gal ta take her place. These hookers always hanged out at the Bonfire 'cos the truckers was ferever lookin' ta get their peters off in some splittail 'tween their long hauls, and the ways it was set up, that big-tookus lot with all them semi rigs parked alls over, Lud could propersition a gal right quick and have her outa there without no one bein' the wiser.

Walkin' down, though, he sawed all them rubbers layin' on the pavement, like a whole lot of 'em, an' this made Lud right sad. Didn't fellas know nothin' these days? Didn't fellas ever use their brains fer more'n skull-filler? The dicksnot, see, was fer more than just feelin' good whiles it was comin' out'cher peter. It was a 'lixer of life it was. It was a special gift The Man Upstairs gave ta fellas so's they'se could have their peters in gals proper the way He intended an' get ta makin' critters once that good spunk got up there inna gal's baby-makin' parts. Givin' life an' all, that's what the dicksnot were all's about, see? Droppin' new rugrats onta the earth ta carry on with things the way ol' God wanted. An' it was a blammed shame seein' all's this good spunk wasted just fer the sake of havin' a nut. Weren't supposed ta be shot inta some infernal conderm! These little things layin' all over the lot, they was like a slap ta the face of The Man Upstairs in a way of reckonin', a way mankind'd figured on cheatin' the ways things was supposed ta be. Lud had a mind ta collect up all these rubbers each night an' empty 'em like maybe inta a soup bowl er somethin', then git hisself a turkey baster so's he could give each of his gals a good squirt without havin' ta do it hisself. Acorse, that might not be such a hot idea considerin' all the devil-made diseases goin' 'round these days. Just seemed a cryin' shame fellas'd see fit ta wastin' their dicksnot like that, kinda in a way of like puttin' a little bit of God in a bag an' flushin' Him down the crapper or throwin' Him down on some dirty trucker parkin' lot—

"Hey, pops, for twenty bucks I'll suck your cock so hard your balls'll slide out of your peehole."

Lud gandered this little stringbean who'd came outa the shadows. They'se was all mostly rack-skinny like this one an' all had theirselfs lank straight hair on 'em an' mostly little-type hooters 'cept acorse fer his September gal with that big ol' pair of the chest melons. "Well, say there, missy, that sounds like a right fair deal ta me," Lud enthused. "Just foller me yonder to my truck an' we'll have ourselfs a dandy ol' time."

They gots in the pickup an' Lud had his peter out even 'fore she could pussy-pocket that double saw-buck he gave her. Then she opened her yap an' got ta work lickety-split. Lud figured he'd let her suck awhiles, not that he was plannin' ta waste a perfectly good load of his critter-goo on her yap but just ta let her get on it awhiles so's he'd be good'n boned up fer later when he were givin' his August gal her beddy-bye pop. Lud in fact 'preciated it, it made things easier later ta have his stiffer all hot'n bothered by a gal who still had her arms an' gams connected to her, yessir, a right nice change ta be with somethin' other'n a brain-jiggered blabberin' torso with a girlhole full of the K-Y. An' this little stringbean here was just a-smokin' his pole like a regler trooper she was an' kindly givin' his ballbag a good feelup whiles she was goin'. Lordy can this gal suck a peter! Lud exclaimed in thought. A regler machine she is, like ta suck the peterskin right off my bone! Then she stopped sucking a speck an' kinda snotty said, "Hey pops, I been doing this a while. You getting close?"

"Well, try ta be patient, missy. Ol' fella the likes of me sometimes takes awhiles ta get his nut out."

She sucked awhiles more, harder an' faster with that little hand of hers just a-pumpin' away on his sac like it were a full-up milkbag on a cow, an' she was a-slurpin' an' lickin' an' really goin' ta town down there on his meat an' makin' more noise than a coupla thousand-pound Hampshire hogs havin' a row in the mudhole, but then she stops again an' bellyaches, "Come on, pops. Hurry up and come, will ya? I ain't got all night."

"What'choo *got,* missy," Lud kindly corrected, "is yer whole life now ta turn from the errah of yer ways an' starts ta doin' what gals was meant ta do in the eyes of The Man Upstairs, like havin' critters an' perpetcheratin' the species. What I'se talkin' 'bout, missy, is the purpose of the whole ball of wax we calls life," an' just right then lickety-split Lud gave her a thunk fierce on the bean with a empty Carling bottle an' put her little lights right out. He stuffed her down inta the footwell an' droved outa the lot with his peter still out'n stickin' up all high an' mighty from that humdinger of a suck she were givin' him, an' it kinda seemed a shame, ya know, what he'd hafta be doin' ta her shortly.

Way he'd do it, see, is he'd take 'em downstairs an' make 'em swaller a bowl of cornmash full of horse trank, so's they'd be out deep fer a good spell. Then he'd glue up their eyes an' poke their ears an' 'botermize 'em with the scratch awl so's they wouldn't have no sense no more an' not be confused an' all. Then he'd lop off their arms an' gams with his field adze, which were like a big ax only the blade went crossways, and acorse before he'd do that he'd tied off each arm an' gam right close with heavy sisal rope so's the gals wouldn't bleed ta death once he had off with their limbs.

And that's just what Lud did when he gots back ta the house with that little suckjob gal he picked hisself up at the Bonfire. Each time looked a little neater, 'fact by now ol' Lud could have off with a gal's arms an' gams just as neat'n clean as you'd ever want, provided acorse that you'd ever in the first place *want* a livin' torso in yer basement. The stumps'd heal over just fine ina 'bout a coupla weeks, then he'd be all set ta get ta pokin' her. This one here, now that she were buck nekit, had some right nice little hooters on her an' a nice big clump a'hair down theres on her babyhole, an' she even had a real fine little line a hair goin' from her snatch ta her bellybutton which Lud always thought was just as cute as could be. One think he didn't much care fer though was the tattoos—lotta these gals had tattoos on 'em—like this here brownyhead who sported one just over her right tittie, a silly little heart with a knife in it it looked like. Seemed a blammed shame ta Lud that gals'd have so little respect fer their bods ta scar 'em up like that 'cos the ways Lud saw it, 'least accordin' ta the books he'd read, was the body was a temple of The Man Upstairs and ta scar it up with silly tattoos were just the same as like throwin' garbage in a church or spray-paintin' the swear words on the altar an' bustin' up the stain-glass winders with stones an' such. Didn't matter now though fer this stringbean little brownyhead 'cos now she were well on her way ta some real goodlylike meanin' in the scheme of life. Lud'd wait a spell 'fore gettin' her settled down inta the June trough, an' meantimes he bandaged up her stumps so's she weren't t'get no 'nfections. Then he picked up her arms an' gams'n carried 'em upstairs ta put 'em in the truck fer dumpin' a little later after he burned up the hands an' feet with mercuric acid, an' he's walkin up them stairs his size elevens just goin' *clump clump clump* but, see, he stopped in his tracks on the top landin' 'cos first thing he sawed was some fancified fella inna suit waitin' fer him an' this fella had in his mitt a big-tookus gun that he was a-pointin' right smackdab at Lud's face. . . .

"The blammed tarnations!" exclaimed the old man in overalls. He'd stopped cold on the landing, his arms heavy-laden with—

Limbs, Tipps realized. He's carrying severed limbs.

"Don't move." Tipps stared at the wizened man, astonished. He kept a head-shot bead in the adjustable sights of his Glock 17, whose clip was full of 9mm Remington hardball. His brain seemed to tick with arcane calculations. "Now," Tipps said. "Drop the . . . limbs."

The old man frowned, then released his burden. Two arms and two legs thunked to the hardwood floor.

"Sit down in that chair next to the highboy. Keep your hands in your lap. Fuck with me and I blow your goddamn head off."

Wincing, the old man seated himself in an antique cane chair that creaked with his weight. "Ain't no call fer swear words, son, an' no call ta be takin' the Lord's name in vain."

Tipps kept the gun on him. "You're the guy . . . Mr. Torso."

"That what they'se callin' me?" Mr. Torso sputtered. "Blammed silliest-ass name I ever did hear."

But Tipps's thoughts revolved in a kaleidoscope of wonder, triumph, and conceit. *I got him*, he thought. *I got Mr. Torso.*

"You're a blammed copper, ain't'cha?" Lud asked. "How'd ya find me, son? Tells me that."

"I followed you from the truck stop."

Lud could'a smacked hisself right in the head. *I am just done et up with a case of the DUMBASS! Led this poker-kisser copper in the fancified Ward an' Roebuck suit straight to him! Jiminy Christmas I musta passed my brain out my butthole last time I went ta the crapper!*

But, acorse . . .

Lud believed in proverdence. He believed what he

eyeballed in them there books, an' he believed The Man Upstairs shore worked in some strange ways. An' it was proverdence he reckoned that this here copper'd made him sit in the chair right next ta dead mama's old highboy. And Lud knowed full well that in the top drawer was daddy's big ol' Webley revolver. . . .

Tipps's gaze flicked about. It was an untold fantasy: I'm in Mr. Torso's house! "I want to know what you've been doing."

"What'cha mean, son?"

"What do I mean?" Tipps could've laughed. "I want to know why you've dismembered sixteen women over the last three years, that's what I want to know. You're keeping them alive, aren't you?"

Mr. Torso's white hair stuck up in dishevelment, his chin studded with white whiskers. "Keepin' what alive?"

"The girls! The . . . torsos!" Tipps yelled. "My forensic tech told me the torso you dumped last night had died within the last forty-eight hours, you crazy old asshole! We matched her body to a set of limbs you dumped four months ago, and she was *two months pregnant!* You're impregnating them, aren't you? Tell me why, goddamn it!"

Mr. Torso shut his eyes. "Aw, son, would ya *please* stop takin' the Lord's name in vain? Come on, now."

Tipps took a step forward, training the Glock on the old man's 5x zone. But at that precise moment his flicking gaze snagged on a row of books atop the veneered highboy. What the . . . hell? Many of the titles he recognized, many he owned himself. The chief works of history's preeminent philosophical minds. Sartre, Kant, Sophocles, and Hegel. Plato, Heidegger, and Jaspers. Aquinas, Kierkegaard . . .

"You"—Tipps faltered—"read . . . *this?*"

"Acorse," Mr. Torso affirmed. "What just 'cos I wears overalls an' live in the sticks, ya think I'se just some dumb-tookus rube with no hankerin' of the meanin' of life? Lemme tell ya somethin', son. I ain't no sexshool preevert like ya problee think. An' I'se ain't no psykerpath."

"What are you then?" Tipps's question grated like gravel.

Calmly, Mr. Torso went on, "I'se a perveyer of sorts, ya know? A perveyer of objectified human dynamics. Volunteeristic idealism's what they'se call it, son. See, the abserlute will is a irrational force 'less ya apply it ta the mechanistics of causal posertivity as a kinda counter-force ta the evil concreteness of neeherlistic doctrine. What I mean, son, is as inderviduals of the self-same unververse we'se all subject ta the meterphysical-duality scape, an' we'se must realize what we'se are as transcendental units of bein' an' then engage ourselves with objectertive *acts,* son, ta turn the do-dads of our units of bein' into a functional deliverence of subjecterive posertivity in the ways of The Man Upstairs, see? No, I'se ain't no psykerpath. I'se a vassal, er a perpetcherater of the Kierkegaardian fundermentals of human purpose."

Tipps stared as though he'd downed a fifth of Johnny Black in one chug. Holy fucking shit, he thought. Mr. Torso . . . is a teleologic Christian phe-nomenalist!

"It's takin' things inta our own mitts, see? Like with the gals, livin' in a neeherlistic void of spiritual vacuity. I do what I do ta give 'em the transertive *purpose* that they'd never reckon on their own. I's savin' 'em from the clutches of human abserlutism, son, ya know, savin' 'em from wastin' their potential as posertive units of bein'. All they'd be doin' otherwise is gettin' the AIDS an' the herpes, gettin' abortions, smokin' the drugs, an' gettin' theirselfs problee beat up an' kilt. But all forces in the unerverse is cycliclike, ya know, one unit of bein' feeding the other to a abserlute whole. Shore, I sells the critters but only ta folks who can't have none theirselfs no ways. An' the scratch I don't need ta keep good care of the gals I gives ta charity."

Tipps felt stupefied, locked in rigor. His astonishment caused the Glock's front sights to drift. . . .

"It's all purpose, son. Human abserlute *purpose.*"

Purpose, Tipps paused to wonder—

—and in that pause a size eleven steel-toed boot socked up and caught Tipps square in the groin. He went down—the pain was incalculable. Through blurred and spider-cracked vision, he saw Mr. Torso standing now, rooting through the highboy's drawers.

"Daggit! Where's that big-tookus Webley?"

Tipps's gun hand trembled as he extended his arm. He managed to squeeze off a double-tap—*pap! pap!*—and somehow both 9mm bullets hit Mr. Torso between the legs, from behind—

"Holy Jesus Moses ta Pete!" the old man wailed, collapsing and clutching the blood flow at his groin. "Ya blammed neeherlistic copper bastard! Ya done shot me in the *dickbag!*"

Tipps, still shuddering in his own pain, crawled forward to finish the job. He could scarcely breathe. But when he raised his gun—

What the—

—his foe's crabbed hand slapped up and pushed it away, and at the same time a terrifying arc movement fluttered overhead.

Then came a hideous *kaCRACK!*

Tipps's world blanked out like a power failure.

"Bet'cha got yerself a headache like a Old Crow hangover, huh?" A chuckle. Movement. "Yeah, I cracked ya a good one right smackdab on the bean with the butt of my daddy's big-tookus Webley .455. Took ya right out, it did."

When Tipps woke, he felt elevated somehow, drifting. . . .

"Was all fired up ta kill ya but then I gots ta thinkin'."

To the right and left, Tipps saw a long row of what appeared to be open-ended metal troughs on stilts. Twelve troughs in all, each labeled by masking tape with a different consecutive month. Tipps's throat swelled shut. . . .

Each trough contained a torso.

"Say hello ta my gals, copper."

Each lay naked in her trough, the skin lean, white, and sweating in the basement's heat and incandescent glare. Healed-over stumped hips were visible at each trough end. As the line of torsos progressed, Tipps couldn't help but note an increasing state of pregnancy; the later torsos sported bellies so distended they seemed on the verge of rupture, white skin stretched pin-prick tight against the burgeoning inner human freight. Fleshy navel buds turned inside-out. Breasts heavy with mother's milk.

Immediately before him lay a wan torso with matted red hair. The slack face with sealed eyes twitched, the head lolled. "Gaaa!" she said. "Gaaaaa!"

"This here's my August gal," Mr. Torso introduced. He stood at Tipps's side. "Been spunkin' her up daily since the first of the month so's ta git her good'n preggered."

"Gaaa! Gaaaaa!" she repeated.

"A regler chatterbox, ain't she? Blabbers like that on account I's 'botermized her, ya know, jigged up her brain a tad so's she can't worry an' be confused an' such. Don't seem fair fer the gals ta keep their sense, bein' in such a state. S'why I glued up their eyes, too, an' poked their ears. But don't'cha worry none, 'cos all their baby-makin' parts works just fine."

Now Tipps deciphered the drifting sensation. His vision cleared further, and four shuddering glances showed him that he'd been divorced of all four limbs. His torso was suspended in a harness that hung from a hook over the trough. Eleven more such hooks were sunk into the ceiling rafter before each torso.

"Oh, I ain't gonna fiddle with *yer* eyes an' ears," Mr. Torso promised. "Nor's I gonna 'botermize ya either. See, a fella's sexshool responses are all up in his noggin, so's I can't be jiggin' yer brain like I done ta the gals. Can't very well git yerself a stiffer with yer brain all jigged up, now can ya?"

Tipps groaned from deep in his chest. He swayed ever so slightly.

"It's proverdence, son. Okay, shore, ya shot me right smack-dab in the balls, but see, old as I am I was havin' a rough time keepin' the crane up anyways, and sometimes I just couldn't get a nut outa me ta save my life."

"What," came Tipps's desolate, parched whisper, "did you say about providence?"

"This, son. Me, you, the gals here—everything. This is God's work, ya know, an' I figure that's why he sent ya to me, so's you can continya with his work. Keep up the human telerlogic cycle that proverdence ordained fer us. Ya know?"

Tipps's brain reeled. The hanging harness which satcheled his body continued to sway ever so slightly. He saw that his butchered hips were exactly aligned with the redhead's stump-flanked vagina.

"Ain't much point at all ta life if we don't never comes ta realizin' our unerversal purpose. . . ."

Tipps groaned again, swaying. The word, once ever-important to him, was now his haunting, his curse. And somehow, in spite of what had been done to him, and equally in spite of how he would spend the rest of his life, he managed to think: You asked for it, Tipps. And now you got it. Purpose . . .

"An' don't'cha worry none. That's why I'se here, son, ta help ya," said Mr. Torso as he opened the brand-new centerfold and carefully laid it on the redhead's belly.

GIVE IT TO ME, BABY

Sidney Williams

*B*renner noticed Randi Rhine first in the back pages of *Marauder* magazine. He admired her and was already in love with her, in fact, before he ever got to talk to her.

In that first viewing, she was a "New Discovery" girl spread across six pages preceding the ads. He'd been buying the magazine sporadically for almost two years because the girls seemed more human than the glossy college girls in *Playboy* and *Penthouse* without the seediness of the women in some of the nastier magazines.

While *Marauder* girls were pretty, even sexy, they weren't always goddesses. In his fantasies, it wasn't impossible for Brenner to imagine himself in love with them.

In reality, Brenner was too shy for any women, but he allowed himself the dreams about Nickie Gold, Devon Dare, April Showers and Cinnamon Sweet—

not their real names but that didn't matter. Their imaginary smiles and soft whispers of devotion took the edge off his loneliness and need.

He took Viddie in his hand, grasping him with the love choke while looking over at the pictures, the light over the bathroom mirror casting an irritating shine across the glossy pages so that he had to angle his head to get the right view. Viddie could do wonderful things if Brenner had the right beauties before his eyes.

He mumbled to them as the explosion of relief came, sending milky strings coursing down into the bowl. They were his girlfriends, not like the girls at the office or the ones in his apartment complex who thought he was a troll.

Brenner had studied journalism in school, but after trying it as a reporter for a time, he had quickly moved over to a job as a page designer. It kept him away from people, which suited him. He didn't like conflict.

He had lived with just his mother most of his life, and his weight had prevented him from playing much with other children. Avoiding them was avoiding torment.

Sometimes he watched the girls in the office in their short skirts, but he knew they would never care about him. He felt a greater intimacy with the girls he could see, fully see. Firm calves in sheer stockings could not compare with the revelations the *Marauder* girls willingly offered.

The day he found the issue with Randi, he knew she was something different, and he knew it the moment he turned the page and set eyes on her. The other girls in the magazine were repeats, with Cinnamon on the center spread. He'd always liked Cinnamon, but he had grown tired of her.

Randi, however, was a woman of mystery with soft brown curls, and there was something special about her, maybe the look in her brown eyes or the shyness she seemed to exhibit.

Her large breasts were on display in almost all the photos, and her perfectly rounded bottom was also glimpsed, but in many shots she wore black briefs that, while sheer, only offered an outline of her pubic hair.

"Randi wasn't ready to show us anything pink except her nipples," read the copy which accompanied the layout. "Maybe she'll join us again when she's ready to offer more."

Sometimes Brenner had to thumb through the magazine several times before he picked out a candidate, but there was no question about Randi.

Cradling the issue in his arms as if he were carrying her Rhett Butler–style, he swept into his apartment's narrow bathroom and placed Randi gently on the tile beside the sink.

He fumbled with his zipper, rushing to slip Viddie out of hiding, stiff with just the sight of the soft thighs and hard nipples Randi offered along with her smile.

He flipped through the pages with one hand, taking in as much of her as possible as he felt the lava building inside him. He was looking at a scene of her kneeling on her bed letting her breasts dangle toward the camera when the explosion came.

"You're beautiful," he moaned through clenched teeth as he felt the hot rush of fulfillment.

* * *

He had to wait three months before he saw her again, although he diligently stopped by the newsstand near his workplace on each first Tuesday, the day new periodicals arrived.

Settling for repeats of Ms. Dare and Ms. Showers, he dreamed of a new view of Randi and frequently returned to the June issue. While he usually grew tired of photographs, there was something about Randi— chemistry?—that kept her exciting.

She was in the opening pages of the September issue, and there were eight pages. As he made love to the new images, he felt an attachment growing. She was from Texas, according to the material, and she enjoyed tennis and reading.

A quiet girl, he supposed. He wondered if she liked mysteries as much as he did. Since Brenner had little social life, he spent a lot of time reading paperbacks and library books.

He began to build a personality for her in his imagination, began to dream her soul. By the time he was finally able to speak to her, he was in love in a way he had never been before.

It was in the January issue that Randi was given her first center spread, and the first time she revealed all. Photographed at poolside, she was shown splashing in the blue water, her breasts bouncing, and stretched out on a chaise with her skin shining under a coat of beaded water. The large two-page center section showed her stretched out on a diving board, legs splayed wide, vagina on display with little pearls of moisture gleaming in her dark pubic hair.

That was the photo he had waited for because now all of her secrets were in view. It was as if she was now giving herself to him totally, as if the previous appearances had been courtship and finally she was ready to submit to him.

He lay her beside him on the bed, resting the page with her head gently on the pillow as he coaxed Viddie to firmness.

When he had finished and buried his face in the pillow, imagining it was the soft, tanned flesh of her neck, he noticed the note scribbled in the corner of the page, printed to look as if it had been done with a felt-tipped marker.

He had seen it before on layouts of other girls, but he had never cared before. This time he felt elation as he read: "Talk to Randi Live! 1-900-555-6287."

After her abortion, Denise Wayne moved out of her father's house. He had told her never to come back, and her boyfriend had gone away to school promising to write. Her letters to him had generated no response.

She'd never intended to let a high school sweetheart make love to her, let alone plant a baby in her belly, but his promises had seemed sweet, his kisses warm.

She should have known better, she realized—too late, of course—and had to deal with matters on her own. He hadn't been much help when she asked him what to do, so she'd had to make decisions. She'd handled it as well as she could, or tried to.

Her main objective had been to keep her father from kicking her out of the house, but he'd found out anyway because some concerned friend of his had seen her leaving the clinic.

After her expulsion from his household, she worked at a variety of jobs, finding it hard to land anything that paid more than paltry amounts. She quit the job in the all-night convenience store after the other evening clerk was robbed at gunpoint.

A week later she became Randi Rhine.

She didn't pose. She had an appendix scar from third grade and small breasts—not to mention a slightly, just slightly, pudgy waistline—but Marauder Publications needed a voice for Randi, who had just become their star Marauder Mate. Randi's real name was Janie Wilson, and she wasn't reliable for phone conversations because she tended to phase out mentally from time to time. She was too busy taping Marauder videos anyway.

They gave Denise a computer printout with suggested topics, instilled in her the importance of keeping customers talking, and put her in a cubicle with a beige Touch-Tone.

She recalled the experiences with her boyfriend as she read over her suggested dialogue. Nothing in those moments—her only ones—had generated the kind of ecstasy she was expected to describe.

Give it to me, baby, she was supposed to say. The reality she recalled was more like: *Be careful with that damned thing!*

She found many of her customers were as nervous as she was about the conversations. Sometimes they made attempts at small talk first, though some wanted to get right into the *hot stuff* they were paying for.

She didn't try to imagine faces to go with the voices. She knew she'd be inaccurate. They all thought she was this gorgeous, voluptuous woman, after all.

A Randi Rhine poster hung on the wall just in case she needed help in describing the anatomy the callers wanted. She didn't really need it, though. As long as she said "big" and "wet" most of them were happy.

Calls were frequent the first couple of nights. The magazine with the center spread had just hit the stands, and Randi's fans were in a hurry to couple auditory stimulation with visual. It must make it closer to being with a real person for them, she guessed.

She soon found it wasn't that hard to ad-lib and let her breath come in gasps as she muttered: "Give it to me, baby. Let me have it hard. I want to feel it in me!"

Calls tapered some after a few days, although they remained steady. She started bringing paperbacks to read between calls.

The first call from Joey came on a Thursday, and she knew immediately he was special. He was shy, as many of the callers were, but his voice was also soft and gentle.

She put down the dog-eared Perry Mason novel and curled her free hand into the phone cord.

"Is this Miss Rhine?" he asked.

"Yes it is," Denise whispered seductively.

"It's good to talk to you," the man said. "This is Joey Brenner. I've, you know, been a fan for a while, since you were a New Discovery."

"It's always nice to hear from fans. I really get off on thinking of you out there, looking at me naked and everything. I love to get bare-assed, Joey."

"You're very beautiful," he whispered, his voice almost so hushed as to be inaudible. "I thought so the first time I saw you. Your eyes are so warm, and they said you like to read."

"Um-humm," she moaned. "Love to curl up in something silky with a book. Of course, I'd love to feel what you have for me, Joey. Give it to me, baby."

"Yes. I . . . I, I don't know, I've been scared to call you. I saw the number when the new issue came out, but I was afraid."

"Why, Joey?"

"Just afraid."

"It's not hard to talk to me, is it, Joey?" He might hang up if he got too intimidated. Someone would bitch if they found out she only had a minute thirty with a caller, especially on a slow night.

"No, no. I just feel a little embarrassed."

She could identify with that notion. The first few times she'd gone through the process, she'd blushed to a bright scarlet even though she was only speaking on the phone.

"I feel, you know, kind of weird doing this," Joey said.

"It's okay, Joey. Everybody needs affection. Tell me what you want."

"I thought it was nice that you liked to read. I don't get out much, so I read. I've thought you were special from the first time I saw you."

She felt flattered even though it wasn't her likeness he was talking about. The photo was just part of who Randi Rhine was.

"You sound lonely, Joey."

"Yes. Yes, I'm afraid I am."

He told her a little about his job. She only had to whisper to him a time or two to keep him going, but she listened anyway.

Several times he seemed ready to get off the phone,

and she almost encouraged it because she knew he must be costing himself a fortune. Then something would occur to her, and she would respond and keep the conversation going.

They both needed someone to talk to.

This wasn't phone sex at all tonight, she thought. It was conversation. She didn't have to help him get his rocks off. He wasn't looking for someone just to help him achieve orgasm. He was looking for something more.

"Can I call again?" he asked.

"I wish you would," she said honestly. He was refreshing, not the average client. He was intelligent, forced into calling by loneliness.

Besides, it seemed he liked her, not just because he thought she was the girl he lusted after, but because he enjoyed talking to her.

As he hung up, she sighed. If he called again, he might make her job more bearable.

When he hung up, Brenner felt warmer than he had ever felt. Elation threatened to make him explode. He had actually talked with her, not just in his imagination. No, it had been real. It wasn't just friendly talk he exchanged with women in the office. It was pleasant, intimate.

He took out a copy of Randi's center spread and carried it to the bed, slipping his hand down to his crotch, massaging gently. Her words still whispered in his head, and the ejaculation came quickly, offering more pleasure than he'd ever felt as the mental picture of his imaginary lover became more complete.

* * *

Denise found herself looking forward to Joey's calls about two weeks after they began. She realized he must be pouring out a lot of cash, but she didn't calculate what it must be costing him. It was his money, and his conversations broke up the monotony of the evenings. Besides, she didn't have the dirty feeling when she got off the phone with Joey that some callers left behind. Some of the guys made her want to shower after hanging up.

Joey didn't mind if she talked about her anatomy on occasion, but he wanted a girlfriend, someone to feel close to. He rambled about Perry Mason and 87th Precinct books and another book by a guy in Chicago which he'd just bought by mail order.

She talked about the books she'd borrowed from a friend. She'd read enough of them over the endless hours to sound intelligent.

Sometimes she wondered what he looked like. He probably wasn't nice-looking if he had to call phone sex, but he had a pleasant voice.

She didn't have anybody else, so she told him about her father throwing her out. He wondered if that was why she posed nude.

Sometimes she forgot about the charade, but she skirted it as much as possible. So what if he thought she looked different? That didn't matter. It was she, Denise, who provided the conversation that kept him going and occasionally talked him through sex of sorts. They had begun that after appropriate courtship.

After about a month, she decided to give him her home phone number and address. He hadn't been weird in all that time, so she figured it couldn't hurt. It would save him money. And besides, he lived so far away she couldn't imagine it ever presenting a problem.

It meant a little less for her on the commission end of things, but there were other guys she could keep on the line. She'd picked up the knack of dragging things out, building up the minutes with the fans. If she could keep a couple of guys on the phone just a little longer, she could spare a few pennies for Joey.

Joey was a friend, and she needed a friend.

Brenner found himself looking forward to going home at night. There had been a time when his apartment's oppressive loneliness had been dreaded. Now he rushed to get through with his work so he could get home to Randi. He had put her center spread on the wall at the front of his bed to look at her while they talked.

He stroked Viddie now while they were on the phone. It seemed boring to touch the Vid monster without Randi's voice, and the ejaculations that were produced by her picture alone didn't seem to be as explosive any longer.

It had to be love.

Since she had given him her phone number and address, something she had done for none of the other callers, he was able to write her. She felt bad about him spending a fortune on the telephone, even though he promised he didn't mind. He'd hocked his CD player as well as cutting back on a few groceries to help cover last month's bill.

It was good to be able to jot notes to her while he was at work, or type long missives on the evenings he didn't call. He could update her on little things in the letters, saving the time on the phone for more intimate matters.

When she revealed things about her life, he knew they were drawing closer and that they were kindred spirits. He sensed she was falling in love with him, too.

On his bus ride to work, he began to hum the tune "Brandy," substituting Randi's name. It worked with the rhyme scheme, and he told himself that she would make a fine wife just like the character in the song.

At times, Denise wondered if things were getting too serious. Joey called frequently. Sometimes it seemed all she did was talk to him, but he was her friend, maybe even her best friend.

Maybe he was nuts about her, but he had to understand they could never be more than voices on the phone to each other. They lived far apart, and besides, he thought she was a blimp-chested girl with a narrow waist and firm hips.

Maybe it was best to let his fantasy live. He liked to pull his crank to her voice, so what? It was a weird relationship, but it worked. For both of them. Didn't it?

As Joey stood over the new poster of Randi from the latest *Marauder,* his fluids oozing over his fingers, he wondered what it would be like to really make love to her.

She liked him. He wasn't nice-looking, but he had seen beautiful girls with unattractive guys before.

As he felt Viddie begin to shrink, he wondered what it would feel like for dear old Vid to slide inside her, into the glistening folds of her womanhood. Viddie had given him a great deal of pleasure on his own, but what ecstasy there must be in actually entering her, feeling her envelop him and tighten around him.

Was there any reason for them to be apart? He could move to her city, find a job there. He had the skills to work at any newspaper. It was something to consider.

After cleaning up, he sat down at his typewriter and began a new letter. Soon the division of the miles would be bridged.

Denise had never expected to fall in love with anyone, let alone a delivery man.

She had given up on love after her experiences. If what she'd known was love, she didn't want any more. Loneliness with an occasional consolation from Joey was enough. He at least made her feel alive and needed.

Her new boyfriend was different, though, more than just a friend. He showed up at the door one afternoon with a package for the woman across the hall. Since the neighbor was away, Denise had to sign.

She spoke with him only a few moments but found she liked his wry smile and the way it made his mustache curl. She thought about him for a few days, believing she would never see him again, but he turned up again with a package from Joey.

She offered him coffee, which he accepted even though he was in a hurry. They made a date for the weekend, and they decided to keep seeing each other. It happened quickly, but Denise realized his good qualities. He was twenty-five, handsome, polite, the kind of guy who made a good husband.

* * *

When she spoke with Joey, she thought about telling him about the new man in her life but wasn't sure how to go about it. She just kept the conversations casual, hoping she wasn't giving him wrong ideas.

She still enjoyed talking to him, and since he didn't ask about verbal stimulation, she stopped offering it.

She tried not to think about how he probably still pleasured himself over Randi's pictures. A new feature on Randi had been published because calls were picking up at work again, but she felt more and more detached from the persona.

Brenner spent several days composing his letter. He spoke to Denise frequently without mentioning his plans to propose. He wanted her to be surprised.

Finally, he mailed the letter and waited, counting the days required for it to travel through the postal system to her door. He knew how long a letter took to reach her and even the time of day that her mail arrived. He was patient because he knew the day she would find it, and he planned to call her—just after she'd had a chance to open it—so that they could make plans.

When no calls came from Joey over several days, Denise felt a little relief. Maybe he'd become infatuated with another girl. That was just fine.

She missed him in a way, but not to such a degree that she wanted to call him. She didn't want to encourage him again. He might not understand that, but it was the way things had to be.

She was thinking about moving in with her boyfriend, and maybe she could find a new job that didn't require her to whisper risqué suggestions all the time.

When Joey's letter arrived, she almost panicked. She'd denied the possibilities, and now she felt like crying as she read his desperate, poetic proposal.

She was fighting tears when the phone rang.

"I couldn't wait to hear from you," he said. "I thought we could see about—"

"Joey, I thought we were only friends."

"I know, but there's no reason for us to be separated. I can make arrangements. We can be together."

She was silent, and he felt his heartbeats so intensely he could have counted them without finding a pulse point. He bit his lip, his hand so slippery with sweat he found it almost impossible to hold the handset.

"We can't be together the way you think," she whispered softly, her words coming through the receiver with the same beautiful tone as the first night he'd called her.

"I can move. I can get a job up there. That would be good, wouldn't it? Then we could find a little place. You wouldn't have to work the phone line anymore."

"It won't work, Joey."

"No, really, Randi. You need somebody. I understand you. I'd be devoted to you."

"Joey, please . . ."

He felt a burning agony igniting inside him. It was becoming hard to breathe, and he imagined a horrible black gulf opening inside his soul, swallowing a piece of him, creating a void larger than he had ever known.

"Please, we could try it," he pleaded.

"No, Joey. I'm sorry. It can't be that way."

"I can't just let go. I love you. I need you. My life is so empty. I'm so alone."

"You'll be okay, Joey. You're a nice person. You'll

find somebody else, someone right there in your home town."

"I don't want somebody else. I want you. It's you I love. You're so good to me, and you're so beautiful."

"Joey, you don't even know what I look like. Randi Rhine isn't a real person. The pictures are a girl from God knows where. They hired me to be her voice on the phone. I've wanted to tell you, but I didn't want to destroy the illusion for you. Don't you see? I'm not even the person you think I am. I'm not as pretty as she is. I'm not even as well-read as you think I am."

He swallowed hard. His insides were quivering, feeling as if his body was about to come apart. "What do you mean? You've lied?"

"It's just the way the line is set up."

"Oh, God. You're not Randi?"

"I'm the person you've talked to all along. I don't look like Randi. I'm not that beautiful."

The jolt of pain exploded inside him, and he felt hot tears running down his cheeks.

She'd lied. It had all been a lie. Randi wasn't real. He bit his lip, his teeth digging almost deep enough to draw blood as his lungs pumped harder and harder.

Did it matter that she wasn't beautiful? He forced himself under control.

"I don't care," he said finally. "How you look doesn't matter. I wish you hadn't lied to me, but it's you I've gotten to know. It's you I love. I can't imagine what my life would be like without you. I look forward to talking to you. I care about you. Everything else I do is just going through the motions."

"Joey, please. I'm involved with someone. I didn't want to tell you, but he's what I need. I have a chance to start over. I've made mistakes, but I want to give this a shot. I can't be what you need me to be. Please understand."

He wept, slamming his fist against the table beside the phone.

"Joey, listen to me. You'll be okay. I want you to settle down. We'll still be friends."

He muttered a yes into the phone, listening to her soothing tone until he felt able to hang up.

As soon as the receiver clicked down, the finality of it seemed to drop onto him, heavy, almost unbearable. The tears ran down onto his lip and seeped into his mouth, their taste bitter, the smell of them nauseating.

He wanted to stop hurting, wanted to relax. He had to unwind. He found the new *Marauder* and flipped through it. Viddie always managed to make things better, but none of the new girls seemed interesting. He couldn't stop thinking of Randi, and he turned to her new feature. Her beauty seemed to beckon to him still.

Friends?

He wept as he touched Viddie, his only friend, but Viddie wouldn't respond. The emptiness was too much. The familiar hardness did not come, and he kept remembering that Randi was not the girl on the pages, not really.

He felt his breath dragging through his nostrils in a dry rasp. He would never feel the same again. Girls in pictures were just that, pictures, and for just a little while he'd found something different, even if it had been a lie. How did one turn back to the past?

There was no way, just as there was no Randi. He didn't even know what the woman he loved looked like, didn't even know her name, but he knew he could never love anyone else.

Viddie wouldn't respond, not now, not ever.

Give it to me, baby, she had whispered.

Give it to me, baby!

He picked up the plastic-handled scissors from his desk.

Four days later, Denise was surprised when Viddie showed up unexpectedly. She hadn't been expecting a package.

A MOMENT OF ECSTASY

Graham Watkins

A nything!" Ray Pender declared enthusiastically. "Absolutely anything!" He was speaking to the big, bearded man in the tailored suit, but his eyes were turned slightly to the left. Ever since the man and his red-haired wife had sat down with them, Ray had been unable to stop staring at her almost achingly beautiful face.

The big man—who'd introduced himself only as "Karl"—smiled. "I find that hard to believe, Mr. Pender," he said in a cultured and slightly accented voice. "Anything?"

Ray waved his hands. "Oh, absolutely!" he gushed. "Carol and I—well, we've been into swinging for— God, a lot of years. She's really into it; she'll try anything once. Sometimes more than once!" He laughed and turned, for just an instant, to the striking-ly attractive dark-haired woman by his side. "Isn't that right, Carol?"

The look she returned was rather sour. "You might" —she sniffed—"let me speak for myself, Ray," she said, her voice a little cold. She turned her attention to the big man, obviously sizing him up; after a moment she smiled charmingly. "Ray's right, though," she admitted. "I am open-minded." She paused. "Well, as open-minded as anybody can be, in this day and age, with AIDS and all that, you understand—"

Karl leaned back in his chair and sipped his drink. "Of course," he murmured. His smile was broad, and he seemed to be winning over the initially somewhat hesitant Carol with it. "Marina and I," he said, tipping his head slightly toward his own wife, "are of the same bent. There are many appetizers and many entrees on the table of love, and we like to think of ourselves as connoisseurs; but it is so, is it not, that one cannot be called a connoisseur unless one has sampled whatever the table has to offer; don't you agree, Mr. Pender?"

"Please," Ray interrupted. "Call me Ray."

"Ah, yes, of course." He shook his head. "But as a couple we cannot, I fear, claim your experience," he went on. "In fact, this is the first time we've been to a meeting of this—ah, club. But—if I can take what you've said to mean that you are here on a regular basis—I suppose you know that."

You're damn straight I do, Ray told him silently, although outwardly he merely nodded. He and Carol had indeed been regulars at this club for some years, and they certainly knew all the other regulars—quite well, quite intimately. When Karl and Marina had walked in—when he'd gotten his first look at the devastating red-haired woman—he'd practically trampled some of those regulars to establish a first claim on the newcomers. He'd succeeded, but not without having to fight back a number of persistent competitors.

"Well," Ray said, intent on pushing things along as quickly as possible, "let me ask you—are you into open or closed swinging?"

A very slight frown crossed the man's face. "I'm sorry, Mr. Pender—Ray, I mean—I don't know the meaning of the terms."

"Oh. Well, open means all four of us in the same room. Closed means—more like old-fashioned wife-swapping. Separate rooms—or houses, whatever." He hesitated but then decided to push on, make the assumption. "You and Carol, Marina and me."

"We prefer," Carol put in, "open swinging." Again she threw her husband a cold look, and he sighed mentally. It had taken months of persuasion to get her involved in these clubs in the first place, and even now she almost always seemed a little hesitant, a little distant, a little less than enthusiastic—although there were times when she would suddenly behave with what appeared to be a wild passionate abandon; her "act," she called it, claiming that it was something she did purely because she knew Ray liked it. Still, her more typical attitude had, in the past, caused more than one couple to back off or lose interest; Ray desperately didn't want that to happen tonight. He found himself wishing that she'd decide to put on her "act," but past experience had taught him that there was no way for him to provoke one of these episodes; they seemed to occur totally at random.

But even so, Carol seemed to have captured Karl's attention completely. "Ah," he said, his eyes fixed on hers, his gaze unblinking. "Ah, yes. Then that is what we should do, no?" He glanced at Ray. "It should be," he went on, "as this lovely lady wishes. Additionally, the 'open' mode, as I believe you called it, would be our preference as well."

Still staring at Marina, Ray resisted licking his lips. It is going to work out, he told himself, it is; this guy definitely has the hots for Carol—hell, doesn't everybody?—and, while she's showing no signs of going into one of her "acts," she looks almost like he's got her hypnotized or something. I don't have to worry much about her throwing a monkey wrench into things, not this time. "What about you?" he asked Marina, hoping against hope that she wouldn't express any reservations.

"I'm sorry," she said, speaking for the first time since she'd murmured an acknowledgment to an introduction. Her voice was low and sultry, as befitted her appearance. "I don't believe I understood your question, Mr. Pender."

"Oh, please, make it Ray," he begged. He fumbled for a moment, having forgotten exactly what he had been asking her—or rather, how he'd been phrasing it.

"If you were asking," she continued, "if we would be interested in a liaison with you and your wife— then I can answer you. Yes, we would be, Mr.—uh, Ray. If you and your wife would be so inclined."

"Oh, yes," he almost gibbered, an erection already pushing his pants upward. "Oh, yes, we would, we—"

"Ray!" Carol exclaimed. "You might want to check it out with me! That was our rule, remember?"

Grinding his teeth, he turned toward her. "Sorry," he mumbled. "I know I should have, I—"

Reaching across the table, Karl touched Carol's

fingers; she jumped slightly at the contact. "Let me, my dear," he said, his voice as smooth as velvet. "Do you, indeed, have such an interest?"

She returned his expression in kind. "As a matter of fact," she answered with a giggle, "I do." She tossed Ray another look, a look much less friendly than the one she was offering Karl. "Sometimes," she continued, "I think he forgets I'm here."

"A grave error on his part, I'm certain." Again he turned to Ray. "Is there any sort of protocol," he asked, "that requires us to remain here any longer?"

"Uhm, no," Ray told him. "You mean you want to go, uh, now?"

"If that is suitable to you. And to your wife."

Ray looked over at Carol; she shrugged. They both started to rise from the table. Karl and Marina joined them, and together they headed for the door.

"Our apartment," Karl said as they walked into the parking lot, "is not at all far. May I suggest that we go there?"

"Fine by me," Ray agreed. He started toward his and Carol's car. "Should we follow you, or—"

"No," Karl answered. "If it is suitable to you, we will ride with you. We can direct you."

Ray shrugged, unlocked the car, slid behind the wheel. Marina got in alongside him; Karl and Carol climbed in the back. As they pulled out of the parking lot and onto the street, Marina started giving him directions, her statements brief and efficient. She responded little to his attempts to draw her into conversation, and when he reached over to touch her exposed knee, she merely laid her hand atop his. In a way, her reserve, her coolness, made her, if anything, even more attractive to Ray.

In the backseat, though, things were proceeding much more rapidly. Carol, although she still wasn't behaving the way she did when she went into one of her "acts," had responded immediately to Karl's first touch; a mere block from the motel where the swing club meeting was being held, she'd pressed herself against him, sighing with obvious pleasure as he touched first her legs and later her breasts. The next time Ray glanced in the rearview mirror, though, they didn't seem to be doing much of anything; Karl was leaning over toward her, his lips very close to her ear, talking to her. As for Carol, she was staring fixedly into his lap, making Ray wonder—he could not see—if Karl might be exposing himself. Ray watched for a moment, curious, and saw Carol glance at Karl's face and then at Ray's back; her expression then, to Ray, clearly denoted fear. Grinning, Ray shook his head and turned his attention back to his driving and to Marina. Karl had opened his pants, Ray was sure; he was equally sure that the man was built quite a bit larger than Carol had expected, a circumstance that often drew fearful looks and a certain hesitancy from her. Ray wasn't—he never had been—too sympathetic about this. Almost all women—at least, so he'd always heard, so he'd always believed—liked men with large organs; Carol's oft-repeated statement that she was not one of those, that she preferred men closer to average—like Ray himself—wasn't something he really understood, and more, wasn't something he really believed. In any case, he was preoccupied with Marina; whatever problems Karl and Carol had in this area were, as far as he was concerned, something they would have to work out between themselves.

The ride lasted a little longer than Ray had expected, but after a few miles and more than a few turns, Marina directed him into the parking deck of a modern high-rise; Karl, walking with his arm rather tightly around Carol's waist, led them inside. Ray, matching Marina's pace, trailed along a few paces behind. The apartment Karl showed them to was large, the furnishings speaking of money. Tossing his jacket casually on a coatrack, Karl disappeared into the kitchen.

As the big man left the room, Carol moved quickly toward Ray and, grabbing his hand, drew him away from Marina—who remained by the front door, taking her time about hanging up her coat, smoothing it down with her hands. Almost stumbling from the force of her tug, he frowned at her. "What—" he started to ask.

She glanced first at Marina, then at the kitchen; puzzlingly, she looked downright scared. "Whatever happens tonight," she told him, her voice a breathless whisper, "just go along with it, don't ask any questions, just go with it. I can't explain it to you now, but we've got a—"

She didn't finish; she fell silent as Karl returned from the kitchen carrying a silver tray bearing four glasses of white wine. For a moment, Ray continued to watch Carol's face, wondering if this might possibly be a warning that she was going to go into one of her "acts," and at the same time wondering if she was going to go on speaking; she did not, and when she caught his questioning look she shook her head almost imperceptibly.

"I did not ask your preference," Karl said as he held the tray out toward Ray, "and I must apologize for that. But this is quite special; I'm sure it will meet with your approval."

Ray took one, sipped it—it was, as Karl had promised, exceptional—and watched the big man offer Carol one, watched him turn the tray slightly as she reached for it, directing her hand to a different glass, a slightly fuller glass, than the one she'd initially selected. Carol, who was looking at his face, did not seem to notice, and Ray himself, who was once again focusing on Marina, paid little attention.

While the glasses of wine were being consumed, Ray and Karl made small talk; both of the women were almost completely silent. During these conversations Ray asked Karl several questions about his background, but the big man skillfully avoided each and every one. He was about to comment on this when Marina, the first to empty her glass, suddenly stood up.

"We should be more comfortable," she said. She reached for the straps of her dress, pulled them off her shoulders. "Carol, would you join me?" She pushed the dress down, leaving herself clad in bra, panties, and shoes only. "The men will, I'm sure, find it enjoyable. . . ."

Carol seemed to hesitate, but when Karl urged her on, she looked at him closely for a moment before getting to her feet and stripping off her clothes. She was matter-of-fact about it, as usual, although to Ray it seemed she was a bit overexcited, a bit on edge; again, he found himself wondering if she had something out of the ordinary planned for tonight. Marina, on the other hand, did an expert striptease, leading Ray to ask her if she'd been—or was—a professional dancer.

Marina didn't answer, and neither did Karl. "Your wife," the big man murmured, "is very lovely." He scanned her by now almost-nude body up and down, pausing to study her high, pert breasts and again in the vicinity of her trim hips, smooth thighs, and narrow waist. Finally he focused on her face, on her large dark eyes, her black hair, her tiny nose and full mouth. "Most lovely. And you say I have your permission to do anything I wish with her?"

Ray's own gaze was fixed on Marina, who by now was clad only in her high heels. She was a little taller and slimmer than Carol, and, in contrast to Carol's darkness, her skin was very white; her breasts were large but seemed to defy gravity, and her legs were, in proportion to her height, almost unnaturally long. "Sure," Ray answered, though he'd only half heard Karl's question. "Anything, anything at all. She's all yours."

Vaguely, he was aware that Carol was staring at him and chewing her lower lip, and that there was some strange mix of concern, fear, and disappointment in her eyes. That didn't matter to him at the moment; he was certain he could patch up any problems he had with her later. Watching Marina's eyes and seeing what he hoped was rising lust there, he started unbuttoning his shirt.

Marina came to him instantly, knelt in front of him. "Let me, Ray," she said huskily. He dropped his hands to her shoulders, let her do what she wanted. Her skin, as his fingers began to explore it, seemed almost impossibly smooth. She allowed him to do what he wished while she continued to expertly remove his clothes; once he was naked, she pulled him to his feet, barely glancing at his already-rigid erection. "Come on," she urged.

As she started to pull at his hand, he realized that Karl had opened up the couch into a bed; as Marina directed him down onto it and pushed him onto his back, he saw that the big man had also undressed, and that he was seated, with Carol on his lap, in a nearby padded chair. They were twined together, and Carol was kissing him with evident passion as she toyed with his still-flaccid penis—which wasn't, after all, especially large. Ray frowned. Carol didn't usually refuse to kiss the men she was intimate with in these situations, but even at her wildest she was rather halfhearted about it. She seemed far, he told himself, from halfhearted now—although, in spite of her apparent enthusiasm, she appeared somehow a little stiff, a little tense. For an instant he watched her hand and the big man's rising erection, remembering the car, wondering what—if not Karl's size—had prompted her odd reaction.

But then Marina sat down on the bed beside him, and he promptly forgot about Carol and Karl altogether. The red-haired woman smiled softly, sensually; he reached up to caress her breasts and waited for her to reciprocate.

Minutes passed; she did not, she did nothing whatever. Ray stroked her legs, touched her genitals, raised himself up to kiss her rather large nipples, finally pushed a forefinger up inside her vagina. She was very wet, and she didn't refuse him anything, but she remained totally passive, contributing nothing but a smile.

Ray pushed himself up on his elbows. "Lay back here," he said, "with me."

"Not yet," she answered, remaining where she was. She turned her head, looking over at Carol and her husband.

Ray looked, too; Carol was down on her knees on the floor, her head in Karl's lap, and she was licking and sucking his penis in a near-frenzy. For a moment, he watched; but his pleasure in swinging was not derived from watching his wife with other men— although he knew several men like that—and he turned back to Marina, trying again to convince her to lie down. She would not; nor would she so much as touch his now almost aching erection. With increasing frustration he continued to play with her breasts and genitals, even getting a little rough with her, but she didn't even seem to notice. He sat up on the bed, almost attacking her body. Nothing changed; she didn't complain and she didn't resist, but she wouldn't do anything.

"Ray." Karl's pronunciation of his name was some-how commanding; it cut through the frustration he was feeling. Tearing his eyes away from Marina—but leaving his hands where they were—he looked up.

Carol was by now on his lap, facing Ray; Karl's penis was pushed far up inside her. She was leaning back, his hands were cupping her breasts; her eyes were bright, her mouth slightly open, and she was breathing very heavily. Ray frowned for an instant; her manner, her expression, allowed several different interpretations. The one Ray eventually settled on was that she was really enjoying herself, that she was really turned on, really into it—for once. That, he told himself, was fine with him—assuming he could ever get anything going with Marina. He started to look back toward her, but Karl called his name again, more loudly; turning back reluctantly, he finally answered.

"You've said," the bearded man began, "that I could do whatever I wanted with your wife." Even though Carol was moving up and down on him, his voice was even, level. "Was that true, Ray? Was that absolutely true?"

Ray frowned again. "Well, I said she'd do anything," he noted. "She has, hasn't she?" Somewhat belatedly, he remembered what he'd said while the women were undressing. "Yes," he agreed. "Yes, I did say that, didn't I?"

"Yes. Did you mean it?"

"Well—sure." His frown deepened; maybe a little prudence was needed here, he told himself. "What'd you have in mind, Karl?"

Karl smiled as if he'd been waiting for that question. He let go of Carol's breasts, and both his hands went down to the floor alongside the chair, reaching under his piled clothing. When they came out, he was holding an ornate-hilted four-inch dagger in one and a small revolver in the other. "I want," he said softly, "to kill her, Ray. As I experience my orgasm, I want to feel her life rush out." He balanced the two weapons in his hands as if he were a scale, one rising as the other lowered. "I simply can't decide which I prefer to use—this time—"

Struck dumb, Ray stared at the man. Carol, he told himself, could not possibly have heard his words; she had not reacted to this statement at all. All she'd done was to move her hands down to his thighs to facilitate the up-and-down movements of her body.

"W-what?" Ray stammered at last. "You can't be serious!"

"Oh, but I am, I assure you." He peered at Ray closely from around Carol's shoulder. "Surely," he went on, "you do not mean to go back on your word, Mr. Pender. You did say I could do as I wished with her. And you confirmed your statement, just a moment ago."

"I meant within reason!" Ray shouted. He started to get up. "You know that, I didn't mean—"

He stopped speaking; Marina, suddenly no longer passive, had leaned over to cup his genitals in her hands. In disbelief, he looked back at her; she bent over further, and, after licking the tip of his penis for a moment, slipped it into her mouth. Ray groaned; Carol was skilled, and he'd met other women during their swinging days who'd been accomplished at this, but Marina was like no one else. Bolts of sensation, almost overwhelming, flashed from his groin to every part of his body.

"Mr. Pender," Karl said again, commandingly.

Reluctantly, Ray raised his eyes—and realized that, for a few seconds, he'd forgotten all about what had just happened, about the threat to Carol. With effort, he managed to force himself to attend to that situation again. "No," he mumbled. "Of course you can't kill her, I don't care what I said!" He felt as if he should get up and go to her, but he couldn't seem to tear himself away from Marina; he quickly rationalized his inaction by telling himself that he could not reach them in time to stop Karl if he really meant Carol any harm. "Put those away," he muttered, staring fixedly at the gun and knife and struggling to put some authority into his own voice. "If you don't, we'll have to—"

Again he stopped; this time, because Marina had.

He glanced back at her. She had released him, she was sitting up straight as before, and she was looking down at him with what seemed to be regret. "We can't go on," she said, responding to his unasked question. "I'm afraid you'll have to leave now."

"Leave?" he echoed mechanically, even though that was the word he himself had been about to pronounce.

"Yes, leave," Karl agreed, although Carol was continuing to move on him and he'd shown no inclination to push her off. "It doesn't seem to me as if we can proceed any further." As he spoke he brought the knife up, balancing it on its tip on Carol's breast and moving it about occasionally. At the same time he caressed her side with the muzzle of his pistol. Her expression had not changed; her actions did not either. She was either unaware of or ignoring what Karl was doing altogether.

Ray forced a grin. "This is a joke, right?" he said hopefully. "It's a rubber knife, a fake gun? It's a joke?"

The big man leaned close to Carol's ear. "Could I kill you," he asked her, "with a rubber knife, a fake pistol?" She shook her head; her eyes were closed, she was chewing her lip, and her breathing was very ragged. "No? I thought not." He smiled at Ray. "You see, Mr. Pender. I am quite serious about this. Quite serious indeed."

Ray's head was swimming; if Carol was hearing all this, if she was aware of all this, why wasn't she jumping up and running to him screaming? There was something wrong, something very wrong. While he continued to stare in confusion, Marina bent down again and drew his penis back into her mouth. His

77

already disordered thoughts became more scattered than ever.

"Give him your permission," Marina said, releasing him long enough to speak. "Give him your permission or I have to stop. . . ."

Ray moved his gaze between her and the other couple several times. "Carol?" he asked plaintively. "Carol, what's going on?"

Her dark eyes opened about halfway. The knife by then had come to rest on the smooth curve of her right breast, a little above the nipple; the pistol was jammed into her side. "He wants to kill me, Ray," she said in a thick voice. "He wants to see me die. Let him do it, Ray; let him do it, but make him do it with the knife. . . ."

His expression showed even more bewilderment. "I don't understand!" he whined. "You can't be serious!"

"But she is," Karl insisted. "And so am I. Tell me I can do it, Mr. Pender. Tell me you have no objections."

Ray almost pulled away from Marina; almost. He could not, he told himself wildly, be expected to think clearly with her doing that! The worst of it was that he desperately wanted her to continue, and he couldn't doubt that if he said no she would stop, just as she'd said. He tried to force himself to think, tried to order his tumultuous thoughts. Why, he asked himself, does Karl need my permission anyway? If he really wants to kill Carol, I wouldn't be able to stop him, he has to know that. . . . For several more long seconds, he kept moving his eyes between Marina and Carol, not wanting to believe the threat to Carol was real but not willing to take the chance.

"Mr. Pender," Karl said sternly. "You've not given me an answer, Mr. Pender."

"You're all nuts," he said with a brief forced laugh. "C'mon, now, man; I know those things can't be real!" As if trying to convince himself, he repeated the words—which, he realized, also delayed things while he himself drew closer and closer to a climax.

Karl seemed to understand this as well. "I must have your answer, Mr. Pender," he persisted. "Now." While Ray stared at them, he moved the knife around on Carol's breast again, circling her nipple. Finally, he brought it back around until it was again resting at the same point and, apparently without thinking, tightened it up against her skin a little.

Instantly, he relaxed his hand; but Ray almost laughed out loud. Not soon enough, he told the big man silently; not soon enough! As Karl had tightened it he'd seen, very clearly, the blade start to retract into the handle. Relief flooded through Ray like a cool summer breeze; it was a trick, a fake, a stage knife. Belatedly, he remembered what Carol had told him when Karl had gone for the wine; she must have known all about this, well in advance! The whys he did not understand, particularly why Carol—of all people!—would go along with something like this; but that, he told himself, he could determine later— maybe this was one of her "acts," maybe she felt this would turn him on. The point was, there wasn't any real reason for him not to go along with the joke, sick though it might be—especially considering the apparent alternative. "Okay," he said when Marina yet again raised her head. "Okay, sure. A man has to keep his word, right? If that's what you both want, then go right ahead!"

With a sudden new jump of anxiety, he realized that, although he did know the knife was fake, he had no such knowledge about the gun—although he strongly suspected it. Still, it was best, he told himself, not to take any chances—especially after Carol had seen fit to specifically mention the knife. Continuing to play what he saw as his role, he shook a finger at them. "Just one thing," he said firmly. "Use the knife, okay? That's what Carol wants, and we don't want all the noise from a gunshot. . . ."

"Excellent . . ." Karl murmured, drawing out the final syllable while Marina went back down on Ray. Then Karl pushed himself up into Carol hard and at the same time pushed downward with his knife, to all appearances forcing an inch or so of the blade into her breast.

Blood seemed to well up around the steel; it was fake, Ray assured himself, it was coming from the handle, forced out as the blade slid back. Carol, her face convincingly contorted, gasped and went stiff on his lap. Holding her tightly around the waist, the big man pushed harder on the knife; Ray could hear, very distinctly, a sound like tearing cloth as it appeared to move on down, on in. Carol began trembling as fresh blood, very real-looking, streamed down over her body. Her acting, Ray told himself, wasn't perfect; she should've been fighting him, but other than having grabbed rather weakly at his arm, she wasn't. Instead, she looked as if she was in the throes of the most intense orgasm of her life.

Even so, it looked, Ray had to admit, almost perfect—it really did look like Carol was being stabbed. There did seem to be rather a lot of the fake blood, too much to have been stored in the handle alone; Karl must've arranged some other delivery system, he thought. Distracted by Marina—who was by now swinging herself over his hips and guiding his erection up inside herself—Ray fought with himself, trying to enjoy Marina and at the same time trying to find some logic in all this.

He didn't, he couldn't, and for the moment, he quit trying. He pushed up into Marina and began moving his hips vigorously, knowing that he was not going to last long. He did look back at Carol and Karl; the big man had pulled the knife out of her chest—no, allowed the blade to come back out of the handle, Ray reminded himself—and it looked like her blood was literally squirting out. Groaning with his climax, Karl pushed his erection harder into her, lifting her whole body, and at the same time struck her with the knife again, hard and fast, seemingly piercing her abdomen this time. Carol doubled over it as more red liquid flowed. Leaning back and sighing, he took the knife away and let her go; with a soft moan she crumpled forward, sliding off his lap and ending up facedown on the floor. From beneath her chest and belly, pools of bright redness formed and steadily widened, staining the rich carpet. She squirmed, acting as if she was trying to rise but couldn't.

Smiling, Karl knelt beside her and rolled her onto her right side. He told her to move her arm; she obeyed, and he made a show of driving the knife back into her, in her left side, just at the point where the curve of her breast met her body. Yet more blood erupted; she arched her body against his knees, quivered violently for a moment, then slowly relaxed as Karl removed the blade.

At about that point, Ray's own orgasm started to

rise; he pushed upwards, too, up into Marina, lifting her body. She reacted little; she waited until he relaxed, then quickly got off of him. "I'm going to shower," she told Karl, and she walked off toward the bathroom.

"She's sure in a hurry," Ray remarked, watching her go. Looking down at Carol, he grinned and swung his legs off the bed. "You can get up, now, honey," he told her. She didn't move; he went to her, shook her shoulder. "I know it was a fake—"

He fell silent; only then did he realize that her eyes looked totally abnormal. They were open, staring, unblinking; her pupils had enlarged in such a way that the irises were mere slivers around them.

"Carol?" he demanded again, though now his voice shook. With a trembling hand he touched the wound in her side—and his fingertip went right into it.

Real, he told himself dazedly. Real, it had all been real.

With bulging eyes he looked back up at Karl. "She's dead!" he screamed. "Dead! You actually killed her, you son of a bitch!"

"Of course I did," Karl answered mildly. "I told you I was going to, didn't I?" He smiled and pointed the gun he was still holding at Ray. "As I told her, while we were still in your car."

Ray goggled. "You told her? You told her you were going to kill her?"

"Well, to be truly accurate, no." He laughed. "I told her I was going to kill you. I showed her this gun; I showed her the bullets in the cylinder so that she would be certain. It is quite real, Mr. Pender; doubting that could be fatal for you. I told her that if she cried out or tried to warn you I would shoot you, the moment you stopped the car."

"What?"

"Yes . . . and then, I gave her a choice. I told her she could, if she chose, risk her own death instead; I told her I would give her a drug to reduce the fear and the pain. I told her, too, that it would be necessary for her to behave passionately toward me regardless of whatever fears she did feel." He shrugged. "As you saw, she did so; possibly simply in the hope of dissuading me from violence, and, I think you must admit, possibly for other reasons, as well—many women, Mr. Pender, and many men as well, find dangerous situations erotic." Pausing, he shook his head. "I told her that I would ask your permission; I explained it all, Mr. Pender, all. If you had said no, we would merely have asked you to leave. Your wife would have been allowed to leave as well, unharmed, after she and I had finished our love." He laughed. "But—Marina is quite irresistible, isn't she?" He grinned, held up the bloody knife. "Oh, yes, I quite forgot—I also showed her this. As if by accident I pressed it against her leg, so—" He pushed the point against the chair, and the blade slid smoothly back into the handle.

Ray moved his eyes between Carol's corpse and the knife. "Yes . . ." he mumbled, "I saw that too—but how . . ."

Grinning still, Karl held it out. "It's quite ingenious. Quite ingenious but quite simple, too." Showing Ray what he was doing, he pressed a small switch on the handle and stabbed the chair again; this time, the blade stuck firmly, so firmly he had to twist it out.

Ray hung his head. "You tricked her! You tricked

her, and you tricked me! But—but—she told me to tell you it was okay! She—"

"Part of our bargain. If she had not, I would have shot you right then." He laughed. "And remember, she, too, thought the knife was a fake. A good joke on her, yes? By the time she realizes its true nature, it's too late—shock and the drug do the rest—"

Ray felt as if he were melting. "You set all this up? In the car? You didn't have time!"

"Oh, yes. It does not take long, Mr. Pender. It never does."

"Are you saying you've done this before?" he demanded shrilly.

"Absolutely." He counted on his fingers. "Six times —including tonight—the woman has chosen to take the risk and her husband has allowed her to die. Three times the husband has died. Once—only once, Mr. Pender, only once—have they both walked away unharmed."

"You're crazy! Maniacs! Lunatic sadists!"

"We do not," Karl continued smoothly, "regard the term 'sadist' as perjorative. But we prefer to think of ourselves as students of human behavior." Marina, at that point, returned and dressed in silence; once she'd finished, Karl handed her the gun and started toward the bathroom himself.

"You must admit," he added, stopping near the door, "that our little study is interesting. Your wife was willing to risk her life to save you; you, on the other hand, were willing to sacrifice her—or, to be fair, let us say that you were willing to take a chance on her death—merely to complete a brief sex act with Marina." He shook his head again. "It is much the same, is it not, as the case of the man who risks a happy marriage for one night of passion? This, Mr. Pender, is our study." With that he turned away and walked off toward the shower.

"You aren't doing a study!" Ray yelled after him. "There's no study! You tricked both of us, we both thought it was just a game!" Getting no response, he turned to Marina. "You won't get away with it," he snarled. "I'll call the cops, I'll turn you in. . . ."

She smiled. "I'm sure you will, Mr. Pender," she agreed. "But—though you have our descriptions, you do not know our names. You—"

"I know where you live!"

"No, I'm afraid you do not." She waved a hand to encompass the room. "This is not our apartment. In fact, we do not know the people who live here—we only know that they will receive quite a shock when they return from their vacation." She smiled. "It isn't hard," she told him, "to find such places. Isn't hard to get copies of keys. There are all sorts of ways, and Karl is a very clever man."

Somehow, Ray understood that what she was saying was nothing other than the truth. His eyes began to mist over, and he looked back at Carol's lifeless form, and, trying to visualize life without her, in spite of his efforts, he soon discovered that he could not. "Oh, Carol," he began sobbing, "oh, God, I'm sorry . . . Carol . . ."

IMMATERIAL GIRL

Michael Garrett

I'm not ashamed. I need companionship as much as the next guy, and I've done just about anything to get it. Some guys meet their ladies through the personals or dating services, but I snared the perfect woman for me in just about the strangest way imaginable, when I least expected it. Sometimes the darkest nights can turn into the brightest.

I was out alone again, looking for that special breed of woman who won't snub her nose at me. The smoky dance floor of the Tidewater Bar and Grill was almost empty, the beat of the music slower and softer, with more silent intervals after each song that gave social outcasts like me a chance to hear themselves think.

Yeah, I'm not afraid to say it. *Social outcast*. I know what I am, and I'm not necessarily proud of it, but neither do I try to cover it up. Anyway, I sat there in a kind of whiskey daze and cleared my throat as I checked my watch. It was past 1:00 A.M. already and I was high as a kite, still wide awake and praying for a miracle. You see, I'm a night person by nature, mainly due to my graveyard-shift job as a security guard. There's never anyone to talk to at work, and I usually sleep all day, so on my occasional nights off I'll talk to anyone who'll listen. (My work schedule doesn't do much to help my social life.) But there I was, gazing around the bar at the thinning crowd. The ones who'd gotten lucky had long since departed and were probably humping their brains out by now.

But not me. I can't even remember my last one-night stand. To tell you the truth, I've only had two or three, and they were disasters. You'd think I was a sanitation worker or mortician or something the way the ladies think they're too good for me. But I have to admit, I'm not much of a sweet-talker. I haven't had a lot of experience with the opposite sex, and to be totally honest, I guess I gave up a long time ago on ever having an intimate relationship. Women are too damn unreliable. They're with you one minute rubbing up next to you, using you but making it appear as if you're using *them,* and before you know it they're out the door, without a hint that there was anything wrong. I hate that. It's not worth it.

God only knows why I keep trying.

Anyway, I sat at a darkened corner table draining whiskey sours, about to call it a night when up walks this Plain Jane who sits in a chair across the table from me. Doesn't even ask if she can join me—just plants her ass and stares at me. Hell, I was lonely, though, and miserable, too. I was thankful for conversation of any kind.

I watched her light a cigarette and nervously tap her long red fingernails against the dull sticky surface of the table. She seemed uncomfortable, so right off the bat I knew we had something in common. "I'm Lisa," she finally said with a deep smoker's voice. She peered over her shoulder at a row of vacant bar stools nearby and drawled, "Looks like the party's almost over." Wisps of smoke leaked from her lips as she spoke.

I grunted and shook my head. "I'm Larry," I said. She didn't offer her last name, so neither did I.

She rolled her eyes and blew smoke in my direction. I hate it when they do that, too, but I wasn't about to complain. "I know what you're thinking," she said. "I might not be much to look at now, but you just might be in for a surprise. I can give you what you want. I can give you a night you'll never forget."

It was unbelievable! Someone was actually trying to pick *me* up for a change! Plain Jane Lisa leaned over the table, grinned, and boasted, "I can be anybody you want me to be. Anybody at all." Not only was she drunk, but she was having some kind of delusion, too, it seemed. Probably escaped from a nuthouse nearby.

I finished my drink while she fluffed her hair. She was trying awfully hard and certainly didn't need exaggerated claims to get my attention. But, of course, she didn't know that. "Look, you don't have to—"

"Just give me a chance," she interrupted. "What could it hurt? I can see that you're a man who needs companionship."

She was right about that. I needed it bad, worse than she could ever imagine. But what she was saying didn't make any sense. She had a blank expression on her face as she dropped her purse to the floor beside her chair, folded her arms on the table, and bowed her head as if she were saying grace. Then she closed her eyes and wrinkled her forehead. I glanced around the darkened room, embarrassed that someone might think she was praying to save my soul. Then she leaned forward and whispered, "Think about someone you'd like to be with tonight . . . form an image of her in your mind."

"First things first," I said as I reached for my wallet to leave a tip.

"Wait!" she screeched. She must have thought I was ditching her, but that was the furthest thing from my mind. I'd never do that to anyone. I'm not the type to disappear, like so many *women* are. But she was really upset, and loud. Even a couple sitting across the room turned to investigate the commotion, so I sank back into my chair and stared at the floor, keeping my eyes away from the other drinkers nearby.

"Look, you don't have to humiliate me," I hissed, trying to calm her down. And then I realized there was something genuinely different about her. Not necessarily appealing—just *different*.

Her hands shot blindly toward me, but her arms were too short to reach across the table. With her eyes still tightly closed she begged, "Just think about her. Who's your fantasy girl?"

This is ridiculous, I thought. I had no idea what she was trying to prove, but the sexy Madonna video I'd watched on MTV a few hours earlier came flashing back into my brain, reminding me of Madonna's *Sex* book that I'd stood in line almost an hour to buy the first day it hit the bookstores.

I shook my head and laughed to myself. This lady had absolutely nothing in common with Madonna, but she seemed determined to prove a point as she slumped back into her chair and covered her face with her hands in intense concentration. It was embarrassing as hell, and I hoped no one else could see what was going on, though I admit I don't have much of a reputation to protect. I would've tried to stop her again, but I didn't want to risk turning her against me. Having someone to talk to was one thing, but the possibility of a roll in the sack was nothing short of the miracle I'd been praying for. When I looked back at her, she dropped her hands to her lap and I swear I could see a resemblance to Madonna in her face. Man, that's some strong shit I've been guzzling, I thought. Had I lost count of my drinks? But a hazy blue neon-like glow pulsated all around her, and her hair looked different now—shorter, and wet. Her facial features had shifted, and she looked more like Madonna with each passing second. I don't mind telling you, I was hooked. I practically fell back into my chair.

"How did—" I began, but then she cut me off again.

"I can't do it here," she gasped, trying to catch her breath. "Too much distraction. I can't lock her in." She inhaled deeply and opened her eyes. Her real face stared back at me, just as homely as before.

I glared at her in disbelief. Her eyes were bloodshot, and her hand wavered as she lifted a drink to her lips, a few drops even dribbling down her chin. "What kind of gag is this?" I finally asked, so impressed by her performance that I momentarily forgot where I was. "For a second there, you really looked like Madonna. Did you hypnotize me or something?"

She shook her head and stared me down. "I can *be* Madonna," she sneered. "I can be anybody you want me to be." She lit another cigarette and blew a smoke ring in my direction. "But this isn't the right place. It has to be quiet, so I can concentrate. Somewhere that I won't be interrupted."

I surveyed the lounge and wondered if anyone else had seen the transformation, but it was probably too dark. Hell, I wished I hadn't had so many drinks to know for sure that I'd actually seen it myself. Then I shook my head and checked my watch. "Let's get out of here," I said with a falsely confident shrug.

By the time we got to my place, I was more hopeful than I'd been in years. There was actually a female in my apartment who hadn't slipped from my sight somewhere along the way, but the more I anticipated the events to come, the more I began to get nervous about my manhood. I was horny enough to fuck the proverbial duck, but I was afraid I couldn't get it up for her. I'd heard enough complaints about my performance before, long ago when I managed to have sex once or twice between birthdays, and I wasn't ready to be subjected to more of the same. But, believe it or not, I think it was companionship that I craved even more than sex that night. Suddenly my apartment didn't seem so lonely anymore. Anyway, she plopped down on the edge of my bed and lit another cigarette. "Hey, put that out, will you?" I complained. "I don't like anyone smoking in here."

"You're the boss, Larry," she said with a shrug.

I shook my head and stared at her in wonder. Then she stretched out across my bed and struck the pose again. "Think about her one more time," she whispered.

I did—I couldn't help myself. I closed my eyes, and Madonna danced across my mind just like in the video, strutting her ass and mimicking masturbation, practically fucking herself with the microphone. I still thought Plain Jane Lisa's act might be a fake until I opened my eyes and her hair color had changed. Her chest swelled higher with each breath, and her bra strained to hold her expanding breasts. She wiggled on her ass, unbuttoned her blouse, and reached behind her shoulders to loosen the strap; then her face began to change. Slowly her cheekbones started to rise, her lips growing fuller and her eyebrows darkening, just like Madonna's.

I was hard as a rock!

"This is in-fucking-*credible!*" I said. But then the transformation reversed, and within seconds she was Plain Jane Lisa again. "What happened?" I asked.

"You interrupted me," she complained. "I can't concentrate with you mouthin' off at me. You've got to let me finish."

I scratched the five o'clock shadow at my chin and sat next to her, both of us sinking deeper into the mattress. "Let me ask you something," I said. "How are you doing this? Is it an optical illusion, or what?"

She took a deep breath and sighed. "I don't think so," she said. "I'm no rocket scientist or anything, but as near as I can figure it, when I concentrate on an image someone else is seeing in his mind, I somehow tap into the actual person he's thinking about at exactly the same point in time, no matter where she is or what she's doing."

"What does that mean?"

"Well, once I was Michelle Pfeiffer for a guy, and pieces of my hair kept falling out. Near as I could tell, somewhere out in Hollywood the real Michelle

Pfeiffer must have been having her hair styled. It gets really freaky sometimes."

"Yeah, like back at the bar when you started to look like Madonna, your hair was wet. So you think at that exact moment, somewhere the real Madonna was in the shower?"

"Yeah, or taking a swim. Something like that," she said. "Like I told you, it gets real freaky sometimes."

Erotic fantasies controlled my mind. "Could I create my own dream girl in my head and let you turn her into the real thing?"

Lisa smirked at me. I hate it when they do that, too, but again I wasn't about to say anything. "Has to be a real, live, breathing girl," she said.

"So I guess Marilyn Monroe is out, huh?"

She laughed. "You wouldn't believe how often they still want Marilyn. But no, I can only work with live girls. *Human* girls, that is. No animals."

"Hey, I'm not into that kind of shit." I laughed. "But I can think of a couple of *Sports Illustrated* models I'd like to do doggy-style."

"Yeah, but you might be in for a surprise. When I copy these celebrity ladies, their makeup and clothes don't transfer. You'd be surprised how average some of those sex goddesses look without their makeup. Some of them, you wouldn't even recognize."

I nodded but was anxious to get on with it. I mean, as flashy as those supermodels look, I couldn't get Madonna off my mind. I'd been excited beyond belief when I first thought I might have a roll in the hay with Plain Jane Lisa, but the possibility of sticking it to Madonna, right in my own apartment, was almost more than I could stand. She stretched out across the bed and closed her eyes again. "Wait a minute," I said, interrupting her one last time. "After you become Madonna, how long will you stay that way? I mean, are you gonna change back before we're . . . well, *finished?*"

She looked pissed, and I couldn't blame her. It was an obvious put-down, and I felt ashamed for even asking. But what the hell? Now that my greatest fantasy was so close to reality, I didn't want to be in the throes of orgasm and look into the wrong baby blues, if you know what I mean. She stared at me for a few seconds, and I swear I thought she was about to slap the shit out of me. I honestly feared I'd blown it, that she'd head for the door like they've always done before. But instead she just exhaled and stared at me through glassy eyes. "It's possible," she finally said. "I can't control how long I'll stay that way. As near as I can tell, it must be something that the celebrity lady does that pulls me out of it. Maybe she realizes something weird is going on and twitches her nose like Samantha used to do in *Bewitched*—how the hell should I know?"

"Hmmm. So once you're Madonna, you'll stay Madonna until the real Madonna herself does whatever-it-is that breaks the spell?"

"Yeah. Near as I can tell."

I grinned from ear to ear. I could be in the sack with Madonna all night! "What's the longest you've ever stayed changed?" I asked, my curiosity piqued.

She glanced at her watch and grimaced. "Look, I don't have all night." She exhaled and rolled her tongue across her nicotine-stained teeth, then yawned. "Once I was Julia Roberts for almost twelve hours, but I had a terrible headache and could barely walk.

Maybe the real Julia had a hangover or something. Like I said, how the hell should I know? I just *do it,* that's all."

By now I was tired of looking at her—she wasn't exactly easy on the eyes—and I was ready to get the show on the road. She kept checking her watch, so I knew she was in a hurry, too, and I wanted to take advantage of her good nature before she changed her mind. "Look," I finally said, "just lie back and relax. I'll keep quiet this time."

She did the same as before, closing her eyes tightly and wrinkling her forehead in intense concentration. Even though I'd seen a partial changeover earlier, I couldn't believe the shape taking form in my bed. Her entire body was surrounded by the same eerie blue glow while the color faded from her hair as it shrank to a shorter length. Her breasts swelled, and her facial features shifted, reshaping themselves right before my eyes. It was like watching a horror flick's werewolf transformation in reverse, because this girl was a dog to begin with but turned into a sex goddess right before my eyes.

By the time the change was complete, the blue glow had vanished and I was spellbound. I mean, I've had the hots for Madonna since the first time I laid eyes on her in that "Lucky Star" video, and I've seen every one of her nude spreads in the men's magazines. As I jerked the rest of her clothes off, I could have sworn it was the real thing stretched across my bed. Her body was flawless. Her stiff, dark nipples pointed to the ceiling, and her snatch was cleanly shaven, except for a dark vertical patch of pubic hair that streaked toward her navel. Her legs were muscular, like a dancer's. And even her tattoo transferred! It was spooky as hell, but I didn't care. I was about to become a Boy Toy!

I took her in my arms and kissed those luscious lips, then squeezed her tits, just like in my fantasies—the best pair of knockers in the world. I was breathing hard and heavy as I reached down between her legs and sank a finger inside her, about to shoot my load in excitement. The sensation was unbelievable.

But something was wrong.

She might have been Madonna physically, but not in spirit—this lady was dry as a bone. When I crawled on top of her, I actually had a tough time getting inside her. And she was so lifeless, she wasn't into it at all. She just laid there like a self-service sex buffet. When she finally moved, she had no rhythm, and she actually yawned while I was trying to get in. I mean, I got no idea how the real Madonna fucks, you know? But the way she moves when she performs on stage, you've gotta believe she's a tiger in bed, right?

This lady fucked like she was in stirrups during a pelvic exam! It was frustrating to have such a gorgeous babe under me whose mind was a million miles away. Even in my chronically horny state, I was severely disappointed. After fearing that I'd shoot my load before I ever got inside her, I ended up losing my erection. Before I could get it up again, she jerked suddenly, and Madonna disappeared. When she opened her eyes, she was Plain Jane Lisa.

It scared me, no shit. I almost screamed. I was exhausted and still horny as hell, but limp. It was getting close to daylight, and the idea that I'd been trying to hump a circus freak gave me the creeps.

"Hey, wait a minute. Don't bother," I said when she closed her eyes again. "I've had enough." I couldn't believe what I was saying. Me? Turning down *sex?*

This time she stared at me as if she was bored, rather than offended. "Are you sure?" she said. "I mean, it'll cost you the same, whether you come or not."

Cost? *Cost?*

"Hey, hold on," I said. "Who said anything about there being a *charge,* for Christ's sake?"

She shook her head as she sat up and scooted to the edge of the bed, covering her drooping breasts. "What the hell did you expect?" she snapped back at me. "Do you honestly think I go around fucking losers like you for free?"

And with that, I knew that she *was* like all the others. *You just can't trust women.* They'll turn on you when you least expect it. "Hey, there's been a misunderstanding here," I said. "I didn't know you were a hooker. I thought we were friends. I'm not about to pay you one red—"

"Three hundred bucks," she spat at me. I could tell by the way she wiggled into her panties that she was serious, that she actually expected me to pay three hundred dollars.

"Listen, bitch," I screamed. "I wouldn't pay the *real* Madonna three hundred bucks for a lay. Now you can just get your ass out of here and—"

She didn't budge. I stopped talking in mid-sentence as she lit another cigarette, ignoring my earlier request. "The longer you delay, the more you pay," she whispered. "You see, there's this guy who works for me. Name's Earl. He's sort of a bill collector. And he beats the shit out of deadbeats like you that try to cheat me out of a fair-and-square deal. You'll end up paying double and getting your legs broken, too. So I'd advise you to pay up—*now*—and save yourself some pain." She opened her purse and pulled out a worn Polaroid photograph of a guy who looked like he'd shaved with a chain saw. It was like one of those morgue mug shots. "This guy never paid up," she laughed as she shoved the picture in my face. "I don't guess he ever paid anybody else, either, after Earl got through with him."

I wanted to throw her ass out the door, but then I realized she probably wasn't lying. A girl like her couldn't work the streets alone, or else every guy would stiff her, in more ways than one. This Earl was probably for real, and I didn't know what to do. For one thing, I didn't *have* three hundred bucks. But I didn't want to meet Earl, either. "Wait a minute," I finally said. "Let's discuss this."

She yawned again and glanced at her watch. "When money talks, I'm all ears," she said. "If money ain't talking, then I'm walking."

I wanted to strangle her. She'd set me up for the biggest disappointment of my life. She'd given me hope that after years of rejection there might still be a chance that I could enjoy sex and companionship again, at least for one evening. I couldn't stand it. I wanted to squeeze the fuckin' life out of her, but I knew I couldn't do it.

"Five hundred bucks," she said. I could see the fire in her eyes growing brighter.

"But you said three hundred—"

"I told you, the longer you *delay,* the more you pay."

She had obviously been through this dozens of times before. Sexual extortion! Suddenly it seemed more like buying protection from Earl than paying for sex. I wondered why she resorted to such a scam. With her talent, she could be world-famous—the human Xerox machine! The chameleon woman! She could play Vegas, Paris, anywhere she damn well wanted. But I finally figured it wasn't sex, money, or fame that got her off—it was the power she felt from the threat of violence against her unsuspecting johns that turned her on. I tried to reason with her, but the bitch only became more adamant. She hadn't been into the sex, but she was enjoying the hell out of watching me squirm. Her temples flared, then she grabbed the telephone. "Fuck this," she snarled. "I'm callin' Earl."

As if my prayer had been answered a second time, the perfect solution came to mind as I envisioned a fantasy girl of a different kind. Maybe the bitch's shape-shifting talent could actually restore my faith in women. I concentrated on the image of this special lady, someone I didn't know and had never met, but I'd read about her in the newspaper and I knew she was the perfect woman for me. Someone who would always listen. Someone who would never walk out on me. Someone I could always depend on to be around when I needed her. "Look," I said, "when you do this trick of yours, does it have to be a celebrity that you copy? Do you have to know what the girl looks like?"

She exhaled deeply and yawned again. "I already told you. I can be anybody you want me to be." She paused, then hung up the phone.

My mind started clicking. "Then let's compromise," I said. "There's a girl named Sylvia that I'm interested in. If you'll change into Sylvia for me, I'll give you the five hundred bucks and we'll call it a night." I paused to gauge her reaction but didn't have a clue what she might be thinking. "We don't even have to make it—I just want to see how Sylvia looks naked, maybe feel her up a little."

The bitch hesitated, and I was afraid I'd suffer the wrath of Earl after all. I pulled out my checkbook and began to write, knowing she wouldn't balk at accepting a non-cash payment since Earl would guarantee that rubber checks eventually cleared. Hell, I'd up the price if I had to. But at last she gave me that cold, calculating stare of hers and said, "Hell, it's almost morning. All right, let's get it over with."

During a frightening moment of silence I worried what might happen if my scheme failed. Nervous as hell, I sat on the edge of my bed. "Just relax," I said. When she closed her eyes, I envisioned Sylvia as she appeared in the grainy photograph that accompanied the newspaper article. By now Lisa, the sadistic bitch, was beaming with confidence as she sprawled across my bed, her hair in disarray and her tits drooping off the sides of her chest.

She wrinkled her forehead in intense concentration, and I couldn't keep my eyes off her. First, her tits firmed up, then her arms and legs stiffened and shifted into awkward positions. She screamed, but I covered her mouth with my hand, applying pressure to keep her from biting my palm. Her complexion faded, and tiny blemishes bubbled across her cheeks. Her hair flattened against her head, and her face looked weathered, but peaceful. Her lips moaned a near-silent gasp.

I leaned close to her face and watched her pupils dilate. She wasn't the bitch anymore.

She was Sylvia.

My heart pounded; I was tongue-tied. Her haggard

appearance didn't discourage me in the least. I saw through her exterior shell and gazed deep into her soul, to the inner workings of a woman who could be devoted to me, who could be endlessly faithful.

"Please don't be mad at me," I whispered, noting by the rapid batting of her eyelids that she was mentally alert. "I'll take care of you." For a moment I guess I lost it and believed she actually *was* Sylvia. I stroked her oily hair and tucked the bed sheet around her, then prodded her with questions. "What's it like to be paralyzed from the neck down? How did the accident happen?"

She rolled her eyes and twitched her eyebrows. Her continued efforts to scream finally brought me back to reality, reminding me who she really was, and how she had set me up. But I wanted her anyway. I couldn't help myself.

My hand still covered her mouth, but since that was the only part of her body that she could move, she couldn't put up much of a fight. She could only lie there, a dead ringer of the girl in the newspaper. It didn't matter to me if she was Sylvia or Plain Jane Lisa or the Old Maid from the card game I played as a kid. We were together, and *she would never walk out on me,* at least not in her present condition. I taped her mouth shut and kept her drugged for several days in case Earl came searching for her, but fortunately she had never called him after we left the bar, so he didn't know where to look.

As time goes by, she accepts me more and more. She even jokes about plotting ways to escape. Hell, I know she's only kidding. I can drop my keys on her pillow and leave the front door wide open without worrying about a thing, especially since we moved out of town. She calls me a "crazy son of a bitch," but she can't fool me—I know it's just her pet name for me. And at least now I know that when she lies there lifelessly when we make love, it's not necessarily because she doesn't want to reciprocate—it's because she *can't*.

I bought her a wheelchair for Christmas so she can go outdoors occasionally and get some fresh air. Sometimes she'll carry on a decent conversation with me, and once in a while she even laughs when she lets her guard down. She doesn't scream for help in restaurants anymore—she gave up on that tactic after a couple of embarrassing scenes when I explained to onlookers that she's mentally ill and hallucinating. Who would believe that anyone would kidnap a quadriplegic?

It's been months now since we first met, and I often think about that night in the bar when Lisa sat at my table, when my existence was so empty and meaningless. Now I have a whole new outlook on life, and I worry that the real Sylvia might do something to snap her out of the spell. And heaven only knows what might happen to my lady when the real Sylvia dies. I really care about her, and when you love someone, you've got to be concerned. You've got to be committed for better or for worse.

Till death do us part, that's what I always say.

THE LAST CLIENT

Jeff Gelb

Karen McDonnell let him fuck her body while her mind was on other matters entirely. She was relieved to be thinking that he was going to be her last one: the last client. Tonight she was quitting.

She adjusted her rump so she wouldn't get friction burns from the bedsheets as he continued to pound at her. She reflected that the last year hadn't been as bad as she'd expected when her friend Lynn had first described what it was like, working for the escort service.

"Right," Karen had snorted. "Sell my body to some nerd for a hundred bucks? Not a chance."

She'd been eating at a mall fast food restaurant, families all around them. Lynn Mumaw hushed her friend to keep her voice down. "Actually, it's two hundred an hour."

"Yeah, but you said you have to give back $80 to the service."

Lynn shrugged, her long red hair bouncing around her pixie face. "Hey, they pay for the phones and the advertising. And anyway, it's still $120 in your pocket, tax-free. You can do two, three guys a night for a year and have enough to pay for college or whatever."

Karen bit her lip. To escape an abusive father and an uncaring mother, she'd run away from home the day she turned eighteen. So far as she knew, they'd never even called the cops, probably happy to get rid of her so they could spend more time snorting coke with their rich friends.

Karen had come to the West Coast to seek her fortune based on her good looks. She had gotten a few jobs modeling swimwear for some fashion catalogs, but after three months, there was still no agent, no scripts, no regular work. Everywhere she turned there were great-looking women in Southern California. In Buffalo, with her long dark hair, generous breasts, and slim legs, she'd been an outstanding beauty. In Los Angeles, she was no less common than the BMWs she saw on every street.

In another few weeks, her money would run out and she'd have no choice but to return home, her tail between her pretty legs. It was her worst nightmare.

Karen turned her attention back to her friend Lynn, whom she'd met at an Aerosmith concert. Once they'd learned they were both from upstate New York, they'd become fast friends. It wasn't long before Lynn had confided that she made her living as a call girl for an escort service. Soon she'd begun hounding Karen to do the same.

"So . . . what would I have to do?" Karen asked for the tenth time.

"No more and no less than you want. The guys are

easy, and the ones that aren't, you can pretty well vibe from what they say on the phone before you meet them. And hey, you can always walk away at the front door."

Lynn took a bite of a greasy burger.

"They'll give you zits," Karen teased.

Lynn snorted, "Hey, it's not my face the clients are looking at."

"Turn over, honey," Karen heard the client say. Dan Tierney was the name on the driver's license she made him show her when she'd arrived at the Bel Air mansion. Men who gave fake names had something to hide, and that something could be spelled c-o-p. "I want to do you from behind."

"I don't do anal. How about doggie style?"

"Woof woof," he smirked as he lubed the rubber covering his penis with some Vaseline. When she went on her hands and knees, she felt him trying to enter her anus.

"Hey! I said no anal."

He laughed nervously. "Sorry, wrong hole." He slid into her pussy and began grunting as he pumped what little prick he had into her.

Asshole, she thought, as she considered Tierney, a first-time customer she'd gotten through Ilsa Skinner, the service's owner. Lynn had introduced the two after Karen had agreed to at least interview for a job as an "escort." Ilsa Skinner was a former topless dancer, now in her fifties, who'd continued to make her living off flesh—only now it was the flesh of younger, prettier girls who comprised her stable of talent, otherwise known as the Happy Times Escort Service.

Karen remembered how surprisingly detailed the interview had been. Ilsa wanted to know everything about Karen's family (she hated them and was not keeping in touch), her boyfriends (she had none), even who she hung around with (aside from Lynn, no one in particular). Karen supposed it was to make sure she wasn't actually a vice cop looking for a big score.

Skinner hired her on the spot, and Karen quickly found that she was able to shut off her emotions when she was fucking these lonely jerks. Actually, some, she discovered, were fairly attractive; they were just in bad marriages or had given up on the dating scene, preferring to get something tangible for the money they spent on women.

Karen had endured the job and Skinner for the better part of a year, long enough to sock away money to go to a massage therapy school—it was the easiest segue from her current job to a legal one. The money wouldn't be as good, but at least she wouldn't have to worry about AIDS and other sexually transmitted diseases.

And she wouldn't miss Skinner, who had turned out to be a tough boss, a mean bitch who treated the girls like cattle once she'd reeled them in.

Karen had decided to make tonight her last night on the job. She called Ilsa and, after some hesitation, shared the news. Ilsa seemed to take it in stride.

"Hey, the girls come and go," she chortled, pleased at her own joke. "Like your friend Lynn. The bitch took off owing me her last week's earnings."

Karen sighed. Lynn may have owed Ilsa money, but worse, she'd betrayed their own friendship by leaving town without even saying good-bye. For a while Karen had been worried about her, but she finally got a postcard from Lynn in Hawaii, stating that she had eloped with a regular client and was sailing and fucking her way around the world. Secretly, Karen was jealous of her friend's good fortune.

Ilsa said, "Well, if this is really good-bye, let's see who I can give you for a special send-off tonight." She was silent for a few seconds. "Let me think . . . Ah, yes." She laughed. "I've got an easy last one, honey," she'd said. "Nice guy. I'll vouch for him personally."

Karen had gotten to Tierney's address an hour later, driven up a long private driveway, and was surprised despite the Bel Air address by the huge size of the house. As she knocked on the door, she chided herself for not negotiating a higher rate for an hour of her sexual time, especially tonight.

Which reminded her—his hour was nearly up. Karen pushed up against him more aggressively, her rump slapping against his heavy stomach. He responded with a series of ecstatic groans. She'd make him come in a minute and be out in five, done for the night and finished forever.

The work hadn't hurt her yet, but she wanted out while luck was on her side. Besides the health risk, she didn't want to get so used to screwing men for money that she couldn't relate to them in any normal way. Karen still hoped to have a husband and family someday—though she was beginning to wonder if a man existed who was faithful to his wife. She hadn't met one in California, she thought with a smile.

Tierney misinterpreted her look. "You like this, huh? Little bitch . . . Uh . . . oh, my God, I'm coming!" He squealed like a pig, eyes shut tight, mouth wide open, tongue protruding. It was not a pretty sight, Karen thought as she looked back at him.

When he settled down, pulling out of her, she got up and started to reclaim her clothes.

"Wait," he grunted, sounding like he'd just run a mile in a minute. "Let me catch my breath."

Karen shrugged. What could it hurt? He wasn't really so bad, after all. She was just suddenly dying to put this job behind her and get on with her life.

"Let's do it again," he said.

She laughed. "I don't think you're going to be able to do it again, do you?" She tweaked his flabby penis, still sheathed in the rubber, its reservoir tip now full.

"That's for me to know and you to find out," he answered, sounding a bit more gruff than the remark deserved, Karen thought. He turned away, discarded the used rubber in a nearby garbage pail, and turned back to her. She was surprised to find his dick already starting to come back to life.

"Well, I'll be fucked!" she said.

"You sure will, girl."

She shook her head. "Sorry—you're the last client for the night."

"Wait—I'll pay you an extra five hundred. Not your service—you. I know they make you give up some of your earnings. Well, not this time. And they'll never know."

She considered the proposition. He was right, actually. She calculated rapidly—if she got him off quickly, she'd clear over $600 in less than two hours. Not a bad going-out-of-business sale! She nodded. "I think I can live with that."

He clapped his hands in glee. "Great. Just one thing—let's do it in another room. Doing it in the bedroom again would be kind of, you know, boring."

She shrugged. "Whatever. Let me call the service

first—tell them I'm leaving. Otherwise they get nervous." She smiled. "Can't be too safe these days, you know?"

He smiled back at her as she dialed the service's number and spoke a moment to Ilsa, claiming she was leaving and would stop by with the money after she grabbed something to eat. Which was almost true.

Tierney then took her by the hand, leading her through the house, happy as a little boy showing off his bedroom to a baby-sitter. "Let's see. The bathroom?" He shook his head. "The kitchen?" He smiled and snapped his fingers. "Yes! Right on the kitchen table. What a dinner! I'll eat and you'll clean up!" He laughed uproariously at his lame joke while he led her into the brightly lit white marble and Formica room. At its center was a large bleached wooden table.

She started to climb onto it but he stopped her. "Wait—let me." He jumped onto the table and let his legs dangle over the side. She sat in front of him and placed another rubber over his now fully engorged member and started sucking on it. He tilted his head toward the ceiling and gasped in delight, already breathing faster.

He won't last long, she thought as she continued to slurp at him, her tongue moving up and down the side of his dick, licking it like a lollipop. We won't even have to fuck again at this rate.

"Wait," he gasped. "There's something I've always wanted to try." She stopped sucking, looked up at his red face. "Saw it in a movie once." He pointed to a nearby freezer. "Get an ice cube and run it over my balls while you lick me. They say it'll give me the best orgasm of my life."

She shrugged. Whatever made him come faster . . .

She got up and padded over to the large freezer, opened it, and saw the long red hair, curled around the mottled pixie face, wrapped in plastic. Karen gasped, blinked. *Not Lynn—it can't be Lynn.*

She whirled toward Tierney, but he was nowhere in sight. Heart pounding, she ran toward the kitchen entrance but felt her hair being grabbed from behind. Her eyes teared in fear and pain as she stopped and turned around. Tierney was holding a large kitchen knife in one hand while his other hand slowly massaged his dick. He shrugged. "I admit I have some rather—unique—sexual proclivities. But if you'll keep very still, I'll make this fast and relatively painless."

Without even thinking, she kicked him in the balls. He screamed and let go of her hair, and she ran down the hall, crying and screaming simultaneously. If only the neighbors would hear her . . . but she knew they were too secluded for any sound that escaped the house to help her.

The hallway led back to the master bedroom, where she ran into a large closet, hiding behind a rack of identical woolen suits that all smelled of him. She tried to hold her breath to listen for him and to keep him from hearing her, but her heart was pounding so hard she was forced to gasp in some air.

Omigod, omigod, omigod. It was like a mantra playing in her head. This maniac had killed her friend Lynn. And another thought struck Karen: Who had sent her the postcard?

Then Tierney was in the bedroom, and she could see that he had a gun in one hand while the other massaged his crotch. His face was contorted; it reminded her of his look when he was coming. She bit her lip to keep herself from crying and tasted her own blood.

"There's no escape from this room, you bitch," he hissed. "Come out now and I'll make it painless. Hide and you'll beg me to kill you."

Karen's body shook involuntarily. She was too young to die. She had so much to live for. She hadn't even had her first real orgasm, no matter what her clients thought. She held her breath till her body stopped shaking.

Tierney approached the closet door. Karen saw her only chance. She jumped out from behind the rack of clothes, tossing one of the heavy coats at Tierney, obstructing his aim. The gun fired anyway, the shot going wild, hitting a shoe rack behind Karen.

She tried to run around him to the room's doorway. Tierney fired again, another wild shot striking the ceiling. Chips of plaster fell on them both.

Karen tried to dodge Tierney, but the man matched her movements, bringing the gun up again for another shot. Karen ran at Tierney with a wire hanger she'd unraveled in the closet. She thrust its sharp end at Tierney's face. It pierced his cheek, and he fell back with a shriek of pain.

Still holding the hanger, Karen tried to run past him, but he was blocking the doorway, so she turned and ran toward the bathroom. Maybe she could break a window and jump down to the ground. . . .

She heard gunfire and felt a bullet zing past her head before burying itself in a portrait against a nearby wall. There was movement behind her. Tierney was stumbling to his feet, one hand clutching his cheek, the other holding the gun. He fired, and the bullet lodged in the oak bedpost.

How many bullets were left? Karen slammed the bathroom door shut. Tierney shot through the lock, and the door flew open. He ran straight into the startled Karen, and the two fell across each other. The gun skittered across the floor.

Both lay there for a moment, panting like thirsty dogs, until Tierney grabbed Karen's throat and squeezed.

Karen grasped at his hands, tried pulling them away, felt the pressure tightening. She wanted desperately to scream, but only a gurgle escaped her blocked throat. She kicked against Tierney's body, but the man's greater bulk kept her in place. Karen was seeing stars now—all the colors of the rainbow and then some.

Almost unconscious, she remembered the clothes hanger still clutched in her hand. With every ounce of remaining strength, she brought it up against the heaving face above hers, puncturing Tierney's left eye. Karen pushed with all her might and felt something give as the hanger slid deep into his head.

Karen felt the pressure at her throat diminish as Tierney rolled off her. Gasping, Karen stood up, her legs shaking so powerfully she fell back to her knees. She stayed there for a moment to catch her breath, then tried her legs again and found her footing.

Crying hysterically, she dressed and grabbed the phone on an end table by the bed. She knew she couldn't call the police—they'd never believe her story. Instead, she dialed the service's number. She'd have to tell Ilsa everything and have her erase the computer files of the night's calls. Then, if the police checked phone calls made that evening from the

Tierney house, there would be no proof that the service had actually sent anyone to the house.

Ilsa picked up the phone on the second ring. Karen begged her boss for help.

The line was silent for a moment. Finally, Karen screamed, "Are you there?" and Ilsa barked, "I'll be right over. Don't do anything."

Forty-five minutes later, Karen spotted Ilsa's BMW making its way up the driveway, its lights out. Karen ran to the car door as Ilsa got out. Crying, Karen hugged the woman, who hissed, "Not here. Inside." She pushed Karen back into the house and shut the door.

"Where is he?" she asked authoritatively. Karen, relieved to have Ilsa's help, nearly dragged her down the hall toward the bloodied bedroom scene. When they reached the room, Ilsa stopped and took it all in, gasping involuntarily.

Karen felt her self-control slipping away, tears rolling down her cheeks as she recounted the entire story. Ilsa did not interrupt, merely nodding occasionally. Finally, Karen stopped talking and wiped at her face. "Do you have a tissue? My makeup . . ."

"In my purse," Ilsa muttered as she reached into a leather shoulder bag. "You know, he was my best client."

"Wh . . . what? What did you say?"

Ilsa opened her purse and pulled out a snub-nosed revolver, carefully pointing the gun at Karen's head.

"Tierney," she said. "Oh, I know what he did with the girls. A real sicko. When I first met him, I didn't want to help him. But money talks, and lord, did he pay well. Enough to help me save enough money to get out of this shitty business. So I hand-picked his clients—girls like you with no friends, no family. Perfect pickings for the sick fuck."

Karen could barely concentrate on Ilsa's words; her head spun, and she felt like she was going to vomit.

Ilsa sighed. "I guess it's time to get out of this business while I still can."

Karen backed down the hallway. "I . . . I won't talk. I promise. I want out, too. This was my last client, remember?"

Ilsa just laughed. "Save the sob story for St. Peter, honey." She stopped, blinked. "I guess Dan was my last client, too.

"Oh—anyone you want me to send a postcard to?" And then she pulled the trigger.

REINCARNAL

Max Allan Collins

*W*hy tonight, of all nights, did she have to get her period?

Patsy Ann, in the claustrophobic restroom stall, her petticoats a nightmarish barrier, was doing her best to rid herself of one bloody tampon and insert a fresh one without getting blood on her white prom dress.

She would simply *die* if that happened! She'd saved so long, and worked so hard at the drive-in, to afford the daringly low-cut gown. Was it God's idea of a joke to have her period come a whole week early—on the night of the senior prom? To give her awful cramps and a heavy flow and make her miserable on this night, of all nights?

The night she and Jimmy were finally to go "all the way" . . .

She'd been nervous all evening, from when Jimmy picked her up in his candy-apple-red '56 Chevy, to the dance in the gym itself, with the ancient Glenn

Miller—style big band the parents had foisted on them. Even on the ferry ride to Coronado, she trembled, and not because of the breeze. The couple had stood at the rail looking at the lights of San Diego, the moon full and white, like a big peppermint Necco wafer.

"Here, baby doll," Jimmy said, slipping his white coat with its red carnation around her shoulders. Tall, with a blond pompadour, long-lashed baby blues, and an overbite that Patsy Ann just loved, Jimmy was cute in a gawky way. She didn't even mind his Clearasil-caked cheeks.

"Thanks, honey bun," she said.

How could she break it to him that the *curse* was upon her? He was being so thoughtful—taking her to see her favorite singer at his late show at the Hotel Coronado, that gothic mansion of a fancy resort hotel Patsy Ann had only seen from the outside before.

Now, as she stepped from the hotel ladies' room to rejoin Jimmy at their table, she heard the M.C. introducing the star.

"*. . . Mr. Bobby Darin!*"

The applause ringing in the room, and her ears, she clapped, too, as she moved to the table, and she was happy, forgetting for a moment the disaster between her legs. Jimmy squeezed her hand and smiled at her as Bobby was singing "Hello Young Lovers." Funny—this was a Big Band sound, too, but somehow it seemed so right, so cool, not at all ancient.

What a thrill to see Bobby in person—to see the face on all those pictures she plastered on her bedroom walls come to life before her very eyes. The only disappointment was the singer's refusal to do his biggest hit, "Mack the Knife."

"You're too kind," he said, a thin figure in a black tux with a roundish face, tie loosened, hand casually caressing the microphone, "but considering the current state of local affairs, performing that number would be in bad taste. Here's a new one I hope you'll like even better. . . ."

She thought he was doing "Mack the Knife" after all, but instead it turned out to be a hip version of the old standard "Clementine" with funny new lyrics.

Patsy Ann could understand why Bobby declined singing his trademark tune. Just a week before, the fourth couple in a brutal series of lover's lane murders had been discovered, parked on a San Diego side street, slashed repeatedly; notes sent to the local papers, signed by "Mack the Knife," taking credit for the slayings, had found their way into the headlines, and into popular usage around San Diego—"look out old Mackie is back" was the equivalent around school for "Boo!", if some smart aleck wanted to get you going. Thinking about it, Patsy Ann began to smile . . . *the perfect excuse* . . .

Hand in hand, as they walked to the parking lot, she said, "I *know* I promised . . . but I'm scared."

"Scared? Your Jimmy's right here to protect you."

"Tell that to those four couples that got killed!"

They were at the car. Jimmy opened the door for her.

"Baby doll, all those couples were *old* folks—in their twenties or thirties!"

She got in. "Maybe. But even so . . ."

"And ol' Mack the Knife may be back in town, but he's never been on Coronado Island, has he?"

"Well . . ."

He shut the door.

Soon they were parked at the beach, looking out at the moon reflecting on the water.

"Jimmy . . . we're just going to have to wait a while before we . . . do it."

"Wait! I've been waiting all semester!"

"Well, you're just going to have to wait a little longer. My *friend* is here."

"Your . . . aw. Aw, shit!"

"Jimmy! It'll just be a week or so. Then . . ."

His look of disappointment melted into a smile. He stroked her cheek. "You're worth waitin' a lifetime for, baby doll."

"Jimmy . . ."

"It's just . . . prom night's so special. It's a night for memories."

She loved him so. Impulsively, she kissed him, deeply—thrusting her tongue into his mouth. He kissed her back with urgency, and their tongues dueled, the kiss a heated mixture of pleasure and desperation.

Reaching over delicately, she undid his pants and, with a boldness that shocked both of them, she found his erect penis—so hot, so thick—and caressed it with her hand.

She had never done this before. One of her girlfriends had told her about it, and her reaction had been horror, till her girlfriend explained it was fun, as long as you didn't let the guy "spurt" too soon, and besides, guys liked it even more than the *real* way.

So she kissed him, it, tentatively, kissed the tip, then opened her mouth and slipped her lips over it, suckling, then taking more of it in.

She heard, but didn't see, the car door behind Jimmy open, and he was still in her mouth when her eyes were harshly filled with the glare of the dome light. Patsy Ann reared back, her hand still on Jimmy, and the long gleaming butcher knife swung past her and into Jimmy, just above where he was rising out from her tender hand, and then Jimmy was spurting, but not in the way her girlfriend had warned her about. . . .

The screaming in her ears was hers, and Jimmy's, and she looked up past Jimmy's pain-distorted features to see a face she would never forget—a thin face with one blue eye and one brown eye and a smile so wide it seemed wider than the thin face should be capable of, and sadder than any smile should be.

Then the butcher knife flashed, like a lightning bolt of cold steel, blood splashing, and she was floating like Supergirl, over the car, looking down at it, down through it, with Supergirl's x-ray vision, and seeing the blond-haired husk in a white, blood-spattered prom dress, a husk that used to be her as the thin-faced man flailed with the knife in the moonlight, then slipped his hand up under her prom dress as, high above, she floated away, looking skyward.

"What did I *say?*" Nora Chaney asked.

The lanky brunette, dressed in beatnik black that bespoke some other era, lay sprawled on the couch in her loft apartment. Scattered around the apartment, amidst her fifties deco furnishings culled from second-hand shops, were half a dozen guests, all of whom looked ashen.

Bearded, bespectacled Will Wyman sat in a chair beside her, looming over her, his cowlike eyes filled with concern. The heavyset psychology professor wasn't easily shaken, but he looked that way, now.

"Are you all right?" Will asked.

Nora sat up; she touched her forehead. "Tell you the truth . . . I'm not sure."

"You *should* feel fine. I gave you a post-hypnotic command . . . you shouldn't remember a thing. . . ."

"I don't, Will." She shook her head. "But the memory of it is tugging at me. . . . I know I've gone through something disturbing. It's . . . clinging to me, like a . . . taste in my mouth, from a meal I can't quite remember eating."

Mary, the heavyset lesbian who ran the bookstore downstairs, brought Nora a beer, which Nora took eagerly.

Over the last several weeks, on their regular Friday night get-together, the little group had been eagerly going along with their old psychology prof Will's hypnosis party games. Nora had proven to be the best subject among the group, and just last week she had been stretched out like a board while two-hundred-pound Ted sat on her stomach; had several pins stuck in her arm, painlessly; and responded to a post-hypnotic suggestion in which she placed two bananas in her purse while preparing to leave the party, which *really* brought the house down.

This week she had agreed to let Will regress her to what might have been a previous life.

"No one really knows," Will had said, "whether hypnotic regressions are merely the subconscious playing games, or evidence of reincarnation, or perhaps something else—maybe tapping into the psyche of some ghost who's just passing through . . . but it can be damn interesting, whatever the hell it is."

Now it was time to find out just how "damn interesting" she had been tonight.

"Play the tape," she said.

The party guests looked at one another, as if sharing some awful secret.

"I won't be left out of the fun, when I *was* the fun," Nora said stubbornly, and she went to the cassette recorder, hit "rewind" and then "play," and stood, listening to her own voice, as she identified herself as "Patsy Ann."

The place was quiet as a church as she—and her friends—listened to the bloody tale of Patsy Ann and Jimmy's ill-fated prom night.

She clicked the machine off, glancing at her long-faced guests; even Wyman looked as if his cat had died.

"You guys aren't *buying* this?" she asked, laughing.

Wyman, still seated near the couch, shrugged. "Who's to say you *aren't* the reincarnation of this poor girl?"

"Oh, please!" Nora got herself another beer from the fridge. "If anything, this fairy tale is proof *against* reincarnation. It's obviously my subconscious having a field day!"

Mary was squinting in thought. "You've always had a thing about the fifties," she said, gesturing to a boomerang-shaped coffee table.

Rodney, the rail-thin eternal hippie art dealer, said, "And I guess we all know Bobby Darin is your favorite singer. You've forced his records on us long enough."

"He's been my fave since I was a little kid," she said, nodding.

Wyman stood. "But when you were a child, it was *after* that particular pop idol's period of popularity. Perhaps you were attracted to his music because—"

"Because in another life I cut his pictures out of fan

magazines?" Nora flopped back on the couch. "Please. The Hotel Coronado—isn't that in some famous movie?"

"'Some Like It Hot,'" Mary admitted.

Nora nodded, vindicated. "And as for this 'Jason Goes to the Prom' yarn that I spun . . . we *all* know where *that* comes from."

The local media was understandably obsessed, currently, with a series of similar murders, dubbed by the *Sun-Times* the "Chicago Ripper Murders," and both the papers and TV had likened this serial killer to the "Mack the Knife" slayer who had hit San Diego back in the fifties.

"It's obvious that some part of my brain," Nora said, "assembled these and other elements, forming this *American Graffiti* ghost story—and you ate it up like kids around the campfire. I'm surprised I didn't go on to say that every year since, on the night of the prom, Patsy Ann is seen riding the ferry back and forth between San Diego and Coronado, looking for Jimmy!"

There was general laughter—although Wyman himself never seemed to shake off the moment—and for the rest of the evening, the topic of Patsy Ann and Jimmy did not come up.

Throughout the night, Nora maintained a cheerful, even giddy persona. She dropped it when she was down to her final guest—Wyman.

"I gotta admit, prof—I'm kinda shook up about your little experiment."

"I don't blame you," he said gravely. "My dear, I've witnessed numerous regressions . . . and I've never seen one more convincing than . . ."

She walked him to the door. "Maybe we should come up with a new party game."

"Maybe we should."

She kissed his cheek, and he left.

Now on her fifth beer, Nora sat glumly on the couch.

In explaining from where, in her subconscious, the elements of the "regression" had emerged, she had failed to elaborate to her guests on one possibility.

The sexual nature of the story could have been a reflection of her own sexual hang-ups. Nora Chaney —her background liberal, her life-style less than conservative—moved in circles that included students and teachers from the University of Chicago, other commercial artists like herself, as well as freelance writers and journalists. Living in this loft apartment in Old Town, smoking pot occasionally, hanging out in alternative rock clubs, attractive, with a raunchy sense of humor, Nora Chaney had one terrible secret.

She was a virgin.

A virgin with an interest in, but fear of, sex. She liked men—she was definitely attracted to some of them. She was certainly *not* gay, though she had tried that, to see if it would help; it was, if anything, worse.

She found that no matter how attractive a man, when the petting got below the waist, she would turn to ice. A literal cold would envelop her, a shivering cold that came from fear, as if she were some repressed frigid throwback to the goddamn fifties or something.

That night, Nora had the first dream.

She is a blond woman of about thirty, and she is

fucking a graying man of about forty in the cramped front seat of a sportscar. He is a married man, and she is a married woman, but not to each other; they don't speak of this, but it is there, with them, in the car, like something between them, even as she sits astride him, pumping, pumping, and then waves of orgasm begin, building, and she's screaming. . . .

And through the open car window the butcher knife flashes, slashes . . . the knife enters her, plunges into her chest, and she is screaming, but it's a different scream as she falls back and sees that thin blue-and-brown-eyed face in the window, with its awful smile, as the knife plunges into her lover's body, just above his sex, and he and she are screaming, blood spurting, as a rough hand is reaching for her ankle, slipping off the panties caught there, as she floats away, above the car, looking down through it at her blond self as the slashing continues, though she feels no more pain, and looks away, looks up. . . .

She woke, sitting up *now*, like a jack-in-the-box. She got up, prowled her apartment, fixed some instant coffee. She sat at her kitchen table, sipping the coffee, remembering the dream vividly. Somehow she knew that this dream, unlike most, would stay with her in its every detail.

The dream seemed remarkably realistic, or so she guessed; that *must* be what sex, what fucking, was like. And she'd had her share of orgasms, of course— her sexual hang-ups didn't extend to avoiding masturbation—but this was different than the self-induced variety.

A wet dream—literally. She was sopping between her legs; and the rest of her body was wet, too, glistening with sweat, though the nearby air conditioner was hurling cold air at her.

She looked at the clock: three thirty-three.

The next morning, Saturday, Nora slept in. She was sitting at the kitchen table again, glancing at the *Tribune,* sipping another cup of instant coffee, only half listening to a mid-morning news report on the portable TV on the counter.

"The so-called Chicago Ripper has apparently struck again," the woman newscaster was saying emotionlessly.

Nora looked up from the newspaper.

"The bodies of Teresa Gibson and Robert Haller, both of Naperville, were found in Haller's sportscar, parked in . . ."

She spilled her coffee. Nervously, she got up, found a dishrag, and wiped up the spill, even as the details made her hands shake all the more.

". . . time of death is estimated at three-thirty a.m."

A few hours later, she found a late edition of the *Sun-Times* that included the murder story, and further details: the victims were a married woman of thirty-two and a married man of forty-one . . . married, but not to each other.

She tried to put it out of her mind. She caught the new Scorsese flick at the Biograph, in the company of her divorced friend, Carol Reed. But all she could think about, all night, was the dream.

Carol, blond, thirty-something, her plain features unadorned by makeup, was just enough into New Age sort of things that Nora figured she might get a sympathetic ear.

But as they nibbled carrot cake at an espresso shop after the movie, Carol was dismissive.

"The trouble," she said, "is you don't make a party game out of something as serious as past lives."

"That dream didn't have anything to do with the party."

"Sure it did. Your 'regression' triggered this other dream."

"I dreamed about a couple being murdered by this 'Ripper' at the same time it was happening!"

Carol shrugged. "You and how many other Chicagoans? The media's been bombarding us with 'Ripper' this, 'Ripper' that." Carol touched Nora's hand, spoke softly. "Hey, I'm single . . . I have sex dreams. I wouldn't be surprised if the next one *I* have doesn't get interrupted by our Freddy Krueger-ish media star."

"Maybe you're right."

"Eat your carrot cake. It's as close to sex as either of us is gonna get tonight."

Nora laughed, and so did Carol, but Monday morning, at her kitchen table, Nora found herself staring at two familiar faces: Teresa Gibson and Robert Haller. The photographs in the *Trib* matched the faces in her dream.

"I think you should go to the police," Wyman told her on the phone.

"They'll laugh at me. They'll throw me out a window!"

"You have to try. Besides, even the FBI has been known to work with psychics."

"Is *that* what I am?"

"I don't know. I don't honestly know anything

except I wish I'd never put you under. I blame myself."

"Don't be silly, Will," she said, but secretly she agreed with him.

The first cop thought she was a crank; that much was obvious. He was young, probably mid-twenties, sandy-haired, overweight, and a smoker; his bad health habits would catch up with him. The bullpen area, where this was just one of many desks, was air-conditioned cool, but he had sweated through his white shirt.

But when she had mentioned one certain detail, he had begun paying attention.

"How did you know the Ripper takes the underpants off the female victims?"

"I told you. I *dreamed* it."

At the desk next door, a female detective was clearly listening in. She was in her thirties, heavyset with short blond pixie hair and thick glasses, and seemed on the verge of putting her two cents in. But she didn't.

"I . . . I also, uh, have a drawing," Nora said.

"What?"

She opened the manila folder, took out the pencil sketch. "I'm a commercial artist. I thought this might be helpful. . . ."

She put the drawing of the thin-faced man on the desk.

"I used watercolor because of his eyes," she said. "One's blue, one's brown. . . ."

He looked at the sketch briefly, then at Nora for a long time. "Thanks for your time, Ms. Chaney—we have your address. We'll be in touch. I wouldn't go on any extended trips, if I were you."

"Do you want this?" Nora said, picking up her drawing of the Ripper.

"You keep it . . . for now."

At the elevators, Nora waited, fuming, angry at being treated so condescendingly, but mostly angry at herself.

"You made Wayne suspicious."

Nora turned, and it was the chunky pixie-haired female cop. A name tag said DETECTIVE LISA WINTERS.

"And why is that?" Nora asked.

Winters shrugged. "You knew a key detail that's been suppressed from the media. That makes Wayne think you might be connected to the murders somehow."

"What do *you* think?"

The detective smiled, barely. "I think you're sincere. Psychic, maybe. But Wayne and me, we agree on one thing."

"And what would that be?"

"We neither one know exactly what to do with, or about, you." Winters dug in her breast pocket for a card. "This has both my work and home numbers. But there's another number on the back."

Nora took the card, glanced at the back of it. "Dick Mathis? Who writes for the *Reader?*"

Winters nodded. "He's bylined several damn good articles about the slayings. He just might print your story—and that drawing you did."

"I'm not looking for publicity."

"I know you aren't. My hunch is you're trying to do the same thing I am: help stop this bastard."

The chunky cop headed back to her desk.

Nora stepped on the elevator, studying the card.

Nora knew who Dick Mathis was—in fact, it was his article she had read, about the similarity of the Chicago Ripper to San Diego's Mack the Knife of thirty-some years earlier, that could have fueled her "regression."

"We have some mutual friends," she said.

"Yeah, I buy books from your downstairs neighbor," Mathis said. He was thirtyish, a wide-shouldered six-footer with a homely handsome face, thinning brown hair, and Buddy Holly glasses. He could have been a cowboy in another life.

"You buy *lesbian* books?"

"There are a couple of lesbian mystery writers I follow, yeah," he said, with a grin. "I *like* women."

They sat sipping espresso in an Old Town café, filling each other in about their backgrounds. She told him about her freelance commercial artwork. He told her about being a novelist and freelance journalist, and working out of his apartment on the Near North Side.

"Lisa Winters says you may have an interesting sidebar on the Ripper story," Mathis said.

"That's right. But when you hear it, you may take me for a flake."

"Maybe. But you seem like a nice enough flake, so go ahead."

She knew he wasn't taking her very seriously; she sensed he was attracted to her, but when she mentioned the Ripper tearing off the woman's panties, he perked up, just as the cops had.

"Detective Winters mentioned that detail to me, off the record," Mathis said.

"I guess holding back key info is common in cases like this, huh?"

"Yes, it is." He picked up her drawing of the Ripper. "I want to print this. And I want to print your story."

"I'm . . . I'm afraid you haven't heard it all."

And she told him about Patsy Ann and Jimmy.

For the next three days, Nora worked with Mathis on an article about her experience. The weekly Chicago *Reader* was a giveaway *Village Voice*–style paper that was widely read in the city; in his article, Mathis kept her anonymous, but he planned to print her drawing under the heading "Is This Man the Ripper?"

Working from his apartment, where Nora sat exhausted on the couch, Chaney faxed his final copy over to the *Reader* office, just making deadline. He flopped on the couch next to her and heaved a satisfied sigh.

"What have we done?" she asked.

"Huh? What do you mean?"

"I have the sick feeling I've just made a colossal ass of myself."

"With my help."

She laughed and slugged his shoulder. "I hope you're not exploiting me."

"Can I tell you a secret?"

"Sure."

He leaned near her. His breath smelled of coffee, but it wasn't unpleasant; hers probably smelled the same way.

"Working with you these last few days . . . 'exploiting' you *has* crossed my mind a couple times."

She smirked at him. "Maybe you should put a classified ad in the *Reader.*"

"'Divorced balding male writer seeks female companionship, psychic reincarnated beauty preferred'?"

"Something like that."

He kissed her. It was a sweet kiss. Gentle.

She kissed him back. Not so gently.

Then they were rolling around the couch, sliding their hands under each other's garments, gasping for breath as they necked and petted like a couple of frantic teenagers. . . .

She sat up, as if abruptly waking from a dream, straightening her clothes, embarrassed—not for what she'd done, but for what she couldn't do.

"Dick . . . I'm sorry . . . I'm sorry, I can't. . . ."

"I understand."

She held her arms to herself, shivering. "For some goddamn reason, I just get this icy feeling. . . ."

"I understand. I really do."

"You do?"

He tentatively placed his hand on her thigh; it was not a sexual gesture.

"Think about it," he said. "This . . . difficulty of yours . . ."

"Hang-up, you mean."

"Okay. Call a spade a spade: This hang-up may mean that you really *were* Patsy Ann in a former life, the life immediately previous to this one—"

"Oh, Dick—you can't be serious."

"I'm a journalist—I'm a combination of cynicism and open-mindedness. And I'm merely suggesting that the trauma of Patsy Ann's death, at a moment of sexual discovery that turned into bloody fucking horror, is something she—you—may have carried along into *this* life."

"Suppose . . . suppose there's something to this," she said. "What the hell am I supposed to do about it?"

"Find Patsy Ann," he said.

"What? What do you mean?"

"See if she existed. Maybe if you can come to terms with who you *were,* you can come to terms with who you *are.*"

With a little arm-twisting, Nora shamed Will Wyman into another hypnosis regression session.

"A fishing expedition," he said, "and a reluctant one, at that."

But he put her under, though little substantial information resulted—no last name, no street address.

"San Diego," she said. "Patsy Ann. But we had that before."

Wyman, seated beside her on her couch, tapped a pencil on his notepad. "But we do have a specific year: 1959."

"I already extrapolated that."

"How?"

"By Bobby Darin singing 'Clementine' at the Hotel Coronado."

"Oh. Well, this combination of the specific and the vague is *not* unusual in hypnotic regression—and it's rather typical for regressed subjects to resist giving certain specific details, including last names. And it's *very* typical for a subject to immediately seize upon a traumatic incident in regression, like Patsy Ann's traumatic death."

"But why have I carried this with me? Particularly this . . . connection with 'my' murderer?"

The professor looked very grave. "Sometimes, when a life is cut short . . . according to one theory . . . we can carry an agenda of sorts into our next life. A job left undone."

"You mean, we keep coming back until we get it right."

"Or wrong. Who's to say someone evil, cut short in the midst of his or her evil pursuits, might not try to continue on in a future incarnation—finishing the job that got interrupted. I'm not saying I believe any of this, mind you."

"I appreciate you sharing these thoughts just the same, professor." She nodded at the tape recorder. "Do you think we should try again?"

"I'm willing. But if you truly believe you have some sort of psychic link to the 'Ripper,' I should think the sooner you do something to substantiate this, the better."

"I'd have to agree. So my next trip shouldn't be back in time, should it?"

"There are ways other than hypnosis," the professor said somberly, "to go back in time."

In San Diego, Nora checked in at the Omni. Less than an hour later, barely noticing the beautiful weather, she walked up the steps of the public library, where she soon sat looking through the old newspapers on microfilm, following the trail of Mack the Knife.

She might have waited the week the inter-library loan would have taken to get the San Diego newspaper microfiches through the Chicago library system, but she felt she couldn't wait. She felt the increasing need to *stop* him . . . was it her own need, or Patsy Ann's?

She didn't know. She only knew she had to go to San Diego—had to make this journey into someone else's past, to see if the city itself touched off any memory switches. She would go to Coronado Island, to the hotel, to the beach where a teenage couple had been murdered so long ago . . . but first, the library.

Where it didn't take long at all.

Their young faces were before her, in high school graduation photos that accompanied the story of the latest tragic victims of Mack the Knife.

Patsy Ann Meeker. James McRae. May, 1959.

She read the news account over and over, then moved on, scrolling ahead to the next day, when a gloating note sent to the newspaper, presumed to be from the killer, made more headlines.

Then Patsy Ann's mother made the front page, on the day of her daughter's funeral, by having a stroke.

A wave of sorrow washed over Nora—it was as if she were reading about her own mother. Which, if Dick and the professor were right, might be the case.

The Meekers weren't listed in the current phone book, but there was an address in the decades-old news accounts, and she tried that.

The little stucco home on San Rafael Boulevard was in a neighborhood that had turned Hispanic. It was a nice enough area, though, and she hoped the current tenants might remember the Meekers, or at least have a lead for her.

They did.

Mrs. Cavazos, a pleasant, heavyset woman in her fifties whom Nora caught in the midst of preparing supper, said her family had bought the home from the Meekers.

"Very sad," Mrs. Cavazos said, standing in the doorway, as Nora wondered if the rooms beyond would stir any memories should she have been invited in. "Mr. Meeker, he pass away about ten years ago— took his own life."

"Oh."

"Mrs. Meeker, she had one stroke after another. She's in a nursing home."

Hillview Care Center was stucco, too, a hacienda-style building up in the hills. Nora was glad she'd rented a car—the cab ride would have bankrupted her.

"I'd like to speak to Mrs. Meeker," she told the head nurse.

"You're welcome to try," said the nurse, a tired-looking woman in her forties, "but I'm afraid Mrs. Meeker hasn't spoken a coherent word in years."

Though still in her seventies, Mrs. Meeker (the nurse said) was an old, old woman, far older than her years—less than human, all but a vegetable. She could eat, feeding herself as if by automatic pilot. With the aid of a walker, she could make it to and from the bathroom. But that was the extent of her life.

"That," the nurse said, "and her TV playing soap operas that she may or may not hear."

The nurse led Nora to a little room, where a frail old woman—tiny, balding, a baby bird of a human—sat in an armchair next to the hospital bed, watching a blaring television.

"Mrs. Meeker," the nurse said, loudly. "You have a visitor—"

The old woman turned her head away from the TV, where a young soap opera couple was kissing. Her eyes were dim, cloudy . . . until they fixed on Nora.

Then the old woman's eyes came brightly alive.

Mrs. Meeker reached her quavering arms to Nora, and Nora went to her, kneeling before her, instinctively holding out her arms to the old woman.

Mrs. Meeker looked right in Nora's eyes and said, "Patsy Ann! Patsy Ann . . ."

Nora held the old woman in her arms for a long time. Then she sat, for an hour or more, holding Mrs. Meeker's hand. The old woman said nothing, just the name "Patsy Ann" occasionally, but her smile was beatific.

When the nurse came back around to collect Nora, and Nora rose to leave, the old woman's expression turned desperate.

"Don't go . . . Patsy Ann . . . don't go. . . ."

Nora hugged the old woman.

"I'll be back," Nora said, calming her.

In the hallway, the nurse shook her head sadly. "That was her daughter's name. The poor old woman thought you were her daughter."

"Has she ever reacted that way with anyone else?"

"Well . . . no."

Their footsteps echoed down the hall, the sound of the blaring TV fading.

On the plane back to Chicago, Nora fell asleep; in her dream . . .

. . . she is a red-headed woman, a flight attendant, in her early twenties, in a hotel room getting oral sex

from, while giving oral sex to, a too-handsome man of
about thirty who is (he says) a movie producer.

"Lick me!" she's saying. "Lick me!"

"Suck me!" he's saying. "Don't stop!"

The man is still in her mouth when the butcher knife
falls like a guillotine.

Nora woke suddenly, to see a flight attendant before
her, shaking her gently awake.

Not the same flight attendant . . . not the red-
headed one in the dream.

"I'm sorry, ma'am," the flight attendant—a pretty
brunette—said. "You were making noise . . . I'm, uh
. . . afraid you were alarming some of the other
passengers."

"Sorry."

"Can I get you something? Some soda, perhaps?"

"Ginger ale."

The flight attendant smiled and nodded and went
away.

Nora sat and breathed deeply. The businessman
sitting next to her was looking at her warily out of the
corner of his eye.

She wondered if she'd talked in her sleep.

Nora took a cab from the airport to police head-
quarters in the Loop. She asked for Lisa Winters and
was soon sitting at the sympathetic cop's desk.

"I think the Ripper may have struck again."

"Why's that, Ms. Chaney?"

"I . . . I had another dream."

Winters listened patiently, not even arching an
eyebrow at the sexual nature of the dream, then said,
"I don't think there's much to worry about. You were

obviously influenced by being on an airplane, which is why you were a stewardess in the dream, and—"

"Winters!"

The young sandy-haired cop with the patronizing attitude was walking over to interrupt them.

"We got another one," he said. "Ramada Inn near O'Hare—maid has discovered two bodies with the usual m.o.—missing panties and all. Really caught in the act—in your classic sixty-nine position."

"Jesus," Winters said.

"It's a stewardess . . . sorry; *flight attendant*. And the guy's some Hollywood jerk." Now he noticed, and recognized, Nora. "What the hell are you doing back? Have another dream?"

"No, thanks," Nora said hollowly. "I just had one."

In the police car on their way to the Ramada Inn, Nora drew a picture of the too-handsome Hollywood producer; she also drew a sketch of the woman, though, having been within the woman's perceptions, she was not sure how she knew what the dead woman looked like, except perhaps from some shared memory.

Nora was not allowed within the hotel room, though she knew full well what was in there.

Winters came out, looking pale, shaking her head, Nora's drawings in hand.

"Any doubts I may have had about you," Winters told Nora, "are gone."

"Then circulate the drawing I did of the Ripper to every cop in town!"

Winters laughed humorlessly. "That's exactly what I'd like to do. Far as I'm concerned, it's an eyewitness police sketch. But I can't."

"Why in hell not?"

"Picking up a suspect on that basis wouldn't begin to hold up in court. The guy would walk."

The sandy-haired cop came out, shook a Marlboro out of a pack, and lighted it up. He walked over to Nora reeking macho and sneering.

"Hope you got a great fucking alibi, lady," he said.

Nora sneered back at him. "How does being thirty thousand feet in the air at the time of the murder strike you?"

Winters inserted herself between them and said to Nora, "I don't think you're needed here any longer. Thanks for your help."

"I'll stay in touch," Nora said.

"Do that," the sandy-haired prick said.

In Mathis's apartment, Nora sat beside him on the couch, unloading her frustrations on him. His arm was slipped gently around her shoulder. On the cluttered coffee table before them was a copy of the *Reader* with her portrait of the Ripper.

Nora slapped the paper face. "Why don't the police *do* something? I've handed the son of a bitch to them!"

"Maybe they will, pretty soon."

"What do you mean?"

He grinned at her. "I have some good news for you. We've had several phone calls at the *Reader* saying a man closely resembling your sketch has been seen in Evanston."

She sat up. "You think there's something to it?"

"One caller even spoke of noticing the man had one blue and one brown eye."

"Damn! Do you think Detective Winters would pay attention to that?"

"Frankly, no. But I'll drive out to Evanston tomorrow, myself, and show the picture around."

"The *police* should be doing that."

"Hey. It's what *I* should be doing . . . I'm the reporter who's breaking this case, remember? There may be a book in this, and then I can afford to take in a roommate."

She smiled, stroked the hand that had settled on her shoulder. "Anybody special in mind?"

"I'll run a classified. How did San Diego go?"

She pulled her legs up on the couch and snuggled against him as she told him.

"Now that you've proved the Patsy Ann connection," he said, "maybe you can lay your demons to rest."

"I don't know about demons being laid," she said. "But *I'm* willing to give it a try."

She kissed him deeply, and he slipped his hands up under her sweater, filling his hands with her.

"I . . . I never made love to a virgin before," he said.

"Don't worry about it," she laughed, not afraid at all. "I lost it riding a bike as a girl."

He nibbled her neck. "That's what they all say."

She lay cozily in his arms, in his bed. The thrum of the air conditioning was the only sound.

"The second time was even better," she sighed.

"Just wait'll the third."

"Dick . . . do you think . . . Nothing."

"What?"

"The visions. The dreams. They've all been . . . sexual."

He sat up in bed; his chest, bare, was as hairless as a child's. "I wouldn't describe them as 'sexual,' exactly."

"Sex interrupted by violence. But now that . . . now that you've helped me overcome my sexual hang-up, maybe—"

"Maybe the visions will stop?"

"Yes."

"Possibly. Or maybe they'll manifest themselves in some other way." He shrugged. "Maybe once the psychic floodgate's open . . ."

"God, I hope not."

"Well, try it out. Quit talking and go to sleep."

She nestled against him and did. Her dreams were only of him.

The next day, Mathis drove to Evanston and asked around the neighborhood where the man who looked like Nora's picture had been sighted. Three people told him the same thing: A guy in his fifties resembling the drawing worked as a janitor at the Faith United Methodist Church.

The church was on the corner in a residential neighborhood of well-maintained turn-of-the-century mansions. The church was a massive brick affair that lacked the Gothic character of the surrounding structures.

Inside, Mathis approached a pleasant, round-faced, middle-aged man with black-rimmed glasses, dressed in sweater and jeans, who turned out to be the minister. Mathis asked if he could speak with the janitor.

"Delbert's out running some errands," the minister said. "But he'll be back shortly—he has a little apartment in the church basement."

"What sort of fella is he?"

"Quiet. Devout. Couldn't ask for a better servant of the Lord."

"Well . . . thank you for your help, pastor."

"Should I say a friend dropped by, Mister . . . ?"

"No. I'll catch him later."

But when the minister slipped back into his office, Mathis slipped down a side stairway into the basement.

Off a finished banquet room, the janitor's quarters were adjacent to the furnace. Must be hot as hell in the winter, he thought, down there in the cement-walled space.

And Delbert certainly *was* devout: makeshift cement-block bookshelves were stacked with books on religion and philosophy; no pornography—in fact, no fiction. Not even a television. No evil influences whatsoever. Nothing but a Bible School–style print of a Jesus painting.

A dead end? Mathis wondered, and he poked around further.

Nora had a frustrating morning in her studio, trying to work on a plum assignment for *Chicago Magazine,* but unable to focus.

She had come back last night from Dick's, taking with her the small handgun he insisted she now carry in the wake of the *Reader* article. Even though he'd kept her name out of it, Dick was worried the Ripper might somehow find out who Nora was.

She had humored him, though once she got home,

she put the little revolver away in a drawer. She had no intention of carrying that thing around with her.

Working into the night, she'd come up with several roughs that didn't satisfy her. After several hours' sleep, woken by sunlight streaming in the skylight, she started back in and finally got something but was too tired to do any of the precision work—the inking, the airbrushing—that could turn the penciled drawing into a finished magazine cover.

After a lunch of microwaved soup, Nora took a nap on the couch and began to dream. . . .

She is a man.

She/he is alone in a small room; it's in a basement of some kind. The room is dreary, dank; the chest of drawers she/he's going through is old. In the drawers are clothes, men's clothing, work clothes, a suit, all of it looking vaguely Goodwill. In the bottom drawer, though, are some scrapbooks. She/he opens the top scrapbook and a headline leaps out: MACK THE KNIFE KILLS TEEN COUPLE. She/he leafs through the book.

More bloody headlines; another scrapbook has headlines, circa mid-seventies, of the Detroit Slasher; the bottom scrapbook, the newest one, the one in progress, details the continuing career of the Chicago Ripper . . . so do the stack of blood-spattered panties below the scrapbooks.

She/he glances up at the mirror over the bureau. She/he is Dick Mathis.

Somehow, through sheer will, Nora forced herself awake. Her heart was in her throat.

If she was Dick in the dream, Dick was in danger! But where the hell *was* he?

In that room.

What room?

She grabbed her purse and was halfway out the door when she thought of something. She took the revolver from the drawer, stuffed it in her purse, and hurried down the steps to the street, where she grabbed a cab.

"Evanston," she told the driver.

"Where in Evanston?"

"Just Evanston!"

"Oh-kay . . ."

They drove to Evanston; she heard herself giving the cabbie directions. She told him street names she didn't know she knew. Told him to take this right. That left.

Then, for reasons unknown to her, she found herself getting out of the cab in front of a church.

She threw money at the cabbie and rushed up the steps, and a round-faced man in a sweater and glasses approached her, pleasantly, but she pushed him aside, running to a stairway and running down to a room near the furnace.

She stepped inside and saw Dick on the floor, half-conscious, holding his chest, blood bubbling through; the man with the thin face, in his late fifties now, a coveralled smiling Satan, was bending over Dick, the butcher knife poised to strike again. He looked back sharply at her with one blue eye and one brown.

"Remember me?" she asked.

He turned and looked at her, his eyes slitting, his face as long and narrow and sharp as the bloody blade.

He smiled his terrible smile and came at her with the knife high in his fist, and she took the gun from her purse and shot him in the chest.

Astounded, he fell to his knees, in praying position, the knife tumbling from his fingers.

"I'm Patsy Ann," Nora said, standing over him.

He looked up at her with eyes that seemed to recognize her. It was as if he were awaiting communion.

"Patsy Ann Meeker," she confirmed. "I came back for you."

He glanced at the knife he had dropped, not thinking of going after it, but (somehow she knew this) wondering why she didn't pick it up and make him suffer before he died. Like he had made her suffer, her and all the others.

She answered the unasked question.

"I don't want you to suffer," she said, and she fired the gun right at his forehead, and fired again, and again. An acrid fragrance wafted through the air.

"I just want you to go away," she said. "Just get the hell out of here!"

But he already had. He was on his back, and both the blue eye and the brown one were empty.

She went to Dick, cradled him in her arms as the frowning minister appeared in the doorway.

"Get help," she said.

A week later, Nora brought Dick home from the hospital to Old Town, to her loft apartment, which they now planned to share.

"Make love to a cripple?" he asked.

"Any time," she said, and she helped him disrobe, scattering clothes on their way to the bedroom, where they made love slowly, gently, and fell asleep in each other's arms. Nora, enveloped in a deep, sound pool of slumber, began to dream.

It is a dream unlike the others. She is no specific person. She is a presence in a white room. Doctors are standing around a table; a mother has her feet in stirrups. She is in a delivery room in a hospital. She watches as a baby is born, its first breaths turning into a wailing that builds into what seems almost a scream of rage.

Nora sat upright in bed, waking Dick, who looked with alarm into her wide eyes.

"He's back," she said.

YET ANOTHER POISONED APPLE FOR THE FAIRY PRINCESS

A. R. Morlan

*B*efore Bob had a chance to say word one to me that afternoon, I knew that the Nutcracker Sweet had been holding back on him; I could tell from his eyes-averted, head-hanging shamble into the club locker room, that non-look my way that clearly said *Warning: Man who hasn't had a piece entering the room.*

Wondering what did you do to her this time to make her clamp those legs together, I decided to let him do all the talking; just nod or grunt or uhm-*hum* sympathetically, while he opened himself wide and let his guts dangle. I'd discovered long before that afternoon that asking Bob what was wrong would only elicit guarded praise for her from him ... as if those double-pierced ears of hers could somehow hear him utter so much as one negative word about her miles away.

It was too bad that those bitch-keen ears of hers couldn't pick up the jokes the rest of the guys at the club made about Bob *because* of her; the jokes about Bob, the Ball-less Wonder, or Bob, the Amazing Pussy-Man—had to grow his own so he'd get some once in a while—but even if she could've heard them, I doubt that they would've affected her. Not after all the times she'd called him *"stupid"* in front of the entire tennis club during the annual charity matches, or the times she'd told all the other wives how inept and boring his lovemaking was . . . when and if she decided to allow him into her bedroom. Even though Jeanette made a pretense of speaking oh so softly, her brittle little-girl voice tinkling like wind chimes, that tiny voice had a way of carrying across the courts.

Beside me, Bob tossed his racket and balls into the open locker before him; the metal interior rattled dully, making a sound not unlike two cats trying to hump each other in a Dumpster, just before he slammed the door shut. I calmly began stripping off my whites, concentrating on the knots in my laces while he took off each article of clothing he wore with the sort of seething deliberation that is somehow more furious than flinging away one's shirt, shorts, and socks in open anger. And he folded each piece of clothing the way men who have to do their own laundry do it, before stacking it in a neat, corners-aligned pyramid on the bench before him.

"I have Bob trained," I'd heard Jeanette say on more than one occasion. "I made sure of that after I married him. Just like the other one . . . he did everything for himself."

Jeanette's first husband sure did do everything for himself—including that final blow job on the business end of his .38. And he was considerate enough to do *that* out in the woods, where he wouldn't mess up her spotless floors or pristine wallpapered walls.

Bob was putting his jockstrap (likewise neatly folded, in a tiny soft square) on the very top of his cloth pyramid, a white pinnacle of sweaty elastic, as he finally said, "Y'know, I used to think she was nothing but a witch . . . but I finally have it figured out."

I grunted sympathetically while scooping up my towel and soap on a rope (a rounded globe of tit-shaped pinkish soap, a playful gift from my own girlfriend), before padding off for the showers. No need to ask Bob to follow me; within seconds I could hear the slap-slap of his bare feet smacking against the tile floor. His wife sure did have him trained.

He and I were alone in the locker room/showers; I don't think he would've felt able to speak so freely if the others had been there. I wasn't even sure why he'd picked me to unload on those other times; maybe it was because I was a newcomer to the club and hadn't screwed his wife during those frenzied days between the death of Chump Number One (funny, she'd never mentioned his name—I doubted that even Bob knew it . . . unless the poor schmuck's folks *did* christen him The Other One) and Chump Number Two. Oh, I'd heard about Jeanette's kiss-by-suck-by-fuck climb up the rungs of the membership ladder; whenever Bob couldn't come to the club, the tiled shower walls rang with the stories of her suction-cup blow-jobs and her vise-like pussy, not to mention the intricate things she could do with her tongue. But her prowess between the sheets (or on the car seat, or under the stars) was her undoing; sure, taking a *piece* of something that all but sucks you dry once in a while is okay, but a steady diet of it would leave a man hollow in a month.

Or worse than hollow. Like The Other One with his permanent skylight on the top of his bloodied head.

All the members of the tennis club—be they single, married, or anything in between—had had her; every man knew the taste of her juices, the smell of her, too, but no matter how perfect her icy-blond hair was, or how carefully she applied those graduated shades of makeup to her otherwise slightly puffy and colorless face (Terry Collier once took a shower with her after an extended session and claimed that she was "almost faceless . . . just eyes, a lump of nose and a suction hose below that"), eventually the guy would realize that no matter what she looked like, or what she fucked like, he'd have to actually try to *live* with her—a prospect which sent the majority of the club members running once they'd satisfied their urges.

Until Bob came along. Nobody knew if it was because he'd been the next best thing to a virgin before meeting her, or if he'd had one of Those mothers who'd given him a taste of the whip across his psyche from boyhood on . . . but whatever the reason, she hooked him. *Then* she trained him.

Positioning myself under the shower head, I waited until I saw Bob hovering just at the outer reaches of my peripheral vision before turning on the water. As the fine sprinkling of warm water cascaded down my chest, across my belly and block and tackle, Bob's voice started in again, the words barely audible over the splatter of the shower spray hitting my body and the tile floor below:

"It isn't just that witches are supposed to be as ugly as they are powerful . . . although you wouldn't believe what she looks like without the makeup. 'Course, when I was a kid, that's all you ever heard—that witches were so full of power, the power to make people do whatever they want them to do. Witches had command over *themselves* . . . to fool people, and lure them into doing . . . things. The stories never said anything about their sex lives, y'know, as if women that ugly weren't supposed to want any . . . maybe it was their not ever getting any that made them vulnerable to the fairy princesses. Now *they're* the ones with the real power—"

Caressing my globe of nipple-tipped soap with one wet hand, I worked up a lather while nodding empathetically, all the while fighting the building urge to start caressing myself with my other hand. It wasn't a big deal with the other guys around, but it wasn't the thing to do in front of a guy who was only turning the "cold" knob in front of him and letting the stream of water hit him in his already drooping organ.

"—how else could they survive all the things the witches did to 'em, unless they had the power? Fairy princesses could consume poison apples like they were only covered with candy. Oh, sure, they'd play at being overcome, for sympathy . . . only way to lure in the suckers who'd rescue them—"

Smearing frothy lather across my upper body, I grunted in reply while Bob just stood there, wet dick limp, balls retracting like kicked puppies curling themselves into defensive lumps of quivering fear, and continued to speak to the walls which had echoed with recitations of his own "fairy princess's" exploits:

"She claimed that she couldn't find anyone who really loved her. Her first . . . one didn't. That's why he did what he did. Because he didn't love her. Why he didn't just leave her she never explained . . . only now she doesn't *need* to.

"I think she did to him what she's doing to me . . . and after something like *that*, leaving must've seemed impossible. Leaving means needing to explain, needing to answer questions . . . 'How could you give up a body like hers?' 'The way she flirts, she must want it twenty hours at a pop—couldn't keep up, could you?' 'She wear you out, buddy-boy?' Because they all can see what she is, they've all flirted with her . . . and maybe more. Not that any of 'em will come out and say it, but . . . I can read their eyes.

"But they don't know . . . not at all. Sure, she has the legs, and what's between 'em—*if* it suits her. If not . . ."

Hanging the now-glistening orb of pink soap on the "hot" knob before me, I worked the lather over the rest of my body but did manage to look over at Bob and give him a knowing wink—Sure, pal, every girl pulls the locked-legs bit.

Something in my glance must have connected, for Bob grew slightly agitated, his voice climbing a notch in volume, as he shook his head in protest. "No, no, not just refusing me . . . it's—it's much more than that. I mean, if she doesn't want me to get some, I *can't* . . . you can't get what isn't there at all. All I have to do is say something she doesn't like, or fail to do something she asked me to, and"—here he sucked in his lips until his mouth was merely an indented line hovering on the horizontal under his nose—"*nothing*. Gone . . . no way to get your fingers or tongue or anything in . . . not when there's no hole to stick 'em *in*to."

My eyes must've registered my disbelief, for at that

point Bob shut off his own water, and as he stood there dripping and shivering slightly, he continued, "I'm not kidding . . . she can pull everything *in,* lips, hair, the works. It's more than muscle control . . . no sexercise book for women can teach her *that.* Maybe it's instinctive—maybe it's something she learned on her own. One minute you're curling her hair around your finger, brushing against her wet lips . . . and the next, it's like . . . nothing. Just rubbing a patch of flat flesh on her belly. And the worst part is, how she smiles when she's doing it, just that little tug at the corners of her mouth while her eyes just stare into you. . . .

"'Course, it's not something you can ask a marriage counselor or sex therapist about. Because she'd never admit it . . . and who wants to look like a nut? And I've looked in the medical books . . . no woman has that many muscles there, to be able to do *that.*

"But a fairy princess . . . now *she*'d be able to do that. *Would* do that. How else could a fairy princess stay alive when someone's trying to poison her? All she'd have to do is close up something inside, and keep the poison away from her insides. If she can do it down there, she can do it anyplace on her body."

As Bob blathered on, his words trickling like drops of water until the individual droplets formed a small yet mighty flood, I remembered what some of the guys had had to say about his "fairy princess":

"I'd of sworn she was going to slurp out every drop from both balls, she was sucking on me like my dong was a straw and my whole body was the cup holding the milkshake—"

"Remember those woven thingies you'd stick your fingers in, and then the more you'd pull to get free, the faster you'd be stuck? Well, stick hair on one end, and you've got her."

"She was *all* mouth, like she'd suck your lungs out if you let 'er—"

But that's just shower-room talk, I assured myself. And Bob's so starved for a little pussy he's starting to think there isn't any to be had . . . if he lets himself think about what he's missing, he'll really go nuts. If the food isn't there, you won't be hungry.

"—after the first few times, when I managed to reach over and turn the lights on before she completely pulled herself in, just so I could *see* it happening, I decided that she couldn't do it everywhere at once, so I'd reposition myself, dangle the bait over her other lips . . . but all she had to do was say very softly, 'No, I don't *think* so,' in that tiny voice of hers, and I'd start to get just as small as her voice down there. Couldn't even prime the pump with my hands afterward. Like . . . just her voice had been enough to keep me from firming up."

I'd heard that "tiny voice" many a time, her matte-finish lipsticked lips barely moving as that terse voice nonetheless blasted the air, sending shattering waves of sound rippling outward:

"Bob, you're so *stupid*—"

"The man can't do *any*thing right—"

"The only way to live with a man is to keep him on his own side of the bed as much as possible—"

And that's just supreme-bitch talk, I thought; thousands of other women say the same things, while their men grovel and scrape and put up with it in the hopes of being rewarded with a blow job and a little action afterwards . . . isn't it?

"—'course, what she can do to herself, and to my

body, that's temporary, but what happened to my stuff, now that, *that's* another story altogether," Bob was saying, and at that point, as the soap foam dried with small popping and snapping sounds on my damp body, I reached over and shut off my own mix of hot and cold water. With the sound of the rushing water gone, Bob's words echoed sharply on the steamy white tiles:

"She uses her voice . . . only, when she's really angry, it doesn't stay tiny or soft. Y'know how a dental drill seems to get louder and louder as it comes closer to your mouth, until the sound is *everything?* Just that persistent *drone?* She's something like that . . . only more. I can tell when it'll happen now—her voice goes all sharp and flat at once, and she says my name like it's so much longer than it is: 'Baaahh—ob' before she really gets going.

"Once, we were in the car, I was driving, only she didn't like the way I was driving, she always says I drive too slow, 'pokey,' as she puts it, and she goes 'Baaahh—ob, put your *foot* on the pedal, don't play footsies with it, *stomp* it,' only she was speaking too high to get the pedal itself . . . but when my fingers started to sink into the steering wheel, I knew I'd better get the car moving. It took weeks for the plastic to go back to normal. . . . I stayed away from the club for all that time, because I was afraid someone might see what happened to the wheel and ask what happened.

"Maybe it's their voices . . . maybe fairy princesses can shatter anything that might hurt them, neutralize the poisons in the apple, y'know? Those tight little voices, aimed right at a man . . . or anything he cares about. Tiny, brittle voices, like glass knives or crystal daggers . . . hard, tight voices with no softness in them. Like when she pulls herself *in,* and doesn't leave a bit of softness or moisture . . . and she doesn't even have to close herself up to stop me; I can actually be in her, working up a steady rhythm, then it sort of skids to a stop, no lubrication, you see . . . dry and rigid and unmoving, like trying to hump the hole in a bowling ball, only it's *not* something funny"—he'd noticed the slight smirk on my lips—"not at all . . . and she can make her mouth go dry, too, as if she'd never been able to so much as spit in her entire life. Can you imagine sticking your tongue into a parchment envelope? It doesn't even *taste* like anything. Same goes for the other set of lips. One second, she's a mass of petals and honey, the next—like I'm licking envelope flaps without the glue on them. Worse than nothing. Not even an unpleasant taste in my mouth to complain about afterwards."

I dipped my head to one side, frowning slightly in agreement. Even a slightly salty clam has its appeal, even if that appeal is in the complaining about it afterwards. But to experience . . . nothing? Not even the smell—

As if sensing my flow of thought, Bob leaned forward and went on. "And she won't even allow herself to give off so much as the odor of sweat if she feels I don't deserve to smell her. I suspect it's because that's something about her that I could appreciate without her actually offering it to me, or dangling it like a prize—the brass ring she can keep holding just out of reach. Now it's like . . . I'm not worth teasing. . . ."

Momentarily thankful that Bob had stopped speaking, I quickly turned on the "hot" knob and allowed the water to pummel my skin, rinsing away the drying soap film and Bob's strange words, which seemed almost to cling to my body like a coating of scum.

But my sense of release was short-lived; Bob simultaneously grabbed his bar of deodorant soap and raised his voice while resuming his low-key rant as he lathered his body with sharp, jerking motions of his soap-clutching hand:

"I guess this fairy princess has had her lifetime fill of sympathy, or what*ever* it is she needs. . . . I'm not even allowed to enter her bedroom anymore. Not that she doesn't need stimulation anymore—I can hear that vibrator of hers buzzing through the bedroom wall. . . . Apparently, she likes something she can manipulate at will. I've seen that thing, when she's out of the house and doesn't know I'm in her bedroom. She's . . . melted it, compressed it in spots, to conform to her own cunt. . . . From the little I can remember of it now, I'd say she's turned that trusty vibrator into an exact match to her hole, bump by bump, all the way to the hilt. Like fucking herself *with* herself. . . . I wonder, sometimes, if she'd have done that to me by now, if I'd pleased her enough for her to allow me to continue bedding down with her. Reshaped me to suit her needs, like a flesh-and-blood French tickler. No, not a good idea," he said, almost to himself, "she'd be leaving herself open to too much scrutiny. If it's one thing that fairy princesses must do, it's protect their powers, not let people really know what they're capable of . . . not unless the person witnessing them is so beneath contempt that *no* one would believe them. . . ."

No matter how bizarre his excuse for not getting laid was, that part of Bob's story rang true. The

Amazing Pussy-Man was the ultimate joke at the tennis club; by that time, all someone had to do was mention his name, and that utterance would be greeted with snorts of derision and hoots of laughter. Bob had become the prince to his wife's Nutcracker; all she had to do was move those hinged, clicking jaws, and presto—instant eunuch. I glanced over and down; sure enough, his nuts were trying to re-enter the shell of his body, while his dick dangled like a defeated worm. I was almost tempted to take a second look, but didn't want Bob thinking I was going strange on him . . . but didn't it used to be a bit *longer* when flaccid?

Once Bob finished soaping himself, and his skin was covered with a mucus-like filmy coating of tiny-bubbled soap, he looked me in the eye and said, "I'm not just blowing steam . . . Jeanette *is* a fairy princess. If she was a witch, like so many women are, I would leave her in a minute. Let her have everything, pay her off for life. But doing that would just free her up, let her start searching and hunting again. Like what happened after the other one . . . y'know. At least he was able to taste something in his mouth before he did it.

"Taste or not, though, I don't want to do that—"

Beside him, I nodded vigorously and gave a snort of affirmation, sort of like the "good boy" noise you'd make when dealing with an obedient dog.

"—but leaving a fairy princess like her isn't easy no matter which way you go about it. Stay with her, and you might as well be alone. Leave her, and you wonder who she'll be trapping next. It's not ethical, y'know, knowingly doing that to another man."

"Uh-uh," I answered, thinking of all the would-be

prey that had escaped her clawed clutches before Bob came along.

"Especially after what she did to me yesterday. I was about to pleasure myself in my bedroom, but when I reached over for the bottle of lotion I keep in my headboard bookcase, I knocked over the open bottle, and it was all curdled, like it'd spoiled or gone rotten, which was nuts, because all it *is* is a bunch of oils—safflower, soy, palm, stuff like that, with some vitamin E mixed in. So there I was, looking at the cheesy clumps of the stuff spilled all over my pillow, when *she* walks past my bedroom door and says through it, 'What do you want to use *that* for?' Just like that. Like either she'd been nosing around in my room, or she'd seen me through the wall and the door. . . .

"Her grubbing through my stuff I could take—I do it to her, after all—but for her to go . . . changing everything of mine, especially when she dries *herself* up in the first place"—here Bob slathered the soap around his already withered organ with a vigor born not of self-love, but of self-loathing—"and then won't let *me* have any lubrication for myself!"

I clucked my tongue in condolence as I hurried up and toweled myself off, hoping I could get dry fast enough to get back into my own street clothes, and then out of there before Bob finished his own shower. Yet, even though his words were growing stranger, something in his voice compelled me to stay. I don't know if it was the raw pain, or the first glimmers of regained self-respect in his words, but instead of hurrying out of there, I found myself lingering. And seeing that his audience wasn't about to leave, Bob placed his soap on the small shelf before him and stood under the pulsing stream of water, poking his head under the spray until his dark hair covered his skull in a flat, shiny layer, conforming to the rounded contours of his head like the shiny skin on an apple, as he concluded softly:

"While I was looking at that spilled mess on my pillow, I got to thinking. If she can do something like this to a fluid, what might she do to the fluids inside of *me?* Did she turn the other one's blood to something that poisoned him, *made* him do what he did out there in the woods? Because if she *can* do that, just like she can melt things or suck them in, there's no escaping her—even for a guy like *you,* someone who's been *warned,* once she gets it into her mind to actually *go* for someone—at least not while she's up and moving. But what to do with a fairy princess like her? Give her yet another poisoned apple? She'd just eat it to the core and go looking for more. By the way, have I ever told you that she finds you quite attractive? Claims she likes the 'quiet type.' So . . . I got to thinking, maybe poisoned apples, things like that, aren't the answer . . . not unless you add a little more poison to the apple, whatever. Maybe . . . someone— or a couple of somebodys—might have to do *something* else to her, even be a little less insidious, a little less subtle. Y'know what I mean. Only question is, would you be willing to be the one to help me add a little more poison to the apple—*or* whatever?"

I hugged my towel against my body, unable to answer him, even though I'd understood the question perfectly. And, as if realizing that despite the fact that the question was received, it couldn't *yet* be acknowledged, Bob added, his eyes (for once) level with my own, "I'm not just asking you because you haven't fucked her yet . . . it's because she *has* noticed you already, and, well, being married to The Other One didn't stop her from roaming and looking and *tainting* other men. Given her interest in you, it would be so simple to just let her *go* for you—and no matter what you might think you could do, I doubt you'd have much more luck resisting her than I did. But then again, The Other One never tried to stop her, or even so much as warn the others . . . like I'm warning *you*. Not that I could stop her if she does decide to try for you . . . but a warning is a warning. And maybe the two of us could turn a warning into an end to a need for all future warnings about her. I'm only doing this for *your* sake. Won't you do something for yourself, while you still can? Or, if not for yourself, then for the next chump she'll adhere to after *you?*"

That speech called for more than a grunt or a nod or an "uh-huh" or "uh-uh." With a few sentences, a scattering of casually uttered syllables, Bob had crossed over from speculation to supposition to surety. But warning to me or not, I didn't think I was ready to follow him *that* far into his personal plan for combined revenge and prevention—so I began to slowly shake my head no (after all, I could always find another tennis club, in another town) when the moist echoing stillness of the shower room was shattered by the shrill jangle of the phone in the locker room a few feet away. Since I was basically dried off, I wrapped my towel around my waist and padded, my soles smacking against the damp tiles like dozens of loud kisses, over to the ringing phone.

I heard Jeanette's voice the second I lifted the receiver, even before I'd had a chance to place it against my ear and mouth:

"Baaahh-ob? Is Bob there? I have to speak with him. Baaah—"

Her voice was almost loud enough for him to hear without coming any closer to the phone, but he did so anyway, walking head down and privates bobbing in time with his slow, defeated steps forward. But just as I was about to hand the receiver to him, I happened to glance at the earpiece, in time to see the formerly tiny holes dilate, then close with infinitesimal slowness after her voice had blasted through the tortured, malleable plastic—and before I gave him the still-contracting receiver, I realized that a fairy princess *that* powerful, that . . . *omnipotent,* might very well find a way to do anything to me, to *any* of the men at the tennis club (or *beyond* the confines of this club), *especially* when she found herself free of Bob. And Bob was so close to unleashing her, either intentionally or by accident (yet he did say *she* found *me* appealing . . . *me,* she'd specifically singled *me* out), and if he was subjected to even one more indignity— so, as I handed the receiver to him, I managed to catch his eye before I reluctantly nodded yes to his question about me helping to add more poison—or something less subtle but more foolproof under our combined effort—to that apple. . . .

SEX STARVED

Edo van Belkom

I now pronounce you man and wife."

Marv Sullivan grinned at the preacher, his eyebrows arching as if he were asking the man if it were really true.

The preacher nodded. "You may kiss the bride."

Marv turned to his new bride and smiled. When he raised the white veil he'd bought minutes earlier in the chapel's lobby, Rosita Juanita Sullivan returned a polite smile and offered her left cheek for him to peck.

It wasn't much of a kiss, but it was enough to give Marv a slight boner. Standing five foot ten and weighing close to four hundred pounds, Marv could count all the relationships he'd had on the fingers of a fisted hand. That's why he'd jumped at the chance to marry Rosie. She was a voluptuous Mexican woman with flowing black hair, dark skin, brooding brown eyes and fat red lips that were permanently turned out in a pout. She had a full, womanly figure, with big round breasts, wide flaring hips and long strong legs that were every bit as shapely as the rest of her body.

The only thing wrong with Rosie was that she didn't give a shit about Marv. She had approached him in a café in Tijuana saying she needed somebody to talk to. An hour into their conversation he flippantly suggested that she'd make someone a good wife someday, and she said, "How about you?" That got the ball rolling, and before Marv knew what hit him he was dressed in a baby-blue tuxedo with crushed velvet lapels and standing at the altar of an all-night chapel in Vegas. He knew he'd been manipulated, perhaps even used. But even though their marriage was one of convenience that would allow Rosie to remain in the United States, Marv couldn't help thinking that over time she might *learn* to love him. At the very least, she might feel grateful to him for what he'd done for her, and if he was lucky, she just might show her gratitude by having sex with him.

"I have other couples waiting," said the preacher, ushering them out toward the lobby. "Don't forget to visit the souvenir booth on your way out. We have over fifty items in stock to help you remember this special moment in your lives, all of them reasonably priced."

Marv shook the preacher's hand and followed Rosie into the lobby. Before they left the all-night chapel, Marv shelled out more than $150 for trinkets like souvenir pouches of confetti with the "Love Chapel No. 9" logo printed on the cellophane, and coffee mugs with their wedding photo on one side and their names and wedding date set inside a heart on the other.

They had dinner back at the hotel and sat around the bar until eleven when Rosie suggested they go up to their room. "I'm tired," she said in her breathy, heavily accented voice. "I want to go to sleep."

"Really?" Marv said in surprise.

"Yes, really."

Marv paid for their drinks and escorted Rosie up to their room. It was well-appointed, with a thick-piled dusty-rose carpet, powder-blue drapes and a huge king-size bed. On one wall was a large painting depicting a dozen Elizabethan ladies and gentlemen in various stages of undress and embrace. On top of the dresser was a bottle of champagne set in an ice bucket, and next to it was a large floral arrangement— consisting primarily of roses—with a card that read, "Congratulations Marvin and Rosita."

Once inside the honeymoon suite, Marv optimistically hung the DO NOT DISTURB sign on the outside doorknob, then locked the door behind him.

Before he was even in the room, Rosie had locked herself in the bathroom and was readying herself for bed. Marv felt a knot of anticipation gather in his chest and another one of arousal tighten between his legs.

He backed up to the bed, bent his knees slightly, and carefully lowered his tremendous bulk onto the edge. A dozen bedsprings moaned and creaked in protest.

As he heard the water come on in the shower, Marv got undressed. His powder-blue tuxedo was drenched and stained with sweat and had to be peeled from his body like a second skin. Once he was naked, he stood up and looked down. He could just make out the tip of his erect penis peaking out from beneath the expansive curve of his belly. He stepped in front of the mirror and turned sideways. His manhood jutted horizontally from his body but was dwarfed by the enormous white gut that hung over it like a bloated sack of whale blubber. "Still there," he said under his breath.

When he heard the shower stop he quickly slipped into his navy blue bathrobe. A moment later the bathroom door opened, and Rosie stepped out wearing a light pink bathrobe of her own.

"Your turn," she said, her eyes pointed down at the floor as she stepped around him on the way to the bed.

"I'll be right out," Marv said, closing the door to the bathroom. After squeezing into the shower stall, he quickly soaped up and rinsed off, then spent several minutes primping in front of the mirror. He combed his hair, brushed his teeth, shaved, trimmed his finger- and toenails, put on deodorant, and splashed on some cologne. Finally, satisfied that he was neat and clean, he sprinkled his body with baby powder, donned his robe, and opened the door.

Rosie was asleep on the bed, lying on her back wearing a modest teal-colored polyester sleep shirt. For a moment Marv stood in the middle of the room, just watching the rise and fall of her chest. He couldn't help but be mesmerized by the sharp points of her long stiff nipples as they poked up from beneath the silky fabric of her sleep shirt. The garment was also hiked up high on her legs, and he could see she wasn't wearing any panties. Her legs were slightly parted to expose a hint of her dark and mysterious sex, a part of her body Marv desperately wanted to explore.

He looked down once more and saw the entire head of his manhood bobbing up and down beneath the outer rim of his belly.

He approached the bed, let the bathrobe fall to the floor, and slowly crawled under the covers. After struggling to move across the bed to be closer to his bride, Marv reached over with his right hand and placed it over one of her breasts. He couldn't believe how full and round it felt in his hand, bigger even than his own. He caressed the breast for a minute before taking her long hard nipple between his fingers and giving it a gentle squeeze. He had just mustered up enough courage to pull down the top of her sleep shirt and touch the naked breast flesh-to-flesh when Rosie suddenly opened her eyes and screamed.

"What are you doing?" she said, clambering off the bed. She stood in the middle of the room pulling the sleep shirt tightly around her body in a way that suggested she'd been defiled.

"What do you mean?" Marv said, a little bewildered.

"I never said I would have sex with you."

"But we're married now, and I thought maybe—"

"We are married, but I won't have sex with you. At least not . . ." Her voice trailed off as she looked at the floor.

"At least not what?"

"At least not as long as you're so fat. You're *too* fat. You look more like a pig than a man."

Marv was hurt, but not surprised. And if the truth be told, he didn't blame Rosie in the least. Marv had a hard time believing that anyone could find him sexually attractive, and sometimes he even had trouble looking at himself in the mirror. "Is that the only reason you won't sleep with me?"

Rosie took a deep breath. "You are a nice man, Marvin Sullivan, and I like you. But I can't have sex with you until you lose some weight."

"How much is *some?*"

"How much do you weigh now?"

"Three hundred and eighty-seven pounds."

Rosie gasped at the number. "Lose a hundred and fifty pounds, and then we'll see."

Marv looked at Rosie a long time. He had no doubt she could make him a happy man, and he was willing to do almost anything to make it happen. He'd always wanted to lose the weight, and now seemed as good a time as any to give it a try. One thing was certain: He'd never have a better reason to go on a diet.

"All right," he said with conviction. "I'll do it!"

They spent the night together separated by a foot and a half of mattress. Marv lay awake all night, watching Rosie sleep and feeling his testicles slowly turn an electric shade of blue.

Despite his being hungry all the time, married life agreed with Marv. Gone was the shy, soft-spoken, introverted boy who masqueraded through life as a generally reluctant and socially inept man that people called "fatso." He was still fat, but he felt more confident now, assertive . . . almost macho.

His new demeanor was also noticed by the people in the office of the software firm he worked for. Coffee machine conversations with Marv didn't center solely around computers and data points anymore. His fellow programmers and technicians, and even some secretaries, treated him differently, exhibiting a mild interest in his life and sometimes going as far as to ask him the odd personal question.

It was as if he'd suddenly been handed the keys to a club he'd been barred from all his life.

Of course, when Marv talked about Rosie, he never mentioned that he was cut off from sex until he lost a hundred and fifty pounds. He preferred to show the guys around the office snapshots of her—especially the one of her in a one-piece swimsuit—and then recount to them one of the fantasies he'd culled and refined over the past few weeks. His favorite story had him sneaking up on Rosie while she worked at the stove preparing dinner. Without a sound he would hike up her skirt, enter her from behind, then fuck her while he ate from one of the pots simmering on top of the stove.

Looking at Marv's enormous bulk, then at the photos, no one had much trouble believing him.

He was a big man around the office now, a different kind of big man.

At home, Rosie was an almost perfect wife. She kept the house clean, always had dinner ready for him when he came home, and was an excellent companion who always had time to talk. He never felt as if he were missing anything by *not* having sex with her because he'd never had sex and didn't have a clue as to what he was missing.

But what about Rosie? She'd told Marv that she'd willingly lost her virginity in her early teens, and he knew she'd supported herself by working for a time in the bordellos of Tijuana. Now she was a voluptuous thirty-year-old woman in her sexual prime. How did she manage to go without sex?

Or did she?

About a month after the wedding, as Marv sat at the dinner table munching salad, Rosie looked up at him and said, "I met a man today at the mall."

Marv looked at her in heartbroken disbelief and was unable to speak. He wiped the sweat from his brow. "Oh?"

"He offered me a job."

"Did he?"

"He said it was in hu . . ." Her English had improved, but she still struggled with the word. "Human relations."

"Is he a personnel manager or something?"

"I think so. He said he was *into people*."

Marv was skeptical. Jobs were hard to come by these days, and people rarely got jobs when they weren't looking for them. Still, it wasn't that hard to believe that Rosie's good looks and fairly decent English could make her valuable to some company in Los Angeles. She'd be perfect for demonstrating products in supermarkets, or some other sort of sales.

"What would you be doing?"

"He didn't tell me, exactly, but he did say it was a part-time job, and that I could probably work as much as I like. He said there was work for me tomorrow if I wanted it. Do you think I should take the job?"

Marv was reluctant to say yes but couldn't bring himself to say no. He couldn't deny Rosie an opportunity when she'd come to America—the land of opportunity—for just such a chance. Besides, in his heart he knew she'd take the job even without his approval. More than once, she'd made it clear to him that she wouldn't start acting like a *real* wife until he lost the weight. And although that hurt him, he couldn't let it prevent him from acting like a *real* husband. A real husband would support his wife and encourage her to pursue things outside the marriage.

"Go ahead," he said, trying to hide the reluctance in his voice with a feigned smile.

"Good," she said with a smile of her own. She got up from the table. "Would you like more salad?"

No! a voice screamed from deep within his mind. What I really want is a fat T-bone steak that I can sink my teeth into and feel rivulets of grease and barbecue sauce dribble down my chin. He shook his head and sighed. That wouldn't help him lose the weight; that wouldn't help him get laid.

So far he'd lost ten pounds, not a lot considering what he was putting himself through, or how hungry he felt. *One hundred and forty pounds to go.* It was such a big number, it made him sick just thinking about it.

"Do you want more salad?" Rosie asked again, this time placing a hand gently, almost lovingly, on his shoulder. It was the first time she'd touched him in days.

Marv was speechless for a moment as her touch permeated his body like a shiver. When the shiver reached his groin, he felt himself getting hard.

"Yes, please," he said.

Marv pulled on his pajama bottoms and pulled the waist string tight against his stomach. After the first try he pulled back the excess fabric gathered around the front of the waistband and pulled the strings tight again. He'd lost forty-seven pounds in the past ten weeks—almost five pounds a week—and had another six months to go to achieve his goal.

God, that sounds like such a long time, he thought.

Especially since the hunger had begun to affect him. Not just his body, but his mind as well. It was getting clouded, as if his diet were starving his brain of energy. He was slow on his feet and constantly late for work. It took him days to create programs that used to take hours. He was past deadline on four reports and threatening to be late on two others. Worst of all, he began having mild hallucinations. Circles sometimes appeared to him as doughnuts, computer manuals became TV dinner boxes, and the paper-clip tray at the edge of his desk looked more and more like a cheeseburger with each passing day.

He slipped into his pajama top, rolled back the sleeves, and tucked the drooping bottom into the taut waistband of his pants. Then he went to the closet for his robe. As he reached for the robe hanging on the inside of the door, something on a shelf at the back of the closet caught his attention. It was a dark and frilly thing he'd never noticed there before. He switched on the closet light and reached back into the shadowy corner.

When his hand came back there were skimpy lace panties clenched in his beefy fingers. For a moment he stood there dumbfounded; it was the closest he'd ever been to women's underwear before. He stepped out of the closet and sat down on the edge of the bed. Then he laid out the panties on top of the bed and took each one in his hand. With a delicate touch that belied his still-stubby fingers and impressive size, he held the underpants before him as if they were made of gossamer and wind. As he looked at them he imagined what they might look like on Rosie. Sexual energy and hunger coursed through him, making his stomach growl and his penis stiffen.

He gathered the lingerie up off the bed and went back to the closet. He reached a little deeper in the same spot and pulled out more lingerie: G-strings, garters and stockings, lace teddies and merry widows. A final grab had him take hold of something long, hard, and cylindrical and another thing that was squat and flat like a box. He took out both items and stepped out of the closet.

In his left hand was a ten-inch-long plastic dildo, in his right was a videotape of something called *Taco Belles: Hot New Talent from South of the Border.*

Marv was even more dumbfounded than before. Anger roiled up within him. "How could she?" he said under his breath.

But then it suddenly made sense, and all he could feel was sympathy for Rosie and what she must be going through. Obviously, she was getting impatient about waiting so long for him to lose the weight and was resorting to masturbation to satisfy her own healthy sexual urges. The lingerie was obviously meant to be a surprise. She was keeping it hidden until the day she could wear it *for him.* That would also explain the need for all the vaginal medications and douches in the bathroom medicine chest. Rosie was just making sure that when he was ready, she would be ready . . . *for him.*

Marv's dick throbbed between his legs like a sore thumb, and his head felt light and hazy. Six more months would be brutal on him. He couldn't possibly wait that long, not now. He vowed to lose the weight faster, starving himself if he had to. Rosie couldn't satisfy herself forever; sooner or later she'd want—no, *need*—a man.

Just then he heard Rosie come in through the back

door, and he hurriedly tossed the lingerie, dildo, and videotape back into the closet.

"Hi, Rosie," he said, his back to the closed closet door as she entered. "How was work today?"

"I'm sore," she said with a long tired sigh. "And my legs feel like rubber."

"Tough day, huh?"

"Yes," she said, tossing a black gym bag in the closet and stepping out of her sweats on the way to the bed.

"Anything I can do for you?" Marv asked, watching her walk awkwardly across the room in her plain white bra and panties.

She flashed him a seemingly warm and genuine smile that acknowledged he was being sweet.

At that moment Marv almost felt loved.

"Yes, there is," she said, crawling into bed. "Close the door on your way out."

"Yes, dear," Marv said.

It wasn't the first night he'd spent on the couch.

He vowed it would be one of the last.

After Marv stopped eating altogether and began starving himself, the pounds rolled off his body like hot wax from a candle. The first few weeks were the toughest as his stomach continuously boomed, panged and growled, causing more than one embarrassing moment in the office elevator.

Eventually, he began taking the stairs to the sixth floor. Although he always felt weak and on the edge of passing out by the time he got to his desk, he was losing up to three pounds per week, a full pound more than he did on weeks he took the elevator.

He didn't get much work done, or rather, couldn't get much work done. When he sat down at his desk in the morning, he became too distracted by the smell of coffee and doughnuts wafting through the air. The same thing happened around lunchtime with stinky, greasy deli sandwiches from Katz's across the street.

In the hours between coffee breaks and lunch, Marv tried to settle down and get some work done, but he found he couldn't concentrate on anything that didn't have to do with food or sex.

Every day he went without food made his hallucinations worse, more vivid. Pens and pencils became licorice whips, markers became hot dogs, and the keyboard of his computer became a huge submarine sandwich. Elsewhere in the office, real pieces of food became body parts. Doughnuts and sandwiches, especially those made with kaiser buns, became breasts; carrots and celery sticks became penises; tacos and fajitas became vaginas.

One day, as he spent an afternoon break in the lunchroom with a current issue of his favorite software magazine, Marv caught a glimpse of Vivian Lorti, a buxom blonde who worked in accounts receivable, munching on some carrot sticks that she'd brought with her in a cellophane bag.

As Marv watched, Vivian held the stick firmly in her hand, ran her lips over the length of it, then lapped at the swollen end with the tip of her tongue. A moment later, after sliding it in and out of her mouth several times, she swallowed it whole.

Marv's hand slid down and nestled between his legs. As Vivian pulled another dick from her bag and began sucking on it, Marv leaned back in his chair and began rubbing his hand against his crotch. When she held the bag out and offered sticks to the three other women at the table, Marv let out a long loud moan.

He didn't realize everyone in the lunchroom was watching him fondle himself until Jack Conroy, his immediate supervisor, placed a hand on his shoulder and asked, "What the hell do you think you're doing?"

"Huh?" Marv said, pulled only halfway out of his daze.

"I said, what the hell are you doing?"

"What?" Marv suddenly realized what he'd been doing. He pulled his hand away from his groin and crossed his legs to try and hide the erection straining against his fly.

"I think we better have a talk in my office," Jack said.

Marv tried to get up, but his erection wouldn't allow him to stand up straight.

"I'll be there in a minute," he said.

"I'll be waiting for you."

When he got to the office, Jack was sitting behind his desk drumming his fingers on the desktop. "I checked with personnel. You've got a week of sick leave built up. I think it would be better for everyone if you took it now."

"But—" Marv sputtered.

"It's either that or look for another job," Jack said matter-of-factly. Then his tone lightened. "You've changed since you got married, Marv. At first everyone thought the change was for the better, but now nobody knows what to make of you."

Marv didn't answer.

"You're a good programmer, and you've done well for the company in the past. Take your week. Hopefully you'll feel better when you get back. . . ."

Marv's gaze was fixed, his eyes locked on the jar of

jelly beans on the edge of his supervisor's desk. To Marv, it was a jar full of brown and pink nipples.

"Did you hear anything I said?" Jack asked.

"Yes," Marv said, without having a clue as to what he'd just agreed to. "Absolutely."

Marv kept on starving himself while he stayed home and did odd jobs around the house. The weight came off even faster. Limiting himself to just a glass and a half of water on a really hot day, Marv could lose as much as five pounds a week or more. Sometimes, he could actually feel the fat burning up under his skin, sizzling into vapor and then sweating out his pores.

His stomach had given up its grumbling and complaining long ago, but his hallucinations continued to get worse. Sometimes he'd look up and see that his house was made of gingerbread, or that the sky was filled with marshmallows.

Sometimes, his hallucinations weren't so harmless. One afternoon he was cutting the grass in the backyard while Rosie sunned herself on the back porch. She hadn't worked in a couple of weeks, and Marv had noticed her becoming restless. Marv was restless himself as well. After all, it was hard to concentrate on cutting the grass with Rosie lying back on a deck chair with two tiny triangles of yellow fabric over the nipples of her full round breasts and a slip of a tanga brief just barely covering her forbidden fruit.

As Marv looked at his wife with a bit of a lolling tongue, he ran over a rock with the mower, and it stopped dead in front of him. The jolt brought Marv out of his daze, and after a moment he turned his attention away from his wife and onto the stalled mower.

The blade, while dented, was not broken. And more importantly, the shaft had not been bent. He switched the electric mower back on and watched the blade turn to make sure nothing else had been damaged.

As he watched, the spinning blade slowly turned into the swirling arm of the candy floss machine he had so loved as a kid. With almost childlike abandon, Marv got down on all fours and stuck out his tongue. Slowly, he moved his face closer to the twirling steel blade. . . .

"Marvin!" Rosie screamed.

Marv saw the candy floss machine blur into lawn mower blades and recoiled in terror.

The machine cut out as Rosie switched it off.

"What were you trying to do?"

Marv didn't answer. His heart had leapt too far up into his throat for him to speak.

Later, after Rosie had convinced him to indulge himself in a cup of tea, they sat together at the kitchen table.

"You have to eat something," Rosie said, pleading with him as if she truly cared about him.

"But I still weigh two hundred and fifty-seven pounds. I still have twenty pounds to go."

Rosie looked at him for the longest time, her eyes moving from head to toe and side to side, as if sizing him up.

"I'll tell you what," she said. "You've been so good about losing the weight, why don't we forget about the other twenty pounds and have sex? Today. Right now."

"You mean it?" Marv said, his eyes wide and his jaw hanging slack in disbelief. "What about the rest of the weight?"

"You can lose it after."

Marv knew she was giving in early because she felt sorry for him, maybe even pitied him, but he didn't care. He needed sex as badly as he needed to eat something, and he wasn't particularly worried about how he got it, just as long as he did.

"Give me ten minutes," she said. "Then come up to the bedroom. I'll be waiting for you." She flashed a sly smile and left the kitchen.

Marv's mouth was dry, his knees were weak, and his hands were trembling. The only part of his body that wasn't shaking was the part of him between his legs. Down there he was rock steady. Hard and ready.

Marv stepped out of the bathroom and slipped across the hall into the bedroom. The curtains were drawn, but the bright midday sun still shone through, illuminating the room in a soft red glow.

Rosie lay on the bed with the covers drawn down.

With a gentle touch, she traced her fingers over her naked breasts and belly, then slid her hands between her legs. She spread her legs slowly, pushing them apart with the open palms of her hands.

Marv stood there watching Rosie for the longest time. Her hands moved expertly over her body, as if she knew just how to touch herself to get the maximum effect from a man. Obviously, she'd been practicing. Marv felt his erection strengthen and his body weaken with each passing second.

"You don't look too bad without all that fat on you," she said, inserting the index finger of her right hand suggestively into her mouth.

Marv couldn't help seeing a breadstick disappearing between her lips.

"You don't look too bad yourself," he said. Then, after a moment's hesitation, "Almost good enough to eat."

"Well"—Rosie smiled—"that would be a good place to start." She adjusted herself on the bed, making herself comfortable as she spread her legs wider to expose her neatly trimmed bush of thick black hair. She pulled her pussy lips apart with the tips of her fingers.

Marv approached the bed slowly, blinking his eyes, unsure about what he was seeing.

He settled down between Rosie's legs and happily began licking and kissing her there. Rosie moaned and squirmed against his touch.

After a few passes of his tongue, Marv's craving for sex was overtaken by hunger of another kind.

He wasn't looking at her pussy anymore. But he bared his teeth and kept on eating just the same.

Rosie screamed and thrashed violently beneath him, but he overpowered her with his bulky mass and continued munching.

She stopped squirming by the time Marv reached her breasts.

THE ROSE

Jack Ketchum

She was his earth, his ground. He had cast his seed to her again and again.

He awoke feeling that he knew what was necessary, that what she needed was a kind of light both real and metaphoric, that she needed to get out into the world far more than he had allowed himself to trust her to do.

He decided he would take her.

When they stepped off the bus into early afternoon sunlight he saw how the city had changed, none of it for the better. It was only a town, really, that had tried to bloom into a city during the fifties and arguably had succeeded for a while, but now the war babies who had driven its boom years, who had caused its schools to rise out of vacant lots and farmland and crammed its movie palaces and soda shops, had fled and left its potholed, littered streets to time and waste.

Still he felt at home here.

He took her to Mabel's Coffee Shop, where as a boy he had sat over Coke and crumb bun waiting for Miss Lanier, his accordion teacher, to finish with the pigtailed little redhead who had the lesson just before his on the third floor across the street. They had lunch there at the counter—she a hamburger from the grill and he a tuna sandwich with a thin slice of pickle.

Miss Lanier was gone. Cancer. Miss Lanier had gone to earth. And he had not seen his accordion in thirty-five years.

The faces in Mabel's were mostly black now. But they seemed to him the same tired faces he had always seen there, working people's faces bent over working people's food.

He realized that Mabel's always had depressed him, even angered him somehow. It had not just been the accordion lessons.

But the girl didn't seem to mind.

He took her arm and led her past a shoe store, a dress shop, a thrift shop, and the Arthur E. Doyle Post of the Veterans of Foreign Wars, to the Roxy.

The Roxy was boarded up. It had probably been closed for years. Graffiti was sprayed across rotted boards thick and colorful as the patterns on a Persian rug. He walked her across the street to the Palace.

The Palace was open.

"How about a movie," he said.

She brushed a clean fine strand of long blond hair off her pretty face and nodded.

They sat in the dark, alone but for three other patrons slouched low and scattered in front of them, and watched Jean-Claude Van Damme fight his way through a double feature, and he thought how they were the only couple there. At intermission he bought

popcorn. Midway through the second feature he unbuttoned her blouse and massaged her naked breast
and rolled her pale wide nipple between his fingers,
letting it harden and then go soft again, feeling the
nipple beneath the palm of his hand and thinking, if
only I had gotten this thirty years ago. Jesus.

When it was over it was nearly dark. They had
dinner at a place called Rogerio's a few blocks over.
He thought the place had served Chinese takeout
once, but now it was Italian. He ordered a double
scotch for himself and iced tea for the girl and then
ordered himself another. They ate pasta and thick, hot
crusty bread, and she was very quiet.

They walked out into streetlights shining.

Across the street he saw the sign.

Like so many others the shop had not been there
when he was a boy. He would have remembered it.
But someone was inside. The place was all lit up.

He felt the flush of pleasure and the swelling of his
cock inside his baggy trousers.

"Come on," he said.

She sat on the wooden bench in front of him naked
to the waist, nipples going hard and then soft just as
they had in the movie theater, while the bearded man
sat behind her working on her shoulder blade, his
needle buzzing like a barber's electric trimmer over
the soft rock music on the radio.

The music was meant to be soothing. The man had
warned them that there would be more pain than
usual because the bone was so near the surface of the
skin in this location. He could see the pain skitter in
her eyes. She had been under the drill for over half an
hour now.

"What's it like?" he asked her.

"Feels like . . . cat scratches," she said. "Hundreds of little cat scratches. Then it's like . . . he's *peeling* me. And then . . ."

The tattooist smiled. "Like a dentist's drill, right?" he said.

"Yes," she breathed.

He saw the sweat beaded on her upper lip.

"Scapula," he said. "Can't be helped. You're a helluva subject, though, you know that? You don't move a muscle. You're like workin' on a canvas. I'm gonna give you something special. You'll see. A rose is just right for you. Just a few more minutes."

From the hundreds of drawings that lined the walls he had chosen for her a simple red rose no more than an inch and a half in diameter. He thought the rose was beautiful and that the man had quite a delicate hand. You could see veins in the green leaves, the creamy blush of red, the thorns that studded the graceful stem.

The buzzing stopped.

"There now," said the man. "Give me your hand. Hold the gauze here and press. Not hard."

She did as he said. The man stood up from the bench.

"You want to see?"

He got up and walked over behind her. The tattooist lifted her hand away. He was very gentle.

Beautiful, he thought. The rose looked even better than it did on paper, more detailed and more delicately formed, its stem tracing precisely the natural curve of bone as though it belonged there, as though it had grown there in her silky flesh.

The man looked at him, nodding, appraising his

reaction. He had a long bushy beard, and his graying hair was tied back into a tail as long as a horse's tail, and his eyes were unreadable. But he saw no judgment there. Though it was impossible that he had missed the marks along her back and shoulders.

He saw no judgment there at all.

"Anything else I can do for you?"

His eye drifted to the glass display case by the register. There were rings and studs of gold and silver and semiprecious stones.

"Yes," he said. "Yes, there is."

She had not sat so well for the piercing.

On the first try she had flinched despite the topical anesthetic, and her flesh slid free of the instrument that was similar to a paper punch just as he had begun to apply pressure. The man had cursed and then apologized to her for cursing. The girl said nothing, though it had hurt her and tears streamed down her cheeks. The man had reapplied the anesthetic and tried again, holding the tip of the nipple more firmly between thumb and forefinger and pulling so that it was possible to see that that hurt, too, telling her soothingly that it would only be a second, just a second, then squeezed the handles together.

She gasped and then was silent.

He was surprised there was so little blood.

The man threaded her flesh with the thin silver band he had chosen from the display case.

Then bent to the other breast.

The lights went out behind them, and he heard the tattooist draw his shade as they stepped out into the street.

He took her arm and led her to the corner.

On the bus trip home he was annoyed with her. It was as though she didn't want the nipple rings. She had shown no reluctance about the rose tattoo. It was as though she accepted that. Whereas to him they were one and the same. Both rose and rings marked her as his—they would for the rest of her life. And if he could not bring her fecundity, if he could not bind her to him by fucking a girl-child into the hot depths of her womb, he could at least do this. Children were the glue, his mother had said, and he thought it ungrateful of the girl to wish to deny him.

It had been such a good day in the city.

He opened his flask and drank. In the darkness there was no one to see. Towns faded by and dark suburban homes. He drank some more.

The towns grew smaller. Houses yielded to woods and thicket and stands of pale birch trees and old weathered stone fences.

Finally they were home. He got off the bus ahead of her and held out his hand. She took it, and they walked up the unpaved road in the moonlight. He could see the small gray spot on the back of her blouse where the tattoo had bled through the gauze. There were no such spots on either of her breasts, but he thought that the blouse would still need washing before the blood had set, and that annoyed him, too, for some reason he wasn't aware of. He tilted the flask and finished it as they came to the door, and he took out the keys and opened it and turned on the lights as they walked inside.

"Get ready," he told her.

"Why?"

"Why? Why are you *asking?*"

Her face looked pained.

"Get ready. And put that blouse in some cold water."

He walked behind her to the kitchen and watched as she ran the water in the sink and stripped off the blouse. He could see the outline of the rose on her shoulder beneath the thin layer of gauze. The man had said it would scab for a few days and then heal. That was fine. He wouldn't touch her there. Nor, for the moment, would he touch the rings.

"Turn around."

He reached for the short leather riding crop on the pegboard behind him on the kitchen wall hanging amid the pots and pans.

"Raise your arms," he said.

He began on her stomach.

He lay across his sheets drunk with too much scotch on top of too little of the greasy Italian food and heard her shift in the box he'd built for her beneath the bed. He knew that it was hard for her to sleep. Her nipples would hurt. Her back would hurt from the tattoo. Her thighs and stomach would still be stinging.

It was nothing new. In the four years since he'd found her in the parking lot at K-mart and bluffed her into the car with his toy pistol pain had become something she was used to. There had been a thousand such nights. Tonight was only different, really, in that he'd had hopes again in fucking her. Perhaps his arousal would translate into her own, and arousal into a baby. He wanted the baby because it would be a continuation of her when she was gone. But it hadn't happened. He knew it hadn't.

It was dark as the grave inside the box. He knew

that, too. He'd tried it out himself to see if the casters worked and found that it was darker even than the basement where he'd kept her the first two years of her captivity, listening to her whine to please, *please* set her free! to let her call her parents or go to the toilet or loosen the wire coils around her wrists—until finally there was no more whining and no more talk at all for a long time.

The box was better than the basement and darker. It was what she deserved. To be buried there.

It was a sin that he loved her.

"Barren," he muttered. And finally he fell asleep.

The following day was Monday, and he went to work as usual, leaving her bound naked inside the box beneath the bed. The bonds were not really necessary. The bonds were merely custom. It was over three years ago that she had attempted to escape him twice over the period of a single month, and he had discouraged her with the red-hot blade of a kitchen knife and the suggestion that he had contacts everywhere, that he was part of some vast vague criminal machine and that should she try a third time, first her mother and then her father would meet with accidental death, reinforcing this by showing her that he had their address and her father's business address in his Rolodex and even knew the make, model, and year of the car sitting in their driveway.

He told her stories of this criminal network frequently, mostly of their viciousness in matters of retribution. He told her that her name was registered in their central computer and that should anything happen to him, should he die or be arrested, they would be honor bound to find her and torture her to death according to their code. In his stories he described these tortures in loving detail and saw that she soon came to believe them.

She no longer tried to run away.

He returned from work at noon to let her feed herself and use the bathroom and saw that she had her period again. Her first day's flow was always heavy. He had her change the thin gray sheets in the box before he put her back inside again. The period meant that he probably wouldn't want to touch her for a few days. He'd probably just watch cable.

Nights he'd come home to a liter of scotch and "Nick at Nite," and he'd be able to forget that she was there doing the dishes, the laundry, even the vacuuming if he turned the sound up loud enough. He'd be able to forget his phone installation route and his goddamn supervisor and the long-dead woman whose home he was living in even though her ghost was everywhere. He'd get a little smashed and think, Ma, if you could see me now.

On the fourth night he fucked her.

He had to have been blind drunk to fuck her because there was still some bleeding, some residue inside her, but fucking her blind drunk was nothing new either, and he pulled and tugged on the rings in her nipples until she screamed, and he came in her from behind with a power that astonished him. And he must have been pretty blind drunk indeed because as he fell away from behind her across the bed and she stepped away he thought he saw not one rose but two branching off the same central stem that curved along her shoulder blade.

He even thought he smelled them.

* * *

The following night he *was* blind drunk, no question, and raging.

"You want to call your parents? We're back to that shit? You're giving me *that* shit again?"

He had all kinds of whips all over the house just for times like these when he needed one instantly and did not want to go looking for one, and this one in the living room on the mantel was long and thin. It was meant to produce pain, and it was studded to produce blood.

She knew that about the whip but didn't run away—just stood there looking at him, defiant. He'd thought they were long past defiance.

"Take off your clothes."

She didn't move.

So he whipped them off her.

She was wearing just a light summer skirt and blouse he'd picked out for her at K-mart, and when he was done they were just tatters hanging off her hips and shoulders, spackled and streaked with blood.

He put her in the bathroom and ran a tub for her and closed the door.

By the time she came out again he'd killed the bottle. He watched her crawl meekly into the box and roll herself under the bed just moments before he fell asleep in the heavy overstuffed armchair in front of the television.

She was naked. The welts across her body looked like runners, like heavy creepers—serpentine, overlapping and intersecting inside her flesh—the ripe red wounds that the metal studs had made like the small blossoms of flowers.

* * *

And then it was the weekend again.

On Saturday he left her alone, feeling bad about the beating of the night before. Though she'd provoked him.

The girl kept her distance. She made them lunch and handed him a shopping list, and when he returned with the groceries she was on her knees scrubbing the kitchen floor. She wore an old red sweatshirt and sweat pants which had once belonged to him but which had shrunk with repeated washings so that they were even tight on her now, and because the front of the shirt was wet and he could see the outlines of the nipple rings when she stood to change the water. Still he left her be.

That night they watched a movie together—*Poltergeist*—about a family battling supernatural forces which threaten to drive them apart and winning. The children were the glue, he thought. He looked at her sadly.

"That could be us, you know," he said.

"What could?" she said.

He drank his whiskey.

By Sunday night he was still feeling tender toward her.

It was partly because she didn't look good. Her face had a gray-brown cast to it that he didn't like. She needed sun. But Sunday was as overcast as Saturday had been. Rain threatened. So there was no point in letting her sit out in the backyard deck sewing his buttons on or mending his socks.

Plus she was off her feed. She'd never been one for breakfast, but she usually had a little lunch at least and a fairly decent dinner. Chicken was normally her favorite, but tonight they had chicken and she barely touched it, seeming to prefer the vegetables—though she didn't do much with them either.

He wondered if she were coming down with something.

Or if that beating Friday night had been more extreme than he'd remembered.

It was possible that she needed a treat, some kind of pick-me-up. A boost to her morale.

So when it was time to go to bed he told her as she came out of the bathroom in her pajamas that she did not have to sleep in the box tonight, tonight was special, she could be beside him on the bed. She said nothing but crawled in next to him and rested her head in the crook of his arm.

He smiled. The girl smelled of musk and roses. He wondered how she had managed that. He was not aware of having ever bought her any such perfume, but perhaps at some time he had. It was considerate of her—even loving—to wear it for him now.

She slept in the moonless night.

He could tell by her breathing.

He almost fell asleep, too. It had begun to rain, and he lay listening to it patter on the roof for a long while, and then he thought about her young girl's body, marked by his hand and bearing his sign, so wet and soft inside, which he had not seen or even touched in nearly two days now, and he felt himself begin to rise.

Perhaps tonight, he thought. He knew nothing about a woman's fertility, only that it was there, and that somehow he might touch it if he were to go deep enough to dig it out of her.

He turned her toward him in the dark. He unbuttoned her pajama top and felt something prick his middle finger as the third button slid through the buttonhole and thought that she would have to replace that in the morning, that it was broken and jagged and might hurt her.

He drew the bottoms down off her legs, felt the welts like thick coils along her thighs. She stirred and in her slide across the sheets he heard a sound like the rustle of leaves.

He heard the distant thunder.

And it must have awakened her, or else his stripping her had, because she put her hands to his shoulders as he parted her legs and entered her, feeling the welts along the insides of her thighs as she gripped him inside her and moved, swaying gently, beneath him.

It was like nothing that had ever come before.

She had never been so responsive to him, pulling herself up onto him, urgently close to him while the thunder rumbled, and he saw flashes of lightning beneath the closed lids of his eyes and then opened them so he could see her, could see this sudden phenomenon that was clawing at him, fingernails scoring the skin of his back and shoulders, this amazing phenomenon as his slave of love in every way now plunged in moonless black, which tore and bit and moaned as though tossed in a savage wind and who suddenly seemed to be everywhere around him at once, her fingers a thousand raking tendrils, her teeth a thousand thorns, her body a billion petals all falling together and himself the author of this destruction, this overwhelming flowering.

The lightning flashed twice.

He heard the rings drop off the bed and roll across the floor as her wide soft nipples opened, bloomed, and parted, smelled loam and fresh-turned earth as a strand of briar turned twice around his neck. He felt her cunt like a crown of thorns gripping him tight and tearing and felt himself throb and shoot suddenly deep within her, blood and semen, runners crawling over him, their thorns sinking deep, felt himself bleeding into her, veins, arteries pricked and severed as he looked down at the body which was no longer her body but the tangled garden of wild blood-red roses that he had made of her blossoming and erupting from tortured flesh.

She was his earth, his ground. He had cast his seed to her again and again.

And the creepers grew, nourished.

FOR BETH AND RICHARD

RELEASE OF FLESH

Steve Rasnic Tem

Stop moving.

"Stop moving, I said." He sounded angry. She'd had them angry with her before, she'd had them furious, but not like this. He was like no other john, like no one she'd ever met.

"There. There you have it. It is the teeth, you see. The nip and the tug of them, the way they grate the skin and bring it alive. Teeth remind us of where we came from, and where we are going, where we will all end up. In the mouth, chewed and swallowed. The teeth abrading the skin, just so. Just as you are doing now. Takes us through skin, and into blood, until it is food that we have become. You know what I am saying. Munch and nibble, we are all cheese, crackers, soup."

At first he was paying her to stay with him. Then somehow he found out that she never spent the money. She hadn't wanted him to know. It embarrassed her; it wasn't professional. She was a *whore,* for chrissake. What the hell was she doing? She didn't understand either. "Why did you take the money in the first place?" he asked her.

"I don't know," she said. "It's funny. I guess I take the money so guys don't own me. It's opposite what you'd think. I take the money and you just think I'm a prostitute, and that way you don't know how I really feel. And that's the way I like it. Keeps me independent."

"In my limited experience with women, this seems to be atypical," he said. He always talked like that. She asked him where he had grown up, where he had gone to school, but he refused to be specific. She didn't press him. Maybe he was just an odd duck.

He just needed her to stay with him. He kept saying this. He used words like "need," "stay," and "safety" all the time. A running theme.

"I really have not thought beyond that—what we would do, what we would talk about, what specific acts we might perform. These aspects of a relationship are far beyond anything I have ever known." She would have to tell him everything, teach him everything.

He watched a lot of TV. He watched more TV than anyone she'd ever known. He said it kept him "focused." He said it taught him important things about himself.

The talk show host looked sad. She almost expected him to cry. He had shiny white hair, and neck wrinkles so that he reminded her of her dad. But she'd hated her dad—he'd raped her over and over again from the time she was five until she was fourteen, before she'd rammed the fork he'd been eating beans with into his big fat belly and ran away from there. She guessed that was the reason the talk show host made her nervous, even though she really wanted to believe everything he said.

The talk show host was talking about the decrease in Americans' sexual desire. "Some have called it the designer disease of the decade," he said. He sounded like he really cared about this, like maybe he had the same problem. "One in five adult Americans," he said. "An estimated thirty-eight million of us"—his voice got low and kind of sexy—"don't want sex at all."

She tried to get the john to change the channel. She figured this probably wasn't putting him much in the mood. She tried stroking his balls. He said this was important information. That she should pay attention —it would help her understand him better. "Well, it's your nickel," she said, then she felt sorry she'd said it that way, like she didn't give a damn.

"Meanwhile nine million more suffer from uncontrollable sexual desire, indiscriminate in their pairings, masturbating uncontrollably."

He turned off the TV and looked at her. "Tell me about masturbation," he said.

"Oh, you'd be surprised what guys will do it to," she replied. "You just have to make the right picture for them. I've been a nurse, a teacher, Little Bo-Peep. Once I was supposed to be a cat this guy had lost when he was nine years old. Another time I was supposed to be this fellow's dead mother. I mean, I was supposed to dress up like his mother. But I was also supposed to be dead."

"When they masturbate, do they like you to touch them?"

"Almost never. I guess it breaks the mood."

"So they are lonely creatures," he said. "Isolates. Aliens."

"Sure. Most of them tell me they can't relate much at all to regular women. Not to their wives, not to anybody. I guess that's why they come to me. Damn sad, damn lonely, just plain damned, sometimes. I used to spend a lot of time wondering how they got that way, just like they were asking me why I'd become a prostitute. I finally stopped wondering because none of them ever had an answer for me, just like I never had an answer for them."

"Masturbation is not what I want," he said softly, somewhat sadly. "It makes it worse. With the friction beneath my hands, I start changing, and then there is no stopping it."

He was a little under six feet tall when she first met him. Although he'd felt much taller. Now she didn't know how tall he was. Sometimes she wondered about his shoe size. His shoes seemed different, like he must have had them specially made. His naked feet seemed even stranger. Once she'd gone through all the shoes in the bottom of his closet looking for the sizes, but they'd been worn away, like they'd been rubbed a lot, or burned, even.

"Move there. Hold it, there," he'd say. She'd never had a john order her around quite so much. He had the right, of course—he was paying for it. Even if she never spent the money. Still, there was always something just a little scary about the way he talked to her.

* * *

"You came highly recommended," he once said. "They tell me there's no one quite like you."

She smiled. "It's nothing. We're all only human, aren't we? We're all different people."

"Do not say that," he said. "What a sad, sad thing that is."

"It's a growing epidemic," the young blond woman on the TV said. She looked overly sincere. It was her first day hosting her own show. "Too much sex, too little sex. And beneath it all, psychologists tell us, is a terrible, debilitating loneliness."

She moved over him with as much control as she could. She tried to be precise, like a doctor would be. He had explained to her that he hated "abandon." He said he felt at ease only when her "faked passion remains within certain bounds." But she was afraid she wasn't faking it anymore. Her feelings were real. But this was something she could never tell him. She'd fallen in love with him.

"Not so quickly, please," he said, struggling with his own breath. "Do not let me, do not let me lose my mind."

She forced herself to slow down. She looked down at him and was scared by the way his skin looked, all rough and red. "You've got a rash," she said softly.

"Ignore that."

"But maybe you're sick. . . ."

"Who in your world is not?"

Hurt, she said nothing more to him for hours. But she touched him, she held him, and gratefully he said she provided a "wonderful focus."

* * *

"Just tell me what turns you on," she said. "You tell me to hold you like this and like that, to touch you in certain ways. So I hold your dick, and I touch you hard between your balls and your asshole, but it doesn't turn you on much. It relaxes you, I guess, but it doesn't really turn you on. You should be telling me what turns you on."

"You mean I should be getting my money's worth. You are afraid of being a bad businesswoman, not giving satisfaction to a customer."

"It's not that at all!"

"Everything you do 'turns me on,' as you say. I am here, now, with you, and that is the most I could ask for. But go too far and I will no longer be here. I will no longer be able to control myself."

"That sounds like a threat."

He looked surprised. "It is simply a warning."

"Sometimes it's good to lose control. Sometimes it's good to let go, to let go of all your tension, of all the stuff you are. Isn't that what good sex is all about?"

"No, no—you have no idea. You know nothing about losing control. You prostitutes, you are all about control. Why do you think I hired a prostitute if not for their legendary control?"

The young woman on the screen was a performance artist. She had sex live on stage three nights a week. "I want to show the great masses out in suburbia that they needn't be afraid of sex, that they needn't be afraid of their desires, whatever form they might take. I want to shake them up, force them to experience their own breasts, vagina, cock and balls."

She thought the female performance artist was just

a slut with a lot of crazy excuses. She was embarrassed by her. But the john couldn't stop talking about her. "The way she is able to concentrate on the act," he said, "while everyone is watching her. It amazes me that she does not fly apart."

"She's vulgar," she said. "That's what my mom used to call it. I may be a whore, but at least I do my act in private."

"But her vulgarity is her strength, I think." He turned off the TV and began rubbing and holding her as she'd taught him. He said it helped him to have her body, her passion to concentrate on. She found it hard to hold herself back. "But she is wrong in her basic premise," he whispered warmly into her ear. "Fear is not the problem; it is just another symptom. Loneliness is the problem, and the condition of being a monster."

"What would you like me to wear?" she asked softly.

"Wear what you like. What would you like me to wear?"

"My skin, my hair, my breath."

"Be careful what you ask for, prostitute. When you receive it you may find it was not what you expected."

"What part of my body do you like the best?" she asked.

"It depends upon the occasion."

"Okay. What part of me do you like best when you're about to come?"

"But I do not want to 'come.' I told you we cannot let that happen. I must be brought close to that point, to the point where I am the most intensely aware of *your* body and not my own. But orgasm must never occur."

"I know. I understand that now. But when you're *about* to come, what do you like best about me?"

"Your eyes."

She laughed. "Well, I didn't expect *that* answer!"

"But your eyes keep me in my place. When I feel the orgasm approaching, I can see myself in your eyes. I can see how you expect me to be, and that alone is enough to keep me from changing. You see I must not reach orgasm. I *must not* change. And yet when I am not feeling pleasure with this body I lose focus, and then I surely will change. And that would be disastrous for both of us. That is why you must give me pleasure, but never too much pleasure. That is why we must make love as often as we can."

She smiled, puzzled. He had never used the word "love" with her before. "What do you mean by 'disastrous'?"

"I would wear you," he said. "I would wear you like a tattered rag." And he showed her his teeth.

She had learned that he liked her in lingerie. He said it was the anticipation the garments encouraged which he loved, the fact that the "final participation" might be delayed an almost indefinite length of time. He continued to talk strangely like that, but more and more there were times when he talked just like any other lover. She taught him words like "balls," "fuck," "clit," "cunt," and "pussy." They sounded funny in his mouth at first, but eventually he began talking as if he liked those words.

But he said the words sometimes made him feel "physically uncomfortable." She thought it was like a disease; he'd been holding back for so long. She wondered sometimes if he'd even thought much about sex before he'd met her, if he'd even let himself. What was he so afraid of?

Sometimes he had her stay in her stockings and garter belt, her straps and belts, for hours before he would let her take something off. He would rub her underwear and grind his teeth. Sometimes he would grind his teeth awfully. She was surprised he had any teeth left.

"Anticipation is always best," he said. "Sometimes when the final act arrives, and the curtain falls, the real tragedy begins."

"At one time I had a serious interest in pornography," he told her. "The variety of poses possible with a relatively limited number of fleshy angles and parts. The better photographs exhibit a rather complex geometry and perspective, I think.

"Sometimes I would gaze at these photographs for hours, admiring their fixed changeability. What a wonderful thing it is, to be able to freeze a pose before a mistake might be made, before climax has been achieved. To stop short of transformation and remain so, what a wonderful thing."

"A john I had once said the best sex he'd ever had was with dead women. They don't change, and they don't complain. I wouldn't see him anymore after that night."

He looked at her with what might have been a smile. She wanted to ask him if he'd like to go out and get something to eat. He looked like he hadn't eaten for a while.

He didn't like to dance, though she tried to talk him into it.

"It frightens me," he would say. She forced herself not to laugh. He was so strong—she had felt muscles under his skin which were harder, firmer than any she'd ever felt before, and he felt so solid—that it was hard to believe he could be afraid of anything.

"Give it a try," she said. "Dancing makes you better at sex. I hear all the sex therapists say so."

So sometimes she would get him to his feet—he moved like he just didn't want to argue anymore—and she would guide him naked around the room in time to some soft music. He was actually pretty good, she thought. A natural.

But he never really seemed to like it. Like most things she saw him do, if he began to enjoy something even a little bit, his face would begin to change, he'd start smiling or frowning, and then he would stop what he was doing right then and stomp away.

"Tell me about the first time . . . you did this," he said.

"It was with my dad. I was his whore. That's all there is to tell," she said.

"And this made you sad. You did not feel in control."

"I was helpless. I've never liked that feeling."

"There is much that is sad in sex, I think. There is much that is sad about losing control."

"He was a monster," she said. Then, as if he wouldn't understand, "My dad."

"Do you ever fantasize? Do you dream? About sexual matters, I mean. Or is this merely your vocation?"

"It's a job, but I fantasize. Now you're making me pretty uncomfortable, you know."

"Fantasize that I am the monster," he said. "Put a stake through my heart, cut off my head, dig out my liver and bury it at a darkened crossroad. Kill the monster and perhaps you will not have to dream."

"Make love to me," she said.

"We do so every day. With 'cock' and 'balls' and 'pussy.'"

"No, I mean let yourself go. Lose yourself inside me. You've told me how much you like my lips, my 'labia,' how dark, how red they are. Now dream that I'm kissing you, and that my lips are taking you inside, and that suddenly you're wearing me."

"I cannot."

"Love me."

"No."

"Let go. Let yourself go."

And so it began. She wouldn't stop. No matter how much he screamed at her. She wouldn't stop. Even when he said he was losing focus. Even when he said he was losing himself. She wouldn't stop. She wouldn't stop. For he was the monster she loved and not the monster she hated. She wouldn't stop until he came. She wouldn't stop until he changed.

And when he came he did change. He changed inside her. He let go. He released his flesh. And the body which flowed through her vagina and through her vagina wall and filled the cavity of the rest of her was sad and lonely and nothing human at all.

THE NUMBERS GAME

Bentley Little

*H*e kisses the computer screen and the glass feels good, cold and unyielding beneath his warm pliant lips. He lets his tongue press forward, and it, too, encounters the barrier of cold glass, straining against the same solid plane. His hands caress the terminal, feeling the uninterrupted smoothness of the plastic frame surrounding the screen, moving on to the ridged air vents on the side and the textured touch of the greater casing.

He can feel himself becoming hard, and he unbuttons his slacks, freeing his growing erection. Released from the restricted confines of his pants, his hard penis points upward toward the computer. He pulls away from the terminal and turns it around until its backside is facing him, tilting it forward until the round seductive jack hole is revealed. The cable that is supposed to be inserted into the hole is much smaller than his penis, but the thought of a tight fit makes him even more *excited, and he lubricates his erection with spit and presses it against the opening.*

The shock, when it comes, knocks him out.

When he comes to, it is later, much later. The semen on his leg and on the terminal has dried, and he can see several small puddles of it on the floor between the edge of the work station and where he's fallen. The tip of his penis is blackened, burned, and the agony is tremendous.

But he still wants more.

Five, he thinks. Six, eight, one . . .

Cooper looked away from the computer screen and surreptitiously pressed down on his erection, trying to force his penis back into a state of nonarousal. He glanced slowly and casually around the room to make sure that none of the other programmers or researchers had seen him. None had. They were all staring intently at their own terminals or writing notes on sheets of loose note paper. He thought of his mother, thought of rap music, thought of unpleasant things until his erection subsided. He looked again at the screen.

He was instantly hard.

How was this possible? He read again the lit green numbers that had suddenly appeared on his terminal. The fact that the numbers had appeared there at all had amazed him—to his knowledge, security had never before been breached this far into the system— and when his screen had gone blank and the numbers had appeared, he had simply stared in shock, reading the series of numerals.

And he'd gotten an erection.

He forced himself to look away from the screen. It was an effort. He wanted to continue reading, wanted both the new feeling inside him and the organ between his legs to continue growing, but something was way out of whack here, and he knew he had to find out what it was. Once more he looked around the room.

Should he tell Deats?

He should. He should tell his supervisor, have him order a trace on the security breach, see if it was in-house or out, track it through a dedicated phone line if that's what was being used.

But . . .

But he wanted to stay right where he was.

He paused for a moment, then turned down the intensity dial on his terminal so no one else could see what was on his screen. He leaned forward to read the numbers.

Five, six, eight . . .

"Jesus. What the hell's he doing?"

Rosenthal looked over to where Deats was pointing. Gil Cooper was sitting in front of his terminal, pants unbuckled, fly unzipped, penis in hand, staring intently at the screen and masturbating furiously.

His first thought was that Cooper had snapped, had cracked under the pressure. But this was not like any breakdown he'd ever seen or read about, and he followed Deats as the supervisor moved forward, sharply calling out the mathematician's name. "Cooper! Cooper!"

A flood of white semen shot out of Cooper's penis, spurting over his pants and exposed thighs, but he did not seem to notice, and his movements did not even falter. He continued to stroke his organ at the same rapid pace, eyes focused on the screen in front of him.

"Cooper!"

Rosenthal followed the supervisor across the room, amidst the stares of the other researchers. Cooper had been quiet, and until now no one had noticed what he was doing; but Deats had drawn attention to his actions, and now everyone was watching in stunned silence.

"Cooper!"

The mathematician gave no sign that he heard them or even knew that they existed. This close, Rosenthal could see that Cooper's penis was bleeding, the skin rubbed raw.

Deats grabbed his arm, yanked him up and out of his chair, and Cooper's glazed eyes flickered for a second. The hand still rubbing his penis stopped, pulled away. "Screen . . . printout . . ." he said.

Then he was stroking himself again, mumbling lowly. "One, three, nine . . ."

Rosenthal knocked on the door of Cooper's room before walking inside. The nurse had told him he could just go in, but he wanted to give his friend at least a courtesy warning. He didn't want to catch him in an embarrassing situation.

Not that it could be worse than what he'd already seen.

"Come in!" Cooper called.

He walked into the hospital room. Deats was already there, as was Kiegelman. The two men nodded to him.

Cooper grinned wryly. "Afraid you'd catch me pulling my pork?"

Rosenthal smiled. "Been there. Done that."

"Going to give me an I-told-you-so on the numerology, huh?"

Deats looked over at him sharply. "What?"

"Oh, yeah. Our Fred's a big believer in the power of numbers." His smile faded slowly, his gaze became less focused. "I guess I am, too. Now."

"I don't *believe* in numerology," Rosenthal tried to explain. "I just study it. It's a hobby of mine, an interest." He looked from Deats to Kiegelman, shrugged. "What can I say? I like numbers."

"Shit," Kiegelman said. "Astrology."

"If this hasn't made us *all* into believers," Cooper said, "then we shouldn't be calling ourselves scientists. You can't ask for a better cause and effect than what happened to . . ." He trailed off, looked toward Deats as he suddenly thought of something. "Has . . . has anybody else read those numbers?"

The supervisor nodded grimly.

"Same result?"

Deats nodded. "Same result."

Rosenthal cleared his throat. "I think we've discovered something here. Something really important. Numerology may be a load of crap, but I think this proves once and for all that numbers are not just numbers, they're not merely written symbols for quantification. They have power of their own. The fact is, in cultures throughout history, numbers have affected everything from the way buildings are built to the way people think—"

Kiegelman snorted. "The way people think, huh? Spoken like a true mathematician."

"That's the one thing that numerologists have always had over mathematicians. They realized the philosophical and sociological importance of numbers. Numerological symbolism is and always has been very important. Three, for instance, is connected with the Trinity: the Father, the Son, the Holy Ghost. Three is also important sexually. The male genitals are tripartite—one cock, two balls. The female has two breasts and one vagina—"

"Or three holes," Cooper said.

"Exactly. The female pubis is covered by a triangle of pubic hair. A triangle has three sides. These symbols recur throughout history, throughout cultures, and they have power—"

"All right, Kreskin. Enough of the psychic mumbo jumbo." Kiegelman crossed the room toward him. "What's all this have to do with what's happened?"

"Well . . ."

"What's sociological significance have to do with Cooper beating off on his fucking terminal? We're not talking term paper or journal article fodder here. This is real-world shit. Hell, this is national security."

Deats nodded. "Yeah. And what's this 'we'? *We've* discovered something here? I don't think *we* discovered anything."

They were silent.

"Who *do* you think transmitted those numbers?" Rosenthal asked. "Who do you think could've gained access to the system?"

"Glickman," Cooper said quietly.

The others looked at him.

"I removed his ID and password from the security system, but when I looked over the report this morning, I saw that he was back in—"

"And you didn't say anything?" Deats glared at him.

"I was going to, but you weren't there yet, and . . . and then the numbers came in on my screen."

"Glickman. Shit."

Kiegelman shook his head. "I knew we should've had that guy taken care of when he left The Agency. Fucking loony."

Rosenthal looked at Cooper, saw his friend's troubled gaze, thought of Glickman, and for the first time since this had all started, a shiver of cold passed through him, and he was afraid.

The calculations are performed automatically, built into the program. He does not even have to see the numbers.

He breaks the new access code, transmits the data to The Agency. Rosenthal's terminal, if he remembers correctly, but he is not sure.

He laughs to himself, thinks for a moment, then gives himself a treat, calling up a short, limited sequence of the numbers on his own screen.

Thirty-five, eighteen, sixty-two . . .

He screams as he shoves his erection against the disk drive and climaxes.

Rosenthal sat in Deats's office with Deats, Kiegelman, Langley, and an unnamed member of The Agency's upper echelon. It was Deats asking the questions, but it was clearly the Agency man who was pulling the strings. Cooper, he knew, had already been questioned in the hospital. Hamilton and Green would be called in after him.

They wanted to know about Glickman.

There wasn't much he could tell them. There wasn't much that he knew. Sure, he'd worked with Glickman during his first four years at The Agency, but for all intents and purposes he'd been little more than the older man's go-fer, and they could not have been considered, by any stretch of the imagination, buddies.

Hell, he'd thought Glickman was a psycho even before the "incident."

Deats cleared his throat. "One more question before you go: There's no doubt in your mind that Glickman *could* have come up with something like this?"

Rosenthal shook his head. "If anyone could conceive of something this far out, let alone execute it, it would be Glickman. He may be crazy, but he is a genius. And . . . and he'd have the motive to play with us like this."

The Agency man spoke for the first time. "You don't think he might have developed this and then sold it to a competing nation?"

Rosenthal shrugged. "I have no idea. I don't know the man's sympathies. I do know that he has a grudge against The Agency, and I can see him doing something like this to get back at us." He paused. "I just wonder what's next."

Deats nodded grimly. "Me, too."

"Thank you," Kiegelman said. "We'll call you if we need anything else."

Rosenthal stood, started to go, then turned slowly around. "One more thing. Ever think that maybe this is what made Glickman snap? I mean, if these numbers could cause Cooper to . . . do what he did, what about all the numbers Glickman has in his head? I mean, he's sitting there, thinking of these numbers, thinking of others, discarding some, adding more.

Maybe it's like a computer virus in his brain. Maybe the formulas and sequences he has in his mind have been working on him. Maybe they caused him to . . . do what he did."

"Maybe," Kiegelman said distractedly. He nodded toward the door. "Thanks."

Rosenthal left the office feeling vaguely pissed off. He didn't expect to be a player in this. He knew he was on the periphery, involved only to the extent that he was a witness. But if they were going to ask for his opinions, they could at least listen to them.

Besides, like it or not, this was a math problem. If they really wanted to know *what* was happening and *why,* instead of merely knowing *who,* they were going to have to let the researchers in on it.

Otherwise, they were missing the entire point.

He returned to his work station, took out the A-986 project folder, and turned on his terminal.

And saw the numbers on the screen.

He came instantly, the most powerful orgasm of his life, his penis jumping immediately from flaccid to erect and spurting a seemingly endless amount of hot sperm into his pants. He had sense enough to look quickly away, fumblingly reaching for the power switch even as the second orgasm was upon him.

He forced himself to think of something besides numbers. He had seen the numerals on the screen for the briefest of seconds, but he was afraid he'd still be able to recall them, so he purposely cleared his mind of all mathematical thoughts.

His first reaction was to run back into Deats's office and tell those self-important assholes that he was being targeted and they'd damn well better let him in on this. First Cooper then himself? There was a pattern here. Glickman had a plan. He knew what he was doing and was working his way up the Agency ladder.

But his second thought was that he should print out a copy of the screen and save it for himself.

Had anyone caught on to what had happened? He glanced furtively around the modular walls of his work station, but no one was looking in his direction. No one had noticed.

He looked down at his lap. The dark stain on the crotch of his light gray pants was huge and obvious. Inside his underwear, the semen was already cold and jelling thickly. His spent penis throbbed painfully.

What the hell was wrong with him?

Policy stated that all findings were to remain in the lab. Any breach of policy was cause for dismissal and grounds for legal action. All work was property of The Agency. He knew that. He agreed with it. He'd signed updated sworn statements every year to that effect and until now had never even been able to conceive of an instance in which he would be remotely tempted to break his oath.

Until now.

There was something frightening in this sudden reversal of his loyalty and feelings.

He thought of the power of those two orgasms.

What was it Freud had said about sex being the driving force behind all human endeavor?

He'd print his own copy, then he'd tell Deats and let The Agency take over from there. What harm could that do? He wasn't going to share this information. He wasn't going to sell it to another government or attempt to profit from it.

He would just keep it. For . . .

For his own personal use.

He thought for a moment, then turned down the intensity knob on his screen. He turned the machine on again, then pressed the "Print Screen" key on his keyboard. The printer attached to his terminal spit out a hard copy of the numbers. He glanced at the first few, became instantly hard, and quickly folded the paper, shoving it into his pocket.

He'd fold it into an even smaller square later and hide it in his wallet before he left the building.

He took a deep breath, picked up the phone, called Deats.

Amy was in the kitchen when he arrived home from work, and Rosenthal put his briefcase down in the entryway, took the printout from his pocket and read the first ten numbers, blocking out the other six with his hand. He was instantly hard, but still one number away from orgasm, and he folded the paper again, put it back in his wallet, and repeated the ten numbers to himself as he walked into the kitchen.

His wife turned at the sound of his entrance, immediately saw the erection straining against his stained slacks.

"What . . ." she began.

He walked up to her, unbuckled his belt, unhooked and unzipped his pants, let them fall to the floor. He started to undo the top button on her jeans and she tried to pull away, but he held tight and pulled her pants down.

"I'm cooking dinner! What do you think you're—"

"Five," he whispered softly. "Six, eight, one, three, nine . . ."

* * *

The tests were normal, no physiological problems could be detected even after the exhausting battery of extensive examinations that were performed, and shortly after nine that evening, Cooper was released from the hospital. Deats and Kiegelman wanted him to come in, wanted to brainstorm with him about the new information they'd gotten from the trace on the outside lines, but he said he was tired and wanted to go home and get some sleep, and they agreed to put everything off until the next morning.

They did send a car to take him home, though, and Cooper was grateful for the gesture and accepted it.

Once home, he ate a quick microwave dinner, took a shower, and got into bed, but he couldn't seem to fall asleep. He tossed and turned for a half hour that felt like ten before finally giving up and heading over to his study, plopping down in the chair in front of his desk.

Glickman.

What was that psycho doing now?

Cooper stared at the ten numbers he'd written down, the ten numbers he'd remembered, and he found himself wondering if it was the mere physical positioning of these numeric symbols that produced such a response, or if it was human comprehension of their meaning and the sequence of thought triggered by their placement in this order that caused the reaction. On an impulse, he rewrote the numbers on another piece of paper, his penis getting stiffer with each stroke of the pen. He stood, taking the sheet of paper, and walked into the backyard.

"Albert!" he called.

There was the sound of a dog yawn from one of the bushy dark corners of the yard.

"Albert!"

The dog came running toward him.

Cooper patted his pet's head, roughed back his fur, made the animal sit. He held Albert's head with one hand and with the other placed the sheet of paper in front of the dog's eyes.

And felt dog sperm shoot onto his bare feet.

"Gone," Kiegelman said. "He must've known we were tracing him—or that he could be traced—and cleared out."

Rosenthal cleared his throat. "Did you find anything—"

"Shit. We found shit. Groceries, furniture, everyday crap. He took his computers, his disks, whatever papers he has, with him."

"But his car must be registered. There must be—"

"What? There must be what? You think a guy who can break into our security system and get you guys to fuck yourselves by reading a bunch of numbers is stupid enough to leave a credit trail or a traceable computer path? This is Glickman we're dealing with here."

"What can we do?" Cooper asked.

"We can't do anything. Bureau men are out there and ready and'll nail his ass if we trace anything else coming in. You guys can find out what these numbers mean and what use we can make of them in the future." He shook his head. "Hell, if we'd had these during the Cold War, we could've dropped leaflets on Moscow, and the Russians could've fucked themselves to death. This has powerful weapons potential here."

"Who else is—"

"You two. Period. Not a word, not a hint to any of the others. Got me?"

"Hamilton and Green—"

"Don't know shit. You. Period. Got that?"

Both Rosenthal and Cooper nodded.

"All right then. Get to work."

Will they figure it out, and if so, which one? Cooper, he thinks. Cooper is quicker.

But he hopes it is Rosenthal.

Doesn't matter either way.

What will The Agency do with it?

Will they have balls enough to use it?

He stares down at the bandaged stump of what used to be his penis, wishes he had not ripped out his testicles, but he thinks of the Sixth Series, repeating the numbers like a mantra, and somehow it doesn't matter that they are gone.

He can still feel the pleasure.

"Jesus. How can we be such assholes?"

Rosenthal looked over Cooper's shoulder, trying to ignore his own maddening erection.

"Look at them," Cooper said. "They're part of a Fourier Series. I don't know why we didn't notice that before. Each step of arousal is marked by a new set. Multiply the first set by cosine functions of integer multiples of the variable, and you have the next set. And amplification of the original effect."

"So," Rosenthal said slowly. "We multiply it a couple more times. And he'll—"

"—die." Cooper finished for him.

"If we can send it back."

"Are you kidding? If he sends us another sequence,

we can program the mainframe to respond instantly. We don't even need to fuck with it."

"He won't have time to escape. They'll trace back the call, find him dead."

"Exactly."

"You're a genius."

Cooper grinned. "Was there ever any doubt?"

The condition of the body shook even Kiegelman.

Rosenthal took only a cursory glance at the photos, and that was enough for him. There was blood everywhere—black in the black-and-white pictures, a startling crimson in the color—and both hands had been shoved into the body cavity through the abdomen.

All six men in the room were silent.

"This never leaves this office," the Agency man said. "Do I make myself clear?"

They all nodded.

"The numbers are now the responsibility of G sector. They're out of your hands now. I want the data transmitted and all of your records wiped clean. Then you go back to whatever else you were working on and forget this ever happened."

Rosenthal caught Cooper's eye, couldn't read the look on his face, glanced away.

"Any questions?" the Agency man asked.

"The numbers are gone," Cooper said quietly.

"What?" Deats blinked.

"I accidentally deleted them when I programmed the transmission to Glickman."

"Well, they're still on Glickman's machine—"

"No, they're not." Langley shook his head. "We

killed his machine when we broke in. National Security. We didn't know how many of those Bureau men could be trusted, and we figured it was on backup here."

"Surely Glickman himself had a backup disk or some notes or printouts."

"He never did here," Rosenthal said. "He was real paranoid about someone else accessing his information. He kept most of it in his head."

"God *damn* it!" Kiegelman glared at Cooper. "You're going to get those numbers back for us. I don't care if we have to hypnotize you to make you remember them, you're going to give them to us."

"I'll try," Cooper said.

Rosenthal waited until all the others had gone before daring to approach his friend. He glanced casually around, then bent down next to Cooper. "Why'd you lie?"

"Too much power."

"Too much power?"

"I don't think anyone should have access to that kind of power. I don't think . . . I don't think man was supposed to know those numbers."

"You're trying to pull that Frankenstein moral on me?"

"Leave the mysticism to the numerologists and the freaks and the fringees. Let governments stick to science."

"But the two overlap. I mean, shit, this could eliminate the need for weapons of any sort. We're at war? Transmit numbers to terminals, broadcast them over television, recite them over radio. Hell, like

Kiegelman said, drop leaflets over cities. Do you realize the power we have here? Bloodless coups, foreign policy control—"

"Dictators of the world?" He turned around. "I didn't hear you contradicting me in there."

"I didn't want to get you in trouble."

"You know how dangerous this is."

"Yes, I do. But I also know that, if used properly, these numbers could change the world. For the better. Do you know that?"

"Yes, I do," Cooper said.

He turned up the intensity on his screen. The numbers were there.

He shut off the terminal.

"Fuck!" Rosenthal ran to his own machine, turning it on.

"Don't bother," Cooper said. "It's deleted. It's out of the system. It's gone."

"You asshole," he said. He tried to make his voice sound angry, but he wasn't angry. Not really. He still had the printout at home. He could calculate from there. He could . . . he could rule the world.

No, that wasn't what he wanted. That wasn't why he'd wanted to save the numbers.

Cooper probably had a printout, too, he thought. Maybe he was planning to save it all for himself, to control everything, to use the numbers to get him out of the way.

Deats and Kiegelman had a printout, too, didn't they? They could get another mathematician to calculate the next sequence. And the next. And the next.

They could be planning to use the numbers.

They sure hadn't mentioned their printout to Langley and the Agency man.

"It's better this way," Cooper said.

"Yeah." Rosenthal walked away. He thought briefly of that axiom about power and corruption and absolute power and absolute corruption, then he thought of five, six, eight, one, three, nine . . .

And he pressed down on his growing erection as he walked out of the lab and out of the building and across the parking lot to his car.

HERETICAL VISIONS

Claudia O'Keefe

On their way home Wednesday morning, Jack having pulled them off I-5 into a rest area forty-five minutes above Portland, a surprisingly beautiful rest stop, majestic almost, being nestled in a grove of redwoods and surrounded by blackberry, by dogwood, with pairs of tulip trees just blooming, flanking the entrances to both the men's and women's restrooms, an empty spot that morning really, a place more private than it should have been, the only other traveler here a portly man in L. L. Bean sweats walking his grass-stained corgi outside the pet area boundaries, and a soft rain transforming their car windows into shower doors, Eveline came.

It was tropical in the car, their heat changing the season from late winter to early summer. Jack had four or five of the hairs at the nape of her neck wrapped tightly in his fingers and was pulling on them hard, a corset-tightening strength in his grip, pain and breathlessness and the wanting of something very, very close clearly demonstrated in his urgency, in the far-away intimacy his eyes reflected, in the way his thumbs modeled the hollows beneath her collarbones as if her skin were green clay that desperately needed sculpting . . .

. . . and they came. She came.

As a vision went off inside her head.

Purple-red butterfly, royal butterfly, its huge wings rich with the texture of an antique fabric, that precise dustiness, the exact sheen of wealth gone, yet still cherished, so fragile it might tatter in the first unkind wind.

In her mind, at the moment when her heart beat too fast, and her breathing became so frantic that she couldn't hear it anymore, and her senses overloaded so that she was blind, in that darkness she watched the butterfly's wings beating. *Together-open-together-open.* Their cadence was her cadence, *together-open-together,* until her cadence faded and the vision faded and Jack sagged down on top of her, his exhausted, contented breath streaming invisibly around the contours of her face. She had a kiss for the drop of sweat on the tip of his chin. They both felt the need for their bodies to rub together just a little longer, fool's foreplay, physical pyrite . . .

Then it was over. At last. Regretfully.

Rain leaked through the seal around the rear windshield. Taco wrappers behind the seat needed to be thrown out.

"Seattle in time to watch the Seahawks?" Jack said.

"Okay," Eveline said. They pulled on their clothes.

"You drive."

"Okay," she said, got out of the back, got back in the front, took the wheel and drove.

Eveline didn't know why she had the visions when she came. They never had any connection to what she was thinking during sex, or even right before. At one time she thought they could be like dreams, that they might operate in the same way, creating themselves out of the flotsam of her day, an image glimpsed here, a conversation snatched there. But they weren't. She only knew that she would have one each time Jack made her have an orgasm. To be honest, she wasn't even sure that Jack was the trigger. She felt naïve and insecure about it, but Jack was her only. She'd never been with another man, and it didn't work when she masturbated. She'd tried.

One thing about the visions, they were sumptuous. Sumptuous. It was a word she didn't like. It seemed like the type of word an old lady would use to describe a chocolate soufflé, some old lady who left too much cakey red lipstick on her fork, but the word fit what she saw. And it was the only one that did. Sumptuous.

Two days after their rest area tryst and the Seahawks loss, they did it in the big picture window at the back of their house in Wallingford, their nakedness fully on display for anyone who might have been sitting atop the doghouse in the backyard. They didn't have a dog. They had annoying neighbors, who weren't home but out sailing their twenty-eight-footer to Vashon Island, but still . . . it was the idea. Anyone could have seen them.

Jack, her technical writer, middle-management husband, was playing idly with her breasts, examining them abstractly by touch, as if they weren't real, but rather saline implants attached to her rib cage, things you could . . . well . . . play with idly. It wasn't a turn-on for her, but since she was studying her superstore's CD inventory sheets, she wasn't paying that much attention either.

Then.

Instead of continuing to sit astride her bare midriff, he got off and stood beside her and began to arrange her very creatively. He unbuttoned the top and the third buttons of her pale gold shirt, leaving the second one buttoned. She didn't know why, but it excited him, and what excited him began to excite her, as he pushed this wisp of her hair away from her face, combed that one along the line of her chin, then caught the rest up loosely in a rubber band he found on the windowsill. Loose, loose, just so, just the right way, tilting her chin back so that the curve of her neck would have a classical bearing. Then when she was exactly the way she was supposed to be, a minor adjustment, a minor shift in the composition, he slid one arm under her thighs near her knees, the other cradling her back, and he lifted her off the upholstered bench, very slowly, very quietly.

Eveline looked at their reflections in the picture window. Her head had fallen back, her lower legs dangled. It was the pietà in reverse. Madonna and child with the sexes wrong.

It made them both catch their breaths.

She'd never known he could do something like that. She'd never known that he had the wonder in him, the artistry. He was such an ordinary man, they, together, were such a mundane man and wife, a microwave-popcorn, federal-taxes-at-the-last-minute, sometimes-forget-to-clean-the-hair-out-of-the-shower-drain couple, and yet she might have guessed that it was possible that they could be more in those rare moments just by looking at his nose. It was truly aquiline, and expressive, a feature perfect and yet tempered by the rest of his suburban face. It spoke of mysteries in his personal makeup, of potentials that might go ignored if something or some*one* failed to bring them to the surface.

She. Eveline.

He set her down. Just as slowly and without a word. Only a look.

That lasted several tense, tense seconds.

Then she grabbed him and pulled him down on top of her, harshly, lovingly, lustfully.

They had what her baby sister called wild monkey sex.

And in their combined sensorial darkness, at the height of their climb to wild monkey sex, he gave her her vision.

The grand curving staircase of a Victorian theater. Her orgasm took her to a place she'd never been in real life. She saw it all. Red velvet carpet flowing down marble stairs like a corrugated waterfall. A woman's soft, white hands holding up a handful of jewelry for her to see, rubies and garnets and opals, and somewhere in the corner a golden curtain tassel. The sensation of shadows that were a hundred years old.

It was all very symbolic. It was like something religious.

Yet it meant absolutely nothing to her.

"Christ, I've got the munchies," Jack said after they came back down. He curled his toes around the phone cord and yanked it off the nearby table. "Are you going to complain if I order jalapeños on the pizza?"

Her visions were what you saw when God burned your eyes out on the road to Damascus, Eveline decided.

She decided this on Jack's twenty-fourth birthday, and he slapped her before fucking her in the most gorgeous way. Just a little slap, shocking the complacency off their love.

Her visions were the remnants from God's head. Images not important enough for Him to keep. Divine scraps, the threads of heaven unraveling as they fell to Earth. They were soft and colorful and once fallen apart could never be woven together again, but she would keep them in a separate place, a special place.

Not abusive, that slap. Jack tried it because it was something they had seen in a movie. Celluloid danger they wanted to experiment with at home, a frame or two at a time.

He slapped her very close to her left eye. The delicate, sensitive skin there still tingled as he cocked his hand back for another openhanded blow, holding the hand and her apprehension aloft as long as he could, stretching the terror, the mock end to their relationship, a violent end. He had her waiting, waiting for a punishment he never intended to deliver. But wanted to. Wanted to.

Was that what his eyes said? Were they joking?

It was like a movie. It was like a movie where you knew in your mind that everyone you cared about would be alive at the end, and yet in your heart you feared.

His fingers trembled as he held the blow back. She watched his wrist cramp visibly, the fine guitar-string tendons in agony, and she shuddered into long, emotive silence. Giving up. Giving in.

When he dropped down on her. Working himself into her, in time to her hypertensive pulse.

Their love was arrhythmic.

Yet with a vision tied to the end of it. A soaring, otherworldly balloon that popped and left her drifting down to a vaguely French countryside through a honey-colored sky. Not blue. Not gray. Not summer white. Not even the unpredictable Cézanne palette of sunset, with its gold and lavenders and orange-tinged pinks. But honey. Milky near the heavens, pollen pale. And at the horizon, a plume of smoke rising, puffing, and twisting on itself.

She saw a sky that was as rare as a cloud of gnats caught in amber.

Then her heart ticked and the world in her head turned and she landed back in their bedroom again, worrying.

It was a small worry, niggle-sized.

But it was a worry. *Why did he want to hurt me?*

"I have to fly to Sacramento tomorrow," Jack said, then he opened his briefcase.

Eveline loved her visions. Even totally devoid of meaning, they gave her meaning. Her orgasms were the Sundays of her life. She and Jack were a religion of two. It was even more special because it didn't have to be a set day of the week, because she didn't need to be trapped for two hours in a church, and because she didn't need a sermon to hear the voice of whomever or whatever was out there.

Her visions were apostolic.

It wasn't until her twenty-fourth birthday, however, almost a month later, that they made love again. It was her day, she should have had anything she wanted from him, but she found herself having to initiate sex.

After their orange roughy and shiitake mushroom salad, after the lazy bottle of Château St. Michelle fumé blanc, a meal with more idle stares than conversation, an ipso facto celebration if she'd ever seen one, instead of hurrying home, or maybe taking a stroll along Puget Sound and engaging in a standing screw as they had once done under the Parisian Arch near Pioneer Square, Jack insisted on going to a drug superstore to look for Armor-all, a new filter for their heater, and batteries for his travel alarm.

Savon stayed open till midnight, but it was nearly deserted. Stockers refilled the shelves from cardboard boxes stacked haphazardly in the aisles. Eveline followed her husband from boring aisle to boring aisle, saying nothing until they accidentally found themselves in the section farthest from the cash registers and stockers, a strip of store where all but one of the fluorescents had blown out, near the pool supplies and Styrofoam surfboards.

Jack turned abruptly when he realized they had wandered off target and nearly knocked her to the floor. He caught her and steadied her, offering profuse though somewhat annoyed apologies, and would have moved on were she not already unbuttoning her dress.

He stopped, filter, antifreeze and vinyl restorer in hand, and watched her, and in a few seconds his face took on that expression she'd seen on actors in porno videos when they were offered snatch in unexpected places.

Dulled excitement. His acting not quite up to the challenge of looking surprised. He glanced up at the ceiling for security mirrors and cameras, found none in this part of the store, then slowly set down his various items on the floor.

She slipped out one breast, offering it to him as if she was a mother preparing to nurse her child. Let him press his head against her rib cage, and placed the nipple in his mouth for him. Let him pretend to suckle because she was afraid. Not of violence from him—the slap had proved boring after all—but because it was the only thing she could think of to do. Because she was suddenly desperate for something to do for him. She had no explanation for her desperation. She only felt it and suckled him.

For the first time, she came without a vision.

They made love and failed to go to church.

She didn't understand.

How could it happen?

Maybe her orgasm wasn't strong enough. Was that it?

Not every time could be a winner.

Yet she couldn't remember when it hadn't been.

It was colorless love. It was lushless. It whispered nothing, shouted nothing.

It was strange.

It was alarming.

They went home and went to bed.

She couldn't sleep, even after the hours melded and drew themselves out, became alternately dreary and frightening, alien and mundane, because the caverns of her thought were empty, disturbingly silent. Though she waited patiently for her mystic vision until dawn, even closed her eyes and tried chanting to herself to induce a meditative state, nothing happened.

"Who do you have to see in Sacramento again so soon?" she asked Jack the second she saw his eyes flicker open. He would be leaving on the 6:30 shuttle, his third trip in as many weeks.

"What do you mean?" he said, and he rolled on his side away from her.

Eveline cried the next time. Not on the outside. Her cheeks weren't damp, her eyes didn't fill with tears. She was certain to keep her face remarkably turned on, but inside, where it wouldn't show, she was hysterical.

Jack chose the laundry center; it was handy and tight-fitting and the dirty clothes were softer than the workbench where they had started. She hadn't asked, she hadn't dared to ask him for sex after he got back. He didn't want it. She could tell. Yet they found themselves with their tongues in each other's mouths, he stroking the backs of her incisors with the tip of his tongue, she terrified that something would suddenly make her bite it off. Their foreplay was utterly grotesque. His mouth groped her armpits. She licked his upper lip too close to his nostrils. He raked her pubic hair in the wrong direction, over and over until she had to bite her own tongue to keep from screaming.

What didn't make sense was that the uglier it got, the hotter she became. She wanted him to hurry. To enter her before she was ready.

If she didn't get her vision . . . if they'd lost their faith together . . . the worries circulated through her mind on a continuous loop, growing louder and more irrational the closer she came.

Tears she wouldn't let out burned her nose like water going up the wrong way, and he flipped her over, pushing her face down into a mildewed towel to do her from behind. It felt as if she were gently gored.

She came anyway, closing her eyes to a different sort of epiphany than she had ever experienced or asked for. She was strapped tightly into a Chinese wedding chair, a heavily decorated cabinet mounted on wooden poles for bearers to shoulder. Except there were no bearers, and she was alone in near darkness, a room with mold-blackened walls and a single door lying directly in front of her.

She wore clothes so tight they cut her at the waist and she couldn't breathe. The wedding chair wasn't right. Instead of the bright reds and greens and golds with which she knew they were normally painted, rather than the cheerful lanterns, brocade-clothed dolls, good luck symbols, paper dragons, everything about this chair was black and sharp and cruel.

A chill breeze blew against her bare skin in an unaccustomed place.

She looked down at herself.

The crotch had been ripped out of her pants. She was savagely exposed. Helpless as the doorknob turned.

Her eyes knew that someone stood there, but her mind wouldn't register an image. Her ears heard his footsteps as he approached, but her mind was so terrified it wouldn't let her see him standing inches away. She felt him force her legs open, parting her, his hand inserting itself into—

Eveline convulsed, the end of her orgasm leaving her dry, sore, in shock.

Jack had just given her something other than a vision.

Cancer.

He didn't want her anymore. That's what Sacramento had to mean. He wasn't going away on business. He was having an affair. Sacramento was code for another woman. Who was she? What did she look like? Was the woman's name prettier than hers? She didn't want to find the answers. All they would tell her was that he didn't love her anymore and had given her cervical cancer.

Lying on the living room floor, Eveline listened to a late spring storm outside. Shadows of raindrops flowed across her ceiling for an entire afternoon. Normally she loved thunder and wind. Today, though, she ignored her favorite weather and clawed at her abdomen with her fingernails, knowing it was in there, its cells dividing over and over. Jack's tumor.

It was too early for it to show up on a Pap smear, but she knew she had it, just like some women knew the moment they conceived. She sensed the change in her body, the thing growing along her cervix. She had felt him create it and leave it inside her, his desire to get rid of her. Was that impossible? Maybe, maybe not. She'd always believed cancers were connected to persistent unhappiness.

It made sense. Jack had ruined their religion, dirtied her visions. They were tainted now, so why shouldn't the place that made them be defiled, as well?

When he came home that night he had a guilt fuck for her, a hand job. It didn't start out as a hand job. He banged through the front door and slung his briefcase on their Mission-style entry table, walked testily into the living room, switched on a Tiffany lamp, and started when he saw her the way she was, lying on the bare beechwood floor in white gym socks, light red welts streaking her abdomen.

His eyes reflected half a dozen passing changes in his internal weather, an operatic storm brewing inside him made of emotions rather than water or wind. From surprise to shock—*she's on the floor*—he reached confusion—*why*—then suddenly worry, and finally fear—*there's something wrong with her*.

She blinked her eyes closed, like someone with a pleasant buzz on, and then she smiled, inviting him, daring him to react . . . somehow.

He did. From fear, at last, sprang anger.

She's playing with me, his expression read.

And with anger, Eveline had come to realize over the last few weeks, came the only arousal he had left inside him for her.

He yanked her up off the floor and backed her toward the staircase, his erection nudging at his fly. She nodded dreamily and placed her hand there to feel it swell and strain at his Eddie Bauer twills, wondering what visual seeds it contained this time. He shoved her down hard, so that she backed her spine against the edge of one stair.

Eveline prayed this vision wouldn't be tainted. Who was responsible for them? Who controlled them? Her? Jack? Both of them? Someone else? If she had glimpsed the fragments of Heaven, were these new apocalypses scraps from Hell?

Yet when he unzipped his pants, she saw that his erection had been a mirage, like a ghost limb she'd half felt inside her.

He saw she wanted to be balled, and saw she was aware of his guilt, so he finished her by hand.

It was angry, estranged lovemaking, reminding her of the doctor's speculum that morning. As he started, she didn't think she'd come. Fingers just never did it.

He made her come.

Bearing witness to another hideous revelation.

She lay naked under a dock that was old and algaed. Fleas hopped atop the sand, and the water lapping at the soles of her feet was a dirty green. It was almost night. Her stomach was slightly distended, and one of her hands cupped it. Where her pubic hair should have been . . . bees. They swarmed between her legs. She felt their legs crawling against her bare skin, their stingers dragging through her hidden creases, their wings vibrating in her folds. Drawn to the perverted nectar inside her.

She heard herself moaning in pleasure, though, frightened, she called for God. Her voice sounded foreign. Her excited groans had a French accent.

Jack had finally corrupted their church. God no longer spoke between them. They had been given erotic paradise, a modern, new Eden, but instead of immersing himself in her forever, Jack had bitten into the apple, cheating on her. She mourned, not as if He were a dead lover, but as if He had never existed to offer them the quiet euphoria of His thoughts.

"How was Sacramento?" she asked. "And by the way, I have cancer."

"What?" He took a step back from her. "Cancer?"

"I didn't do this," she told Jack. "You did."

Of course, Jack had to call the doctor to find out about it. Of course, he found out that they didn't think she had it. It didn't matter. She began to show soon enough. Another couple of weeks and it became very apparent that something was wrong with her. After seeing her for a consultation on a Thursday, Eveline's doctor wanted her back in his office on the following Monday. He insisted.

In the meantime, the doctor suggested Jack take her away somewhere for a few days' rest. To gather her strength. She would need it. They flew away to Maui.

She supposed the thing that hurt her most was not that Jack had destroyed their love, but that even before he perverted them, her visions were really nothing more than the leftovers from a higher place. Perhaps, if Jack hadn't betrayed her sexually, the oracles would have increased in splendor until she might have actually found her way to God or whatever power suffused this place and others. Perhaps she would have evolved, perhaps both of them would have. She'd felt special. She had been special to have been given such ecclesiastical gifts, delicacies of the soul wrapped in communion lace. Little presents from Him. Now they could only become greater abominations, as had her most recent hypnagogic revelation last night in their hotel suite overlooking Kaanapali Beach.

A pregnant woman with a penis, who excited herself . . .

She'd spent the rest of the evening obsessing over ways to be smaller, lighter, to rid her stomach of every bit of fat possible so she wouldn't be that woman. She'd gone to the ice machine and then sat in the tub numbing her genitals so she couldn't identify with the idea of having an erection.

Now, the next morning, they drove the road to

Hana through Maui's rain forest on the Eastern Shore. Hana lay at the bottom of the island, less of a wonder to get to than the drive itself, three hours to go forty-four miles along a one-and-a-half lane road. Hana Highway had 617 turns and fifty-six one-lane bridges. It had a sultry rhythm all its own. Jack's languid hand at the wheel heightened that music, arranging scores for the groves of banana trees filtered through golden-green light; for the red and pink ginger growing wild, simply blooming everywhere; for the rare species of black and white stiff-legged birds which would have become extinct a long time ago had the road not required such a slow hand. Nothing on this side of the island was ever dry, not the pavement, nor the mutant-sized philodendrons, nor the feral cats so hungry they begged for scraps of lettuce from her and Jack's garbage. Everything was wet, warm. Rain dripped and drizzled straight out of the air without the necessity of clouds.

Eveline let the pikake-scented humidity wash over her through the car window, composed her face into something smooth and unbothered, and dug her fingers into her armrest, sensing the tumor even now, the pincushion made of red leather and filled with blood, grown large, growing larger inside her.

Her anger was as unique and amazing as this rain forest, certainly as vast. She thought about that the whole way. Without this tiny road, this part of the island would have been completely inaccessible, even by boat. Just as that place had been inside her, brought to wondrous life and consecrated by forces outside man's contemplations. This was the perfect place to end the anger. This was the perfect place to reclaim that purity of vision she couldn't live without. This was probably the only place she could think of to do it.

They passed a dozen waterfalls and their bathing pools, maybe more, before they entered the bamboo forest halfway to Hana where Jack pulled off. As they got out, her fingers slipped around the handle of a steak knife she'd brought with her inside her canvas tote bag. It was the fourth time she'd checked to be sure it was there. She rounded the car and joined her husband, giving his hand an affectionate squeeze. She smiled at him the best she could, so phony, and let him lead her down to a river flowing beneath a chalk-white 1912 bridge.

On every side, the slopes were too steep to be climbed, and the ocean, barely visible at the far entrance to the tropical ravine, appeared as no more than a tiny cobalt-blue dart in the fabric of the landscape. They hiked in along the river as far as they could manage, which wasn't far considering the terrain. They were well out of sight of the road, however, when they stopped next to a huge basin fenced by full-grown bamboo. From a distance bamboo looked fluffy, like brilliant green feather dusters. Up close, the poles were phallic, each deep green stage of a tree's growth emerging from a cock-pink outer leaf.

While Jack stripped, Eveline walked up to one, ran a hand slowly up a trunk, then cautiously, experimentally, pulled away one of its fleshy outer wrappings. The trunk was sticky and dirty beneath the leaf, and the impulse to bring out the knife and hack away every one of its sheaths, to expose the filth beneath them was strong.

Don't, she told herself.

Her heart pounded, just *pounded* at her ribs, and her thumb rubbed the serrated blade inside her purse so hard, she sawed her hand open.

Don't! Save it for what you really need to do.

Jack, naked, waded into the pool behind her. She felt the purse's lining blotting up her blood as she turned around and watched his pale tourist's body dive, a bit clumsily, beneath the surface.

She loved him. She thought of the knife in his throat. Quiet Hawaiian water stained with clouds of red.

He surfaced and patted the water. "Come here," he mouthed.

She started to undress, and Jack submerged again. Eveline removed the knife from hiding and quickly entered the pool up to her breasts. Half a minute, a minute passed, and still Jack hadn't come up again. The bamboo trees were so tall and thick and impenetrable that their leaves choked out most of the light, bringing the basin to the level of darkness in a Shinto shrine. She thought of pandas and the ticks that lived in bamboo, how much these things reminded her of the first of her bad visions, the black wedding chair. It brought back their tryst on the road to Seattle last winter, too, that secret, sultry heat. As she gazed up into the bamboo, she wished she would spot a butterfly like the one from the vision she'd had that day.

Jack seized her legs and dragged her under before she could get a breath. He shoved her beneath him and held her pinned flat against the rocks at the bottom of the pool.

Her hand tightened around the knife and she almost struck out, but she began choking on water she'd accidentally inhaled.

Jack went down on her, using his weight to trap her legs, even as she struggled not to drown. Gulp after gulp, she fought to swallow the flood rushing into her mouth, but it was always too much, knots of water so huge they stretched her throat painfully as they went down, faster and faster, until she couldn't keep them out of her lungs, and—

"I can't breathe," she tried to shout through the water, "can't, can't . . ."

Jack bit down hard on her clitoris.

She heard her arms thrashing, their water-baffled hysteria, the knife blade scraping against stone. She heard Jack's excited grunts and knew he used her hysteria to feed the erection nudging against the back of her knee like a nosy bass.

Oddly, near-death brought her harshly to arousal, too. But this time when she came it was different. She was still in the pool when she received the nightmare. She never left the pool. Instead, her vision bled into reality.

Where a giant octopus stabbed its beak into her vagina.

Eveline twitched in shock.

As it settled between her legs, and consumed her until only the roots of the highest hairs showed above its maw. Its mouth was cold, rubbery, clamping down on her with the strength of a bear trap. Its eyes stared into hers, mesmerizing, subjugating.

It raped her.

As if painting her into a watercolor by Masami Teraoka, everything around her took on the colors of Japanese art. Her skin assumed the mildest rice paper glow. Her tears flowed into her hair into stylized Ukiyoe waves, and her toes curled in the greatest, most horrible ecstasy she had ever been tortured to accept.

Tentacles drifted about her ribs and tightened.

Stop, Jack!

The creature's chill, purple flesh rubbed softly against her breasts.

I hate you. Please stop!

Two more tentacles snaked around her legs and forced them wider.

See what you're doing to me.

She resisted, but the mollusk's suckers attached themselves and pulled at the tender area along her inner thighs until her skin tore. She still held the knife but was too weak to lift it. Grains of sand jammed up under her fingernails as she dragged the blade closer to her body.

Jack!

A fifth tentacle slid up over her collarbone and around her neck, strangling her—

I don't want this! I don't want . . . don't want . . .

—as her back arched and the beak dug and scored and bit at the rare flesh inside, ramming its way nearer to the source of her visions—

Jack!

She plunged the knife into her lower abdomen. She sawed herself open and exposed it at last, the tumor. It lay within her, on the altar of herself, wet and briny and glistening with visions to come even more obscene than this one.

Seeing her secrets exposed, she knew now what she had wanted since the visions began, and why she could never have it. The tumor of her obsession was not only impure. It was also the result of her stupidity. Her naïveté.

How could I have fooled myself thinking God was here? And that He would love me? How could I have gone so insane with the grand incest of wanting Him to make love to me?

God was not here. God wouldn't come here. Not to this badly flawed place. He couldn't.

She raised the knife again and stabbed through both the tumor and her altar, destroying them together. Not even pain's blossoming red climax could disturb the final serenity it gave her. She released the knife, and it floated slowly downward, wedging itself into a crevice in the rocks.

Jack wrenched her to the surface, frantic. His fingers pushed at the sides of the wound, urgently trying to close it and stop the blood.

"Eveline!" he said in disbelief.

Her eyes widened in surprise. She saw but couldn't believe who he really was.

"Oh," she said, her voice quiet, childlike. "It's *you.*"

Clasping her fingers in his, she stared raptly into His eyes, while His loving hands unraveled her soul. Then her mind evaporated into a million beautiful visions, the fragments of the dead.

SUFFER KATE

Graham Masterton

There are some guys who have to live right on the very edge, the razor's edge, no matter what. I could never understand that; I never wanted the fear. I always used to think there's enough nerve-jingling experience in life, just waking up close to the woman you love, just walking scuffle-footed down some summer street.

Who needs to live right on the very edge? Who needs to test their mortality, time and time again, as if they can never quite believe their luck at being alive?

Maybe it's something to do with the mentality of certain spermatozoa. Maybe some of them don't have too much confidence, and when they penetrate that ovum, they lie there, trembling, with their tail dropped off, thinking, Shit, I can't believe it, I just can't believe it, man, out of all those millions and millions of other spermatozoa, I actually made it. I'm going to be alive, man, while all of those other guys just fade away, just fade away, like a crowd scene in a 1912 silent movie, like unknown soldiers on the Western Front, disappearing through the mustard gas.

But my friend Jamie Ford, he always had to live on the edge. *Beyond* the edge, in fact, so that his toes were way over the abyss, if you understand what I mean, and nothing between him and falling but sheer chance. My friend Jamie Ford had discovered what it is to choke.

That's what he used to call it, a Choke. Like, "I'm going for a Choke, man; I'll see you in physics." And there was nothing I could do. I mean, what could I do? We were both kids, and we were both at Sherman Oaks Senior High. We were friends, we were blood brothers, we'd cut our thumbs and shared our actual life-substance.

I knew everything about him. I knew the scar on the left side of his head, where his spiky blond hair never grew. I knew the gray-blue color of his eyes. I knew all of the songs that he could remember, and all of his memories. I knew his bedroom as well as he did. I knew where he kept his Superboy comics and where he hid his copies of *Pix* and *Adam*.

I even knew the name of his imaginary friend, the one he'd had when he was three years old.

His imaginary friend whose second name was Kate and whose first name was Suffer.

Suffer Kate.

He used to tell me that it was something to do with his pillow, the pillow in his crib. It had smelled so clean and it had felt so soft, all he ever wanted to do was to plunge his face into it and never breathe, never again. And his mother had leaned over his crib, her face all tight with panic, and said, "No! No, Jamie! No, darling! I don't want you to Suffer Kate!"

She had taken his wonderful pillow away; but he had still found ways to stop himself from breathing. He had wrapped his head in his comforter, round and round, so that it was tight over his nose and mouth. And one day, when he was eleven, his mother had found him naked in the middle of the kitchen floor, with a plastic shopping bag over his head, his features wrinkle-sucked into the lettering of Hallmark cards.

Dr. Kennedy had said that he was lucky to survive. Another thirty seconds and he would have Suffer Kated.

His mother could only remember that he had fought her off. Desperately, as if he wanted to die. His mother could only remember that his penis had been totally rigid.

His mother was pretty. I can picture her now. Petite, with the same blue-gray eyes that Jamie had, maybe a little sad-looking. She used to wear a sky-blue checkered cowgirl blouse that I liked a lot, because she had very full breasts, and when she leaned over to butter my corn-on-the-cob I could see her brassiere.

In the sixth grade, one by one, we all grew physically mature enough to ejaculate. At least, most of us did, and the ones who hadn't quite made it yet always pretended that they had. "Oh, sure, I shot about a pint last night. It went right out the window and landed on the cat. He looked like the cat who got the cream, hunh-hunh-hunh!"

It was then that Jamie started to go for his Chokes. Jesus, it makes me go cold and shivery now just to think about it. If I had been an adult then, I would have stopped him, physically stopped him, and insisted that he go for therapy. But when you're a kid, you don't think that way; you're all inexperienced, you're all slightly crazy, believing in myths and legends and all kinds of weird superstitions, living on hormones and fear and expectations and zits and embarrassment.

What was I going to do? Knock on the principal's door and walk up to that dessicated, arroyo-wrinkled face and say, "Please, Mr. Marshall, my friend Jamie keeps hanging himself and whacking off"?

But, of course, that was what Jamie was doing. During almost every recess, he was locking himself into one of the heads in the science department, which hardly anybody used during recess. He was taking off all of his clothes. Then he was knotting a damp sports towel into a noose, looping it over the coat peg on the back of the door, and putting his head in it. All he had to do then was twist himself around a quarter-turn and lift his feet clear of the floor. He was literally hanging himself, while his cock rose stiff as a board, and the jism jumped out of him and spattered the walls.

Once he didn't appear in time for class, so I ran to the washrooms and climbed over the partition and found him gray-faced and whining, his fingers caught between his crimson-bruised neck and the tightly wrung towel, unable to pry himself free. He was chilly and white, and his thighs were dripping with sperm. I cut the towel with my Swiss Army penknife and lifted him down. He was like Christ from the cross—thin and tortured, a soul in need of rest and absolution. I'll never forget how he shuddered.

After that, whenever he announced that he was

going for a Choke, I used to follow him, as quietly as I could, and wait outside the cubicle while he hanged himself and masturbated. I couldn't bear it. I couldn't bear the choking noises, or the strangulated gasps of pleasure, or the sound of his bare heels knocking against the door. But I was mature enough to understand that if I tried to stop him, he would only do it someplace else, where I wasn't around to take care of him. Maybe he was going to kill himself one day, but I wasn't going to let him do it when *I* was around. I vowed that much.

In a peculiar way, not a homosexual way, I loved him. He was so good-looking, so edgy, so dangerous, a boy's boy. He once asked me if I wanted him to suck my cock, just to see what it was like, but I said no. I had a feeling that all he wanted to do was fill his mouth with penis-flesh, so that he could hardly breathe.

He frightened me. I knew that he would have to die. Maybe that was why I loved him so much.

On graduation day, with the school band playing "Colonel Bogey" and the sun dappling the lawns, I suddenly realized that I couldn't find him. The first students were already lining up beside the rostrum to collect their diplomas, and the principal's voice was echoing, amplified, from the gymnasium wall, and I began to panic. If I wasn't on stage in about a minute and a half, my mom and dad were going to hang me out to dry. But Jamie might have gone for one of his Chokes, and if I did go down to the parade ground, and Jamie died because I wasn't there to save him, then my graduation day was going to be a day of guilt and agony, not only today, but on every anniversary, forever.

I ran to the washroom with my gown flapping behind me. I banged open all of the doors, but he wasn't there. I ran to the locker rooms and shouted his name, but he wasn't there, either.

He was dead, I was sure of it. The very last day, the very last minute when I was responsible for him, and he was dead.

I barged into the senior common room, with its blue pastel walls and its carpet tiles and its posters of Jefferson Airplane and the Grateful Dead. And there he was, lying on the floor, stark naked, his head all wrapped up like a science-fiction mummy in Saran Wrap. His eyes staring. Sucking for breath. Sucking for breath. The cling film misted with lung moisture and sweat.

And, sitting astride him, Laurel Fay, the cheerleader, with her skirt lifted and her bare breasts bouncing out of her unbuttoned blouse, her arms lifted, her fingers tugging and winding at her golden-red hair. Her eyes were closed, and she was ecstatic, and I wasn't surprised that she was ecstatic, because I'd seen Jamie's boners when he was suffocating—tall and curved and totally hard, like some kind of animal's horn.

She twisted around and stared at me. She started to say, "Get the hell—" when I walked across the room and pushed her off him. She fell awkwardly, and between her plump white thighs I saw a flash of pink sticky flesh and gingery pubic hair. The image of it stuck in my mind the way a Matisse painting sticks in your mind. Clashing colors. Erotic yet tasteless. She swore at me: a curse that was strange and vehement.

"Judas! Judas fucking Iscariot! You don't even understand! You don't even fucking understand! He wants it! He needs it! Damn you and all the rest of you! It's death meets life! It's life meets death!"

I wrenched the Saran Wrap from Jamie's head, twisted it away from his nose and mouth. He gave a terrible, throat-racking gasp, and then he coughed and coughed, bringing up strings of phlegm and half-digested Rice Krispies.

Laurel had sat herself up with her back against the couch. She gave me a quick, venomous, disgusted glance, then looked away.

"He's my friend," I told her, trying to make my voice sound totally cold. "He's my best friend, and you nearly fucking killed him."

"I thought that was the whole point," Laurel retorted. She reached out for her bra, and fastened it up, and lifted her breasts back into it.

I cradled Jamie in my arms. His chest was rising and falling, rising and falling, like an exhausted swimmer who knows that he won't be able to reach the shoreline but can't think of any reason to stop swimming.

His eyes flickered from side to side, and the saliva that slid out of the corner of his mouth was streaked with blood.

"You've been playing with Suffer Kate again," I told him, dabbing his mouth with a Kleenex, and then stroking his sweat-cold forehead.

Jamie tried to smile, but all he could manage was a cough. "Everybody needs somebody to love," he breathed.

I held him in my arms, and I knew that I would miss him. But I was so relieved to be free of his Chokes. I was so relieved that I wouldn't have to take care of him any longer, him and Suffer Kate. If he strangled himself tomorrow, I would feel wretched about it, and miss him like hell, but at least I wouldn't feel responsible for him any longer.

It was almost seven years before I came across Jamie again. I had taken a course in journalism at UCLA and then worked for eleven months as a freelance reporter before landing a job on the city desk at the *Sacramento Bee*. It was a roasting morning in August when Dan Brokerage, my editor, parked himself on the edge of my desk and said, "What do you know about the Golden Horses out on Highway 80?"

I shrugged. "Not much. It's not the kind of place you'd take your sainted mother for an evening out. Why?"

Dan unwound his wire-rimmed glasses. "One of my contacts says that the Golden Horses has been pulling some unusually substantial crowds lately, especially on Friday nights."

"Well, they have strippers, don't they?" I said. "Maybe they've found themselves some girl who's really special."

"That's not what my contact was suggesting. My contact was suggesting that there's something bizarre being staged down there. His exact words were 'There's something real sick going down.'"

I looked at the half-finished story on my VDU screen. Mayor Praises Ornamental Gardens. Unlike most young reporters of my generation, I prided myself on my attention to upbeat civic stories. Most of my contemporaries wanted to be gonzo investigative journalists, exposing bureaucratic corruption and police brutality. But I knew what sold papers like the *Sacramento Bee:* constructive, happy, feel-good stories, with everybody's name included and everybody's name spelled right.

All the same, I was pleased that Dan had chosen me to look into the Golden Horses story. It meant that he trusted me to get my facts straight.

"It's Friday tomorrow," said Dan. "Get yourself along there. It won't be easy to get yourself in. From what my contact says, they're shit-hot on security. But talk to a man on the door called Wolf Bodell, and tell him that Presley sent you. And take at least two and a half bills in cash money. And try to look like a pervert."

"What does a pervert look like?" I asked him.

"I don't know . . . but he doesn't look like you. He doesn't have clean-cut hair and an Oxford shirt and Sta-prest pants. I don't know. Just try to look disreputable. Just try to look *shifty.*"

"Shifty," I nodded. "Okay."

The Golden Horses was a low whitewashed building with a shingle roof about a quarter of a mile south of Highway 80, in that flat, heat-hazed no-man's-land between West Sacramento and Davis. I arrived just after sunset in my beaten-up metallic-bronze LTD, and I couldn't believe what I saw. The main parking lot was already crowded with hundreds of vehicles of all makes and sizes—Cadillacs and Jeeps and pickups and BMWs and Winnebagos—some of them dilapidated, some of them gleaming new. Whatever attraction the Golden Horses was offering, it obviously appealed to the strangest variety of people, regardless of age or wealth or social background.

As I drove down the dusty, rutted track, I was

flagged down by a huge man in a white Stetson hat and an ill-fitting black suit, carrying an r/t.

"Evening, friend. Where d'you think you're going?" he wanted to know. His eyes were piggy and blood-shot, and his breath smelled strongly of whiskey and Big Red chewing-gum.

"Presley sent me."

"Presley? You mean *Elvis* Presley?"

"Of course not. I'm supposed to see Wolf Bodell."

The man stared at me for a long, long time, his hand grasping my car windowsill as if he were quite capable of tearing off the entire door with one exerted heave. Then he raised his head and shouted, "Wolf! Guy says that Presley sent him!"

I didn't hear the answer, but I had to presume that it was in the affirmative, because the man slapped the roof of my car and said, "Park yourself as close to that prickly pear as you can get."

I climbed out. The night was warm. The sky was still the color of warm boysenberry jelly. There was a smell of desert dust and automobile fumes and excite-ment. A long line of vehicles was turning off the highway, twenty or thirty at least, their indicator lights flashing. I could hear deep, heavy rock 'n' roll on the wind, ZZ Top or something similar, the kind of music that sounds like freight trains and people walking, hundreds of people walking.

On the ridge of the shingled roof, two neon horses danced. There were flashing lights, too, and smoke, and people yelping in anticipation. I walked across the boarded veranda and up to the doorway, where six or seven muscular-looking men in black suits and dark glasses were vetting everybody who went in.

One of them put out a finger and prodded me right

in the center of my chest. "You got your pass?" he wanted to know.

"Presley sent me. Said I should speak to Wolf Bodell."

A thin man in a blue satin suit emerged from the crimson light and the cigarette smoke. His face was yellowish gray and deeply emaciated. His gums were so eroded that his teeth looked as if they could drop out in front of you. He walked with a slurring limp, and it was obvious that his left arm was wasted or injured, because he kept having to drag it upward with his right arm.

"I'm Wolf Bodell," he said in a distinctive Nebraska accent.

"Presley sent me," I told him, without much confidence.

"Presley, huh? That's okay. How long you known Presley?"

"Longer than I care to admit." I grinned.

Wolf Bodell nodded and said, "That's okay, that's okay. So long as you know Presley. I'm afraid it's still two hundrut 'n' fifty to see the show."

I counted out the cash that Dave Brokerage had given me (and made me sign for). Wolf Bodell watched me dispassionately, not looking at the money even once.

"You seen this show before?" he asked me.

I shook my head.

"You're in for a treat, then. This is the show of shows. What you see tonight, you ain't never going to forget, not for the rest of your born days."

"Seems popular," I remarked, nodding at the crowds who were still arriving.

Wolf Bodell let out a thin, cackling laugh. "What

are the two most salable commodities on this here planet? I ask. And you say sex. And you say vicarious suff'rin'. That's what you say. The fascination of fucking! The fascination of the auto wreck! Death, and sex, and terror, and all of the glee that goes with it, my friend! *Schadenfreude,* to the power of n!"

Wolf Bodell hobble-heaved around me and gripped my elbow. "Let me tell you something," he said, as he guided me into the Golden Horses, through the smoke and the luridly colored lights and the knee-deep rock 'n' roll. "I stepped on a claymore in Vietnam, and I was blown shitless. I was hanging from a tree by my own intestines. Can you believe that? My buddies unwound me, and they saved me somehow, although I still can't help screaming whenever I shit.

"But, you know, I learned something that day. When I was blown up, my friends were *laughing.* They were laughing, when they saw me hanging from that fucking tree; and the reason they were laughing was their gladness, that it wasn't them; and because they'd seen death, which was me, but it hadn't hurt them.

"If somebody had taken a movie of me, hanging from that fucking tree, I'd of been a fucking millionaire by now. People love to see death. They love it. Which is what makes Jamie Ford so fucking popular."

I stopped, abruptly, causing a big bearded guy in a red-checkered shirt to spill his beer.

"Hey, pencil-neck—" he began to protest. But then he saw Wolf Bodell, and he shrugged and said, "What the fuck, okay? It's only beer."

"Jamie Ford?" I demanded.

Wolf Bodell took off his dark glasses. He had one glass eye, as blue as a summer afternoon, which stared right over my shoulder.

"Jamie Ford, that's right. Presley would've told you. Jamie Ford's been doing this for years. Jamie Ford's the one and only. That's why you came, yes?"

It was then that I turned toward the center of the Golden Horses saloon, toward the dance floor. On most nights, a country and western band would have been playing; or couples would have been square-dancing or jiving; or drunken truckers would have been breaking chairs over each other's heads. But tonight—through the drifting cigarette smoke, through the red and yellow lights—I saw the tall, gaunt structure of a gallows.

Jamie Ford. I should have known it. *People love to see death. They love it.* And who could show you death more vividly than Jamie?

Wolf Bodell ushered me up to the bar. "What do you want?" he asked me.

"Anything. Coors Lite."

"You can't face the Grim Reaper on Coors Lite," Wolf Bodell cackled. "Leland—give this man a Jack Daniel's, straight up, with a Pabst chaser."

I took out my billfold, but Wolf Bodell shook his hand to show that he didn't want me to pay. "Any friend of Presley's is a friend of mine; and any friend of Presley's is a friend of death. We're all dying, my friend! All of us! So why are we all so bad to each other? What's the point of snatching a woman's purse when both of you are sitting side by side on a bus that's going over a thousand-foot cliff? Die and let die. That's my philosophy."

I was handed my drinks by a busty barmaid with a white-powdered pockmarked face and a dusty red velvet basque. She must have been very beautiful once. She winked at me, but I saw nothing in her face

257

except suffering. Eyes unfocused, nose not quite straight. A walking casualty of Smirnoff or crack or a violent husband, who could tell? No joy, for sure. Not even hope. I turned away, and she called out, "Don't be so unsociable, lover!"

Wolf Bodell nudged me with his elbow and grinned. "You know what your trouble is? You're too damned nice. All of Presley's friends are too damned nice. Don't play poker, do you? I relish playing poker with real nice people. Lambs to the slaughter, that's what I call it. *Nasdravye!*"

He tipped back his Jack Daniel's, and I tipped back my Jack Daniel's and coughed. He snapped his fingers for two more, and I was about to say no, not for me, when the lights suddenly dimmed, and there was a rough, blaring fanfare on the amplifiers. A thin gingery man in a scarlet spangly cowboy suit stepped into the spotlight and raised one arm dramatically for silence.

"Maize darmsey maize sewers," he announced. "Tonight, for your sheer excitement, for your outright in-cray-doolity, the Golden Horses presents the act of acts, the laughter in the face of Beelzebub himself, the mocker of mortality! The man who seeks his pleasures on the brink of death.

"Yes, folks . . . one more time, Jamie Ford, the Supremo of the Slipknot, is going to risk oblivion for your entertainment and his own sex-you-ell satisfaction. He will gen-yoo-inely hang himself from this here gallows-tree, as inspected and pronounced authentic, and based on the model used for the hanging of Charles J. Guiteau, the assassin of President Garfield, in 1882.

"What you are about to see is one man facing death

for the sheer purr-leasure of it; and he has signed legal documents which hold the Golden Horses blameless should things go awry.

"But be warned . . . the performance you are about to witness is strictly of an adult nature, and more shocking than anything you have ever seen before or will again. So if any of you are having second thoughts, or if any of you wish to have your money refunded, then you'd better do so now.

"Because here he is, maize-darmsey-maize-sewers, the Hero of the Hempen Rope, the Nero of the Noose . . . Ja-a-a-mie Ford!"

We were half deafened by a crackling cornet fanfare on the amplifiers, but scarcely anybody applauded. I looked around the Golden Horses, through the sliding cigarette smoke, and saw that everybody was too tense, everybody had their attention fixed on the gallows. Everybody had that same guilty, mesmerized stare—and I expect I did, too. We were like people driving past a fatal auto accident—horrified, fascinated. The emergency services would have called us ghouls.

"Here," said Wolf Bodell, nudging my elbow and handing me another whiskey. "This is what I call a show. One of the best in the country, though I say so myself."

"You're the *promoter?*" I asked him.

"Well, manager, more like."

"How do you manage a man hanging himself?"

Wolf Bodell tossed back his second drink. "Everything on God's good earth needs managing. You don't think that cows grow by accident? There's always somebody who wants to do something and somebody else who wants to watch them do it. It's as simple as that. But the skill comes in bringing the exhibitionist and the voyeur into the same room, at the same time, and making a profit out of it. That's managing.

"Let me tell you something . . . I was bred and brung up in carny. My grandfather was carny; my father was Henry T. Bodell, the founder of Bodell's Traveling Entertainments and Curiosities. When I was three years old, I was introduced to Prince Randian, the Caterpillar Man, who didn't have no arms and legs, and got about by wriggling. I had nightmares about Prince Randian for years later, but, boy, I never forgot him. Never.

"Of course, those days are gone now, the days of freaks and bearded ladies. Very long gone. But every now and then, you still come across people like Jamie Ford, whose need for attention doesn't fit into any of your usual molds. They're still carny entertainers, even if the carnies are dead and gone. They still have the devil in them. They still have the *need*. What's more, people still have the need to watch them. Deplorable, ain't it? But there's nothing in this whole world more fascinating than watching a human being die, except if it's watching a human being die by *choice*. It's like watching those Booh-dist monks, who set fire to themselves. I saw one or two of those out in Nam. Can you imagine doing that by *choice?* Because I sure fucking can't."

He sniffed and wiped his nose with the back of his hand. "It's just like I can't imagine why Jamie keeps on hanging himself. Don't tell me the high is *that* fucking great. But he wants to do it, and people want to watch him do it, and it's a pity to let a good psychosis go to waste."

At that moment, out of the smoke, Jamie appeared,

my old school friend Jamie Ford. He was much thinner and grayer, and his eyes seemed to have lost all of that bright, vicious sparkle. Now they were dead men's eyes.

His blond hair was greasy and lank and almost shoulder-length now, and he wore a black-and-yellow bandanna tightly tied around his head. He was wrapped up in a faded black cloak that trailed on the floor, but as he stepped forward it parted a little and I saw his thin bare leg, and realized that—underneath the cloak—he was chicken-naked.

"And now!" cried the man in the sparkly cowboy suit. "For your extra delight . . . for your unmatched excitement . . . Mr. Ford's dee-lectable assistant . . . Ms. Suffer Kate!"

There was another scratchy fanfare, followed by a desultory assortment of "yahoos" and wolf-whistles. A tall girl came prancing onto the stage, white-skinned, naked except for black stiletto shoes, a tiny black-sequined thong, and a headdress of nodding black ostrich feathers.

She twirled around, and the spotlights gleamed on her chubby, luminous flesh. Her breasts were enormous and wallowed on her chest like two white whales dipping and rolling in a slow flood tide. Her stomach was rounded, but she had no stretch marks. She had the figure of a girl who drinks too much and eats too many hamburgers and too many taco chips and spends too much of her life watching too much TV in too many Howard Johnson's.

She lifted her arms and blew kisses all around the crowd, and it was then that I recognized her. "Ms. Suffer Kate" was none other than Laurel Fay, the cheerleader from Sherman Oaks Senior High. A raddled, puffy, corrupted version of a once-beautiful "most-likely-to." I could have shed tears, believe me.

But I remembered that curse that Laurel had cursed, on graduation day, the day that I had caught her riding up and down on him while he slowly suffocated in Saran Wrap.

"Judas! Judas fucking Iscariot! He wants it! He needs it! It's death meets life! It's life meets death!"

Now Jamie was circling the gallows, eyeing it up and down, gripping it and shaking it to make sure that it was firm. The hi-fi played "Tie a Yellow Ribbon 'Round the Old Oak Tree."

It wasn't a proper executioner's gallows, for all that the master of ceremonies had described it as an authentic copy of the gallows on which Charles J. Guiteau had been executed. The drop on a proper executioner's gallows is more than twice the height of the man to be hanged. When the trap opens, and the man falls through, the chances are high that he will instantaneously break his neck. But this wasn't a gallows designed for the quick judicial extinction of life. This was a gallows designed for long, slow strangulation.

Watching Jamie shaking that gallows gave me a spasm of utter dread, like nothing I had ever experienced before. I turned to Wolf Bodell and said, "Is there a phone in this place?"

"Sure, next to the jakes. But don't take too long . . . he's just about to do the business."

I pushed my way through the murmuring, mesmerized crowd. As I did so, I think Jamie must have caught sight of me, because he stopped shaking the gallows and peered into the darkness which enveloped the audience, his hand raised over his eyes to cut out the glare from the spotlight. I dodged behind a large red-faced man in a crumpled business suit and continued my journey to the telephone with my face turned away from the gallows and my shoulders hunched.

I reached the booth, closed the folding door, and thumbed in a dime. The phone rang for a long, long time before anybody answered.

"Bryce."

"Deputy Bryce? It's Gerry, from the *Bee*. If I were you, I'd come on out to the Golden Horses with your foot flat to the floor. And bring some backup."

"I just started supper. Can't it wait?"

"Not unless you want a man to die."

Deputy Bryce said something unintelligible, but I didn't wait to hear what it was. I pushed my way back to the bar, where Wolf Bodell had already lined up another Jack Daniel's for me. I was half drunk already, but he wouldn't take no for an answer. "You can't face the Grim Reaper sober," he told me.

With Ms. Suffer Kate prancing and pirouetting around him, Jamie mounted the low gray-painted trestle which stood directly below the noose. The trestle was arranged so that when Jamie himself tugged on a lanyard, the legs would collapse flat and he would be left hanging six or seven inches above the floor. He took hold of the noose and gently tugged it, to test that the rope was running free. The hi-fi music changed to "Stand By Your Man." Jamie loosened the collar of his cloak—and it was then that I saw for the first time the terrible blue and red bruises and rope burns that disfigured his neck. His carotid artery bulged in several purplish lumps, and his Adam's-apple was crisscrossed with deep shiny weals.

He lifted the noose over his head with all the

solemnity of a king crowning himself. I thought I caught the faintest trace of a smile on his lips, but I couldn't be sure.

Ms. Suffer Kate made an exaggerated Betty Boop O with her red-lipsticked mouth, her breasts bounce-delay-bouncing with every step she took.

Wolf Bodell grinned at me and said, "Heart-stopping stuff, ain't it? The odds against him surviving are about three to one. So you see *my* livelihood's going to be hanging by a thread, too."

"Stand By Your Man" was abruptly interrupted by a long, thunderous drumroll. Jamie was standing straight-backed amidst the eddying cigarette smoke, the noose around his neck, staring at someplace far in the distance. I looked for sweat on his face, but he appeared dry and pale and almost saintly. I wondered what he was thinking; but maybe he wasn't thinking anything at all. Did he really want to die? Or was he mortally afraid?

"Maize darmsey maize sewers, burr-ace your-selves!" screamed the master of ceremonies.

Jamie took a tighter grip on the lanyard. The drumroll went on and on. In fact, it went on for so long that I began to think that he wasn't going to do it. Maybe he had lost his nerve. Maybe he had stood on this trestle and faced his Maker just once too often.

But then, with his left hand, he pushed back his cloak, so that it slid off his shoulders and revealed his nakedness. More red-lipsticked O's from Ms. Suffer Kate. She perched on the edge of the trestle and caressed Jamie's scarred and bony legs, smiling up at him and O-ing the audience alternately.

Jamie's penis hung heavy and dark between his

thighs, not yet aroused. Ms. Suffer Kate ran her hands up and weighed his hairy scrotum in her hand. Then she squeezed and rubbed his penis until it began to swell up a little. The drumroll continued, but they didn't really need a drumroll. Everybody in the Golden Horses was staring at Jamie transfixed, their mouths open, their eyes wide, daring him actually to do it, begging him not to do it, fearful and fascinated at the same time.

I found myself pushing my way forward.

"Jamie!" I shouted. "Jamie, it's Gerry! *Jamie!*"

Wolf Bodell snatched at my elbow. "Hey, come on, man, don't break his concentration!"

"Jamie!" I yelled.

I forced my way right to the front and stood in front of the gallows. Ms. Suffer Kate stared at me—crossly at first, but then with growing recognition.

"You?" she said, in a blurry voice.

She looked up at Jamie, and I did, too. He was smiling down at me with a wounded, beatific smile. The Hero of the Hempen Rope. The Nero of the Noose.

"Jamie," I said, as loudly as I could, so that he would hear me over the drumroll, and over the impatient whistling of the crowd, and over his own dreamlike trance. "Jamie, it's over. It's time to come down now. You don't have to do this anymore."

"Hey, mister, mind your own fucking business and get out of the fucking way!" somebody roared at me; and there was a roar of approval and a locomotive-like stamping of feet.

Jamie looked down at me, and I don't know whether he recognized me or not. I like to think that he didn't. Because the next thing that happened was—without warning—he pulled the lanyard, and the trestle table collapsed with an ear-splitting bang. Jamie dropped three feet and then jolted to a stop as the noose tightened. He swung around, spun around, his feet bicycling wildly in the air, his hands clawing at his throat. He made the most terrible cackling sound; and when he spun around again and I saw his face I felt a surge of warm sick in the back of my mouth. His eyes were almost bursting out of his head. He was purple—a dark, eggplant purple—and he kept opening and closing his mouth in a desperate attempt to breathe.

I tried to push my way forward, but I felt Wolf Bodell gripping my arm. "You can't help him, my friend. You can't help him. It's something he has to do. If you save him today, he'll do it again tomorrow."

Jamie was twisting around and around, and the crowd was baying in horror. A woman was screaming, *"No! No! No! No!"* and a man was roaring, "Cut him down, for Christ's sake! Cut him down!"

The whole of the Golden Horses was surging with fear and disgust and a hideous unbalancing fascination. It was like wading through a warm, heavy swell with ice-cold undercurrents.

Jamie kept on gargling and kicking. Whenever he stopped twisting, Ms. Suffer Kate gave him another push, so that he spun round yet again, and again. His eyes were bulging so much now that I could see the swollen scarlet flesh behind the eyeball, and he had clawed at the noose around his neck so furiously that one of his fingernails was flapping loose.

Now, however, came the climax. As Jamie spun

around again, Ms. Suffer Kate stopped him, and steadied him, and we could see that his penis had stiffened into a hugely distended erection. His testicles were scrunched up tight, and the shaft rose thick and veiny and hard as an antler.

Ms. Suffer Kate stood up in front of him and kissed him, leaving lipstick imprints all over his heaving white stomach.

Then she stepped back, so that she was at least six inches away from his rigid penis, and stretched her mouth open wide.

"Holy Mother of God," I heard a man say; and his words weren't a blasphemy; not even here; not even while we were witnessing a slow and deliberate self-suffocation.

There was a second's agonized pause. Jamie's entire body was arched like a bow. He had stopped scrabbling at his noose, and his hands were held up in front of him, his fingers skeletal with tension. He let out one gargling, strangulated breath, and then another. He was so taut, he was straining so hard, that his right eyeball at last squeezed right out of its socket and bobbled on top of his cheek, staring downward without expression at Ms. Suffer Kate.

Then—with a sickening convulsion—he climaxed. His penis seemed to swell even more, the head swelled, and then a thick spurt of sperm flew out of it, right into Ms. Suffer Kate's stretched open mouth. It spurted again, and again, and again—more sperm than I had ever seen a man ejaculate in my life—and it covered Ms. Suffer Kate's lips and cheeks and eyelashes and clung in her black funereal ostrich plumes.

Throughout the whole ejaculation, she hadn't touched him once. He had climaxed from lack of oxygen, from agony, from dancing with death.

Ms. Suffer Kate turned around, and raised her arms, and nodded her plumes, her face still glistening with sperm. Then, with no more hesitation, she stepped up onto one of the trestles and released the locking catch that had prevented Jamie (when the table had collapsed beneath him) from reaching the floor.

Jamie was lowered swiftly down; and Wolf Bodell was right beside him; and so was a man with thinning greased-back hair and a cigarette between his lips and a worn-out medical bag. Ms. Suffer Kate meanwhile was standing a little way back, wrapped in a grubby baby-pink toweling robe, wiping her face with Kleenex. She looked no more concerned about what she had just done than a runner who has just completed the 500 meters in a fairly unspectacular time.

For some reason I looked at my watch. Then I walked stiffly to the bar and said, in a kaleidoscopic voice, "Jack Daniel's, straight up."

I was still trying to lift the shot glass without spilling the whiskey when I heard the double doors crashing open and a familiar voice shouting, "Police! This is a raid! Everybody stay where you are!"

I turned and looked down at Wolf Bodell, and Wolf Bodell looked back up at me. I don't know whether he suspected me of tipping off the sheriff or not, but right at that particular moment I didn't care. Somebody had just said, "He's breathing . . . he'll make it," and that was all I cared about. That, and making sure that Jamie never tried to hang himself again.

I went up to Ms. Suffer Kate and said, "Hallo, Laurel."

She slowly turned her eyes toward me, still dabbing her right cheek with a crumpled-up tissue.

"Hallo, you rat," she replied.

The case never went to trial, of course. The Golden Horses was closed down by county ordinance and reopened eleven months later as the Old Placer Rib Shack, and promptly closed down again after an outbreak of food poisoning.

In lieu of prosecution, Jamie agreed to undergo a minimum of three years' analysis and rehabilitation at the appropriately named Fruitridge Psychiatric Center in Sacramento, a secure institution for the gravely whacko.

Laurel Fay's parents stood bail for her and produced an oleaginous San Francisco lawyer who looked like Jabba the Hutt in a seersucker suit, and who promised such a long and expensive and complicated trial that the district attorney decided that it would be against the public interest for the case to proceed any further. Laurel sent me thirty dimes in the mail, along with a postcard of the Last Supper and a ballpoint arrow pointing to Judas Iscariot.

I went to visit Jamie in the first week of September. The Fruitridge Psychiatric Center had cool white corridors, and a courtyard with terra cotta pots and fan palms, and yellow-uniformed nurses who came and went with pleasant, proprietary smiles.

Jamie was sitting in his plain white room on a plain wooden chair, staring at the wall. He was wearing what looked like judo robes, without the belt. His hair had turned white and was cropped very short. His eye was back in its socket, but it had an odd cast to it now, so that I never quite knew if he was looking at me or not. His skin was peculiarly pale and smooth, but I suppose it was the drugs they were giving him.

He talked for a long time about backgammon. He said he was trying to play it in his head. His voice had no color, no expression, no substance. It was like listening to water running. He didn't talk once about school, or the old days, or Chokes. He didn't ask what had happened to Suffer Kate. I came away sad because of what he had become; but also glad that I had saved him at last.

Two years later, the telephone rang at 2:30 in the morning, when my metabolism was almost at zero and I was dreaming of death. I scrabbled around for the receiver, found it, dropped it, then picked it up again.

"Did I wake you?" asked a hoarse, scarcely audible voice.

"Who is this?" I wanted to know.

"Did I wake you? I didn't mean to wake you."

I switched on the bedside lamp. On the nightstand there was my wristwatch, a framed photograph of my parents, a glass of water, and a dog-eared copy of *Specimen Days in America.*

"Gerry, is that you?"

A silence. A cough.

"Gerry?"

"I need your help. I badly need your help."

"You need my help *now?*"

"There's been an accident, Gerry. I really need you."

"What kind of an accident?" I asked. A cold feeling started to crawl down my back.

"You have to help me. You really have to help me."

I parked outside the Fort Hotel and climbed out of my car. The streets of Sacramento were deserted. The Fort was an old six-story building with a flaking brown-painted facade and an epileptic neon sign that kept flickering out the words ORT HOT. Next door there was a Chinese restaurant with a painting of a glaring dragon in the window.

Inside, the hotel smelled strongly of Black Flag, with an undertone of disinfected vomit. A surprisingly neat and good-looking young man was sitting at the desk, short-sleeved shirt and cropped blond hair, reading *Europe on $60 a Day*. When I asked him for Jamie's room, he said, "Six-oh-three," without even looking up at me.

I walked toward the elevator.

"Out of commission," he said, still without raising his eyes.

I walked up five flights of stairs. It was like climbing the five flights of Purgatory. From behind closed doors, I heard muttering televisions, heard blurted conversations, smelled pungent cooking smells. At last I reached the sixth floor and walked along a dark, narrow, linoleum-floored corridor until I found 603. I listened for a while at the door. I thought I could faintly hear marching music. I knocked.

"Jamie? Are you there, Jamie? It's me."

He took a long, long time to open the door. Security

chains, locks, bolts. At last the door swung ajar, and I heard him say, "You'd better come along in."

I hesitated for a moment and then stepped inside. The room was lit by a single desk lamp, without a shade, so that the shadows it cast were coarse and uncompromising. There was a terrible smell in the room—a sweet smell of urine and decay. On the far side, there was a sofa bed, heaped with dirty red blankets. On my left, a tipped-over armchair, revealing its torn-out innards.

Jamie was naked. His body was so scarred and emaciated that I wouldn't have recognized him. His eyes were red-rimmed, and his hair was sticking up in wild, mad tufts. Around his neck, tied in a hangman's noose, was a long, thin nylon cord. It was so long that he had loosely coiled it, and had looped the coil over his left forearm, like a waiter holding a napkin.

"I thought you were cured of all this," I told him.

He gave me a furtive, erratic smile. "You're never cured. It's the way you are."

"You said there'd been an accident. What accident?"

He limped over to the sofa bed. He glanced at me once, and then he dragged back the filthy blankets. At first I couldn't understand what I was looking at. A white, curved shape. Then—when I stepped closer—I saw that it was Ms. Suffer Kate. She was wearing black lacy split-crotch panties, and the butt of a huge blue plastic vibrator protruded from her hairy vulva. Her stomach sagged sideways. Her breasts were bruised, and her nipples were purple, like prunes. She was staring unblinkingly at the fold in the blanket only an inch in front of her nose, as if she found it totally absorbing. Her face was so white. So white that it was almost blue. Around her neck was a thin cord, which had been twisted around and around with a broken pencil until it had throttled her.

"She's dead," said Jamie.

I covered her up with the blanket. "You know I can't save you now," I told him. "Christ knows, I've tried to save you. But I really can't save you now."

"It was what she wanted," said Jamie, in a matter-of-fact voice. "We talked about it for weeks beforehand. And when I twisted that pencil, and twisted that pencil, she came and she came and she came." He paused. "I wish it could have been me, instead of that . . . dildo thing. But these days, there's only one way that *I* can get it up."

"I'm calling the cops now."

Jamie fingered the noose around his neck. "Sure you are. You have to."

"Do you have a phone in here?"

"Unh-unh. But there's a pay phone at the end of the hall."

I was shuddering, as if I were freezing cold, but I knew that it was only shock. "You'll have to come with me," I told him. "I can't leave you here alone."

"That's okay." He nodded. He thought for a moment, and then he handed me the end of his rope. "You can hold onto this. Stop me from running away."

We stepped out into the corridor, Jamie limping a little way in front of me.

"Are you okay?" I asked him.

He lifted one hand. "Okay as I'll ever be."

I was trying to think what I was going to say to the police when we turned the corner in the corridor. Directly in front of us was the elevator shaft—and it was open. A dark, drafty doorway to noplace at all. Somebody had wedged the trellis gates with a paint-spotted pickax handle. No wonder the porter had thought it was out of commission.

There was an instant when I knew what Jamie was going to do—a stroboscopic split second when I might have been able to stop him. But you and I and most of the rest of the world are doing their darndest to survive—so when somebody is determined to do the opposite, we have a fatal tendency not to believe it.

And Jamie ran—*sprinted*—right to the open elevator gate and threw himself into it, without a scream, without any sound at all. Tumbled, fell, disappeared like a conjuring trick.

The rope that I was holding wriggled and snaked, and then abruptly thumped tight. It almost took my arms out of my sockets. I shuffle-staggered to the elevator gates, straining at it, pulling at it, until I reached the very brink.

With my shoulder pressed against the folded trellis gates to give myself support, I leaned over the edge of the elevator shaft and cautiously looked down. I was panting and sweating and whispering under my breath, "God help me, please, God help me."

Thirty feet below me, in the windy echoing half darkness of the elevator shaft, Jamie was hanging with the noose tight around his neck. His arms were spread wide, his toes were pointed, like a ballet dancer. His head was thrown back in ecstasy. The rope creaked, and paused, and creaked, and paused.

He opened his eyes and looked up at me, and his face was triumphant and gray with oxygen starvation. He had done it. He had done it to me, after all these years. I had worried about him and cared for him and promised to save him, and he had made me the instrument of his own terminal hanging.

Jamie tried to speak, tried to mock me, but the noose was clutching his larynx too tight. He twisted around and around, and as he twisted, I could see his penis rising, pulsing with every heartbeat. His eyes bulged. His tongue suddenly slopped out from between his lips, fat and gray.

I had a simple choice: I could hold on to my end of the rope, hanging him, or else I could let go. In which case, he would drop four stories down the elevator shaft.

I waited, and clung on to the rope, and as I clung on to the rope, it all became clear to me. What is any savior, in the long run? What is any devoted friend? We do nothing except delay the inevitable, for our own selfish ends. We are nothing less than executioners-in-waiting.

I had been so unctuous. I had cared so much. In fact, I had prolonged Jamie's agony.

I should have let him hang himself in high school. Better still, his mother should have let him smother himself in his own pillow.

Thirty feet below me, he twisted and twisted; and then he let out a high, thin cry that was like nothing I have ever heard, before or since. It was pitiful, saintly, ecstatic, sad. Sperm jumped from his penis, two, three, four times, and dropped down the elevator shaft.

I leaned over. I said, "God damn you, Jamie." I don't know if he heard me.

Then I let him go.

THE CONTRIBUTORS

Forrest J. Ackerman

World-renowned editor of *Famous Monsters of Filmland,* Ackerman is the man who coined the term "sci fi." He has won four Hugos, written two thousand articles, authored twelve books, agented two hundred writers, and compiled a lifelong, world-famous collection of horror and sci-fi memorabilia at his home in California.

Max Allan Collins

Iowa's Collins is a two-time winner of the "Shamus" Best Novel award for his Nate Heller historical thrillers *True Detective* and *Stolen Away*. He is the author of four other mystery series, the former scripter of the *Dick Tracy* comic strip, and has also scripted such comic books as *Batman* and *Ms. Tree*.

Michael Garrett

Garrett's first novel *Keeper* has been optioned for a movie. His short stories have been published in numerous periodicals and anthologies, including *Shock Rock 1* and *2* and *Fear Itself*. He is an editorial associate with *Writer's Digest* magazine and is co-editor of the *Hot Blood* series. He lives in Alabama.

Jeff Gelb

California's Gelb is the editor of *Shock Rock 1* and *2* and *Fear Itself*, and co-edits the *Hot Blood* series with Garrett. Gelb's first erotic horror fiction sales were to *Hustler* and *Chic* under the pseudonym Jay Amarillo. Gelb is a frequent contributor to several comics-related publications, including *Comics Buyers Guide* and *Golden Age Update*.

Jack Ketchum

New Yorker Ketchum is the author of *Off Season*, often credited as the first splatterpunk novel, as well as *Hide and Seek, Cover, She Wakes, The Girl Next Door, Offspring*, and *Road Kill*. Short fiction credits include *Fear Itself, Vampire Detectives, Stalkers III*, and *Book of the Dead III*.

Edward Lee

He is the author of nine horror novels, including *Ghouls, Succubi*, and *The Chosen*. His short stories, articles, and commentaries have appeared in *Cemetery Dance, Deathrealm, Afraid, Mystery Scene*, and others, as well as numerous anthologies. Lee lives in Maryland.

Bentley Little

California's Little has had over one hundred short stories published in various horror magazines and anthologies. He worked his way through college selling erotic fiction to such men's magazines as *Cavalier* and *Gent*. Little is the author of *The Summoning*, *Death Instinct*, *The Mailman*, and the Bram Stoker Award–winning *The Revelation*.

Graham Masterton

England's Masterton is the author of twenty-five horror novels, the first of which was *The Manitou* and the latest of which, *Burial*, revives the same characters twenty years on. His short stories have appeared in more than forty anthologies, including *Shock Rock* and *Fear Itself*.

A. R. Morlan

Morlan has two published novels, *The Amulet* and *Dark Journey*, and her short fiction has appeared in over forty magazines and anthologies, including *Weird Tales*, *Night Cry*, *F & SF*, *Horror Show*, *Shock Rock 2*, *Cold Shocks*, and *Obsessions*. Morlan is a Wisconsin-based *Writer's Digest* instructor.

Claudia O'Keefe

California's O'Keefe is the author of *Black Snow Days* and *Gawkers*. She has edited *Ghosttide* and the upcoming *Ghostcliff* and *Mother* anthologies, and her work has appeared in *Shudder Again* and others.

Lucy Taylor

Colorado's Taylor is a prolific short fiction writer, with credits including *Hotter Blood, Northern Frights, Bizarre Dreams*, and publications like *Pulphouse* and *Bizarre Sex and Other Crimes of Passion*.

Steve Rasnic Tem

Prolific short story writer Tem has been nominated for the World Fantasy, British Fantasy, and Bram Stoker Awards for his work, winning the British Fantasy Award in 1988. He lives in Colorado.

Edo van Belkom

His very first short story sale was reprinted in *Year's Best Horror Stories 20*. Since that sale in 1989, he's sold over fifty stories to magazines and anthologies, including *Fear Itself, Shock Rock 2, Deathport*, and *Northern Frights 1* and *2*.

Graham Watkins

North Carolina's Watkins is the author of *Dark Winds, The Fire Within*, and *Kaleidoscope Eyes*. His short fiction has appeared in such anthologies as *Hottest Blood, Shock Rock*, and *Fear Itself*.

Sidney Williams

He has written several books, including *When Darkness Falls* and the vampire novel *Night Brothers*. He is currently working on a mystery/suspense novel to be published under his Michael August pseudonym. Williams lives in Louisiana.

THE HORROR WRITERS ASSOCIATION PRESENTS

GHOSTS

EDITED BY PETER STRAUB

An anthology of short stories from
the best horror writers alive today

**Available from Pocket Books
mid-March 1995**

POCKET
B O O K S

DON'T BE AFRAID TO BUY IT!!

Pocket Books presents
its collection of

EROTIC HORROR

HOT BLOOD ....66424-7/$5.50

HOTTER BLOOD.......70149-5/$5.99

HOTTEST BLOOD.....75367-3/$5.50

THE HOT BLOOD SERIES: DEADLY
AFTER DARK..........87087-4/$5.50

EDITED BY JEFF GELB AND
MICHAEL GARRETT

IT'S TERROR BEYOND THE LAST TABOO!